THE IN

Sarah, straight from a convent, went out wide-eyed with excitement to the West Indies to a job as governess to the small wards of Jason de Cordova. And had the bad luck to fall in love with her employer – who was not only married but had every intention of staying married! How could she cope with the heartbreak?

THE INNOCENT INVADER

BY

ANNE MATHER

MILLS & BOON LIMITED
17-19 FOLEY STREET
LONDON WIA IDR

First published in 1969 by Robert Hale Ltd. under the title The Enchanted Island

This edition 1974

© Scribe Associates Ltd. 1974

ISBN 0 263 71593 0

Made and Printed in Great Britain by
C. Nicholls & Company Ltd
The Philips Park Press, Manchester

CHAPTER ONE

THE pearly, early morning light stole like a wraith across the island, lifting the wreaths of mist from the trees, and, as the sun rose higher, gilding the fleecy clouds with a golden glow. Jason had seen many such sunrises, but they never failed to move him by their complete detachment from the toils and rigours of the world they so beautifully illuminated.

Leaning against his balcony rail, he saw the shadows disappear among the palms that fringeed the coral beach, and the white-surfed breakers that creamed on the sand sparkled iridescently. This was the time of day he liked best, when everything was fresh and unspoilt, and for a few hours at least, before Irena awoke, he was free from the sound of her hysterical recriminations.

He looked inland, over the fields of waving sugar cane, the brightness of the crop interspersed here and there by the dark brown thatched roofs of the huts belonging to the plantation workers. Beyond the estate, below the terraces where the white population of the island lived in luxury, was the small town of El Tesoro, *the treasure,* so called because of the legend that one of the many Spanish galleons, loaded with gold and precious stones, had floundered on the reef on its way to Cordova.

The town, which hugged the small harbour, was densely populated, and living conditions for many of the West Indians were squalid. The birth rate continued to rise and consequently, although Jason tried to help them, little was achieved. Jason's money was tied up in the estate, and besides, they did not always welcome help. They were poor but independent, with the kind of contentment found only among people who have never known the urge for power and money and position in society. At times Jason envied them.

Education was gradually being brought to the people, but as yet the schools on the island accommodated only a small proportion of the children. Those children that did attend were restless and dilatory, only waiting for the bell to be free so that they could swarm into the warm sea, or go out with their fathers in the fishing boats as they had done for generations. Whether it was all worthwhile was a problem that Jason sometimes pondered; would they be happier knowing the outside world and its problems, or was it more sensible to leave them in ignorance to live a life which, if narrow in outlook, was broad in experience?

5

His family, the Cordovas, had governed the island since the first white settlement was made there over three hundred years ago. Only sixteen miles by twelve at its widest point, it had provided little interest for the French or the English, and gradually the white population had increased and today there were over thirty white families on the island. The rest of the near seventy thousand population was made up of Africans, Indians, and Creoles, with a fair proportion of mulattos amongst them.

During the tourist season, a time Jason abhorred, day-trippers from St. Vincent or Grenada came to the island, but as there were no hotels suitable for their accommodation they were forced to leave at nightfall. For this Jason was grateful. He intended that as far as possible the island should retain its individuality. He wanted no neon-lighted, chrome-plated monoliths turning Cordova into another Martinique or Trinidad.

Jason turned now from his contemplation of the view, and reached for a cigarette which he lit before shedding the white bathrobe which was his only garment. He dressed leisurely in the tight cotton trousers and loose shirt which were the usual garb of the planter at his work. He pulled knee-length leather boots on to his feet and after running the comb through his thick black hair which was over-long and brushed his collar, he opened his bedroom door silently, and crossing the wide landing descended the stairs.

The stairs were marble, as was the mosaic floor of the cool hall below. From this hall, corridors led off to the various regions of the house, while the cooking and servants' quarters were at the rear of the building in a separate one-storey dwelling. Everywhere was painted white. and at this early hour of the morning the scent of beeswax filled the air. The floors of the living rooms were wood, and Beulah, the African housemaid, polished them religiously until they shone like the polished surface of a table.

Jason walked along the corridor to the dining room which he and Irena used, and seated himself at the long refectory table. His place had been laid as usual, with the fruit and rolls and coffee he always enjoyed at this time. Romulus, the elderly manservant, came to see whether there was anything else he required, but Jason shook his head and the man bowed and left him.

The wide french doors were open, and through them he could again see the beach and the shadowy blue horizon. A breeze blew in, ruffling his hair, and he ran a hand lazily round the back of his neck, stretching for a moment.

His thoughts turned to the argument he had had with Irena the previous evening, and his expression darkened. As always,

6

to mar the beauty of the day, the problem of Irena was fresh in his mind. He finished his breakfast, shrugged his shoulders as though to lift the thoughts that plagued him and, leaving the table, he went out of the french doors and stood on the verandah for a moment breathing deeply. Then he turned and walked round to the rear of the building, where, beyond the pool, and hidden among trees was the stable where he kept his horses. He kept two hunters, and three ponies for the children.

Apollo, his black stallion, was being saddled in readiness for him as he approached, and he patted the horse encouragingly, and produced an apple for it from his pocket, holding it in the palm of his hand, and allowing Apollo to nuzzle the fruit with his soft mouth.

Jacob, the stable boy, stood back to admire his handiwork, and said: *"Mucho bello, señor!"* in a satisfied voice.

Jason straddled the animal, and nodded down at the boy. *"Si,* Jacob. *Esta bien. Gracias,"* and pressing his heels into the animal's sides he rode out of the stable yard.

The air was like wine as he rode down the steep incline to the beach, and then, giving the horse its head, he galloped swiftly along the damp sand. Apollo, sensing his master's mood, sped on winged feet, until Jason slowed him to a canter and finally to a trot. Wheeling the horse round suddenly, he rode up the bank and into the shade of the casuarinas. Dismounting, he flung himself down on the sand and stretched before reaching for a cigarette. After lighting the cigarette he lay back, looking upwards through the tracery of leaves to the blueness of the sky above him. It was going to be another perfect day. Although he had visited many foreign countries in his lifetime, and had attended school in England, nevertheless there was nowhere to compare with Cordova.

But, as always, when he had time to think, his thoughts turned to Irena and the terrible argument they had had the previous evening about Serena and the children. Their arguments of late were always about Serena and the children. If only Antonio were still alive, things would not have been so bad. As it was, with his brother dead, he felt responsible for his brother's widow and their three children.

The children were aged eight, seven and five and urgently needed a governess. The schools on the island were only for the West Indian children. All the white families employed tutors or governesses until the children were old enough to attend boarding schools. If Antonio had been alive things would have been different. He would have seen that the children were properly educated. As it was, Irena's attitude towards Eloise, Ricardo

7

and Marie forestalled Jason from acting in the matter for the sake of a peaceful life. But finally he had decided that he could not be responsible any longer for their education. He had tried to instil a little knowledge into their heads, and although Spanish was the most widely used tongue on the island, the children could speak English quite fluently already so that later they could attend an English school as he had done. But the short time he had to devote to them every day was not enough and mostly they ran wild. Serena, child that she was, had no idea how to maintain discipline, and her indifference only made them worse. If only Irena had been a normal, healthy human being, kindly disposed to her nephew and nieces, she could have done so much for them. But Irena refused to acknowledge their existence except in moments of anger, and although they all lived in the same house, there were two separate households. For Jason and the children the situation was intolerable, and the children were most frequently to be found down in the cane fields, playing with the children of the plantation workers. But now Jason had decided it could not go on. They must be taught; not only elementary lessons but how to behave, before it was too late.

He rolled on to his stomach and stubbed out his cigarette in the sand, watching a sandfly flitting across the ground in search of some interesting article on which to settle himself. Its steady progress was relaxing.

If only Serena had been the daughter of one of the Spanish families here on the island, things might have been different, more tenable. But his brother had married a beautiful young Creole in Trinidad and had brought her back to Cordova. That was nine years ago, and Serena had been sixteen at the time. Irena had been outraged. Although at that time Antonio had had his own house, it had been near Jason's own, and Serena had thought she would be as welcome there as in her own home. In consequence, she had often appeared at the villa while the men were at work, until Irena and she had had such a row that neither of them had spoken since. Serena had been eight months pregnant at that time, and it had disturbed her so much that the baby was premature. For a time it had looked as though both Serena and the baby would die. Miraculously both had survived, but Antonio had not entered Jason's home from the time on. He remained friends with Jason, and Jason was always welcome at their home, but there was no social life between the two families. It had caused quite a stir on the island, and Jason had despised the whole affair.

And now he was faced with a much greater problem, a problem which had grown worse during the two years it had been his. Antonio had been killed while on a business trip to the United States two years ago. He had left Serena a widow with three young children, and little money of their own. Antonio had only worked for Jason. He had not had any share in the company. He had forfeited that years ago when he left home to live in Trinidad.

After Antonio's funeral Jason had told Serena that he wanted the four of them to come and live at the villa. To begin with she had refused, but circumstances had forced her to see reason, and that was how things stood today, except for the fact that he had advertised for a governess, and had obtained one.

"You must be mad! Stark, staring mad!" Irena had raged at him the previous evening, when he had presented her with the *fait accompli*. "Bringing some strange woman into my house. Isn't it enough that I have to live in the same house as that witch and her brood?"

"Irena!"

"Well! Do you want a stranger in the house? Is there no end to your generosity towards these people . . .?"

Jason had shrugged expressively. "No, Irena, I do not want a stranger in my home, but those children are turning into savages before my eyes. It's for them I'm prepared to have this woman here."

"They're savages!" Irena had clenched her fists in fury. Her temper at times was quite uncontrollable, and Jason had tried to pacify her.

"Irena, please! This will be someone for you to talk to. She's been brought up in a convent – surely that's recommendation enough?"

"She's a Catholic?" Irena was curious. "You're sure of this?"

Jason spread wide his hands. "That I can't say. But what else can she be? After all, convents are not run by Protestants."

"That's true. Nevertheless, Jason, I will not have it. She must go back. You must give her her return fare. You say she's coming from England? She can go back there."

"No." Jason was adamant. "In this I refuse to be countermanded. This woman will come and take charge of the children, and you will accept her. Goodness knows, her situation here will be far more difficult than she has any idea it will be."

Irena had argued for a long time and finally, in weariness, Jason had left her screaming and maligning the fates that had brought her to live in this house.

As he remembered, Jason's fingers sought the scar on his right cheek. A livid thing, it stretched from high on his cheekbone,

9

almost to his jawline. Whenever he was emotionally disturbed, the scar throbbed painfully, and with a muffled oath he got to his feet, determinedly putting all thoughts of Irena out of his mind. There was no more time for soul-searching; it was time to go down to the distillery.

The island's main exports were sugar cane and the rum distilled from the molasses, and Jason himself kept an expert eye on the day's work. It was not always necessary; his staff were reliable and efficient, but it kept him out of the house most days until lunch time and saved him the trouble of trying to find excuses for Irena's ill-temper.

He rode back to the house, and leaving the stallion for Jacob to groom, he went and retrieved the Land Rover from the garage. He drove smoothly down the drive, between the neatly laid-out lawns and flower gardens that Irena found so pleasing, and which the children avoided meticulously. The artificiality of it all did not appeal to Jason; he preferred the rather flamboyant confusion to be found in abundance on the island; bougainvillea rioting gloriously with hibiscus and wisteria; the scarlet beauty of immortelles, the oleanders.

An arched gateway in the high stucco wall which surrounded the villa bore witness to the Moorish influence on all the larger dwellings. Balconies, courtyards, fountains, wrought ironwork; all reflected the Moorish artistry predominant in Spain itself.

The hard track wound down towards the town, its surface throwing a film of dust over the Land Rover. As Jason neared the town, stray animals ran heedlessly across his path, and the colourful African women in there floral cotton dresses became more numerous. Dozens of children swarmed about their legs, and waved excitedly as Jason drove by; they all knew Jason.

Before driving to the Cordova distillery, he drove down to the harbour. This was the only part of the island accessible by sea. A coral reef surrounded the island with only a narrow channel that gave access to the small port of El Tesoro. Here a weekly steamer brought mail and supplies, and the occasional passenger, and in return took the export trade of the island. Besides the sugar cane and rum, there was a small bottling and canning plant, which was owned by another of the Spanish families. This was only a small concern, as most of the fruit grown was used by the islanders themselves.

To reach the quay Jason had to leave the Land Rover and walk the remaining distance. Adjoining the quayside was a busy open market, where all the commerce of the island was executed, and he had to press his way through the crowds of early traders and shoppers. The scents of the market, always aromatic and sometimes overpowering, were none the less exciting, and the throng of people and the noise gave him an exhilarated feeling. Everywhere was the feeling of suppressed vitality, a steel band practising for the coming fiesta adding their sound to the din. Sometimes the sound of drums reverberated round the shallow hills above the harbour and the pulsating rhythm fired the blood and stirred the primitive emotions of the body. The African ancestry, superstitious and tribal, brought its own kind of mystery, and Jason knew that many of the practices in the villages owed their origin to the dark gods of Africa. But this was something the white population had to accept, and Jason knew there were few who would go against the voodoo. Its power was absolute.

The harbourmaster's office which was his destination was a low wooden building, occupied by Abe Smith, a massive Negro, with ebony skin and a thick moustache. He and Jason were the best of friends; and Jason usually found time to have coffee with him at this hour of the morning.

He entered the wooden office, stretching as he came through the door. Abe was sprawled in a chair, smoking a cheroot, and he grinned amiably as Jason came in and seated himself on the side of his desk. "Morning," he said, wrinkling his huge nose. "Coffee?"

Jason nodded and helped himself. "Thanks. I could use some." After pouring a blue striped beaker full of the black liquid, he turned back to his friend and re-seated himself, idly stirring the brew.

"How goes it?" Abe straightened up, and poured himself another mug of coffee. "Have you told her?"

Jason raised his dark eyebrows. "Yes, I've told her."

"I can guess what she said!" Abe grimaced, and raised his eyes heavenward.

Jason shrugged. "What I expected I got." He took a long drink of his coffee, savouring it.

Abe smote one fist into the palm of his other hand. "*Madre mia*," he exclaimed, "that woman is not human!"

Jason lit a cigarette. "The governess arrives on the steamer tomorrow," he remarked, changing the subject.

Abe sighed heavily. "She does, eh? Another woman to cause trouble?"

"Let's hope not." Jason rose to his feet. "I'll meet her."

Abe grinned suddenly. "And how will you recognise her? If she's not the only woman to arrive tomorrow?"

Jason bit his lip thoughtfully, and his fingers sought the line of his scar. "She's a governess. My only criterion is the other governesses on the island. She'll be like them."

Abe chuckled. "Ah, I see! A little grey and long in the tooth!"

"I didn't say that," replied Jason mildly, his eyes smiling. "But yes, that will suit us very well."

Abe walked to the door of the office, and leaning against it, his bulk blocking out the light from the room, he said harshly:

"How long is this to go on, Jason? How long are you going to exist in this manner? No one could call it living!"

"Enough," said Jason, abruptly, but Abe was not to be denied.

"Enough is what you've had," he exclaimed. "You forget I've known you since you were knee-high! I've seen you change these last fifteen years from a man who laughed and enjoyed life, lived it to the full, to a stranger who interests himself only in his work, in business – must you sacrifice yourself in this way? You need a woman in your bed –"

"Abe!" Jason's face was like carved granite, the scar like a pale slash against the dark tan of his face.

Abe moved away from the door, shaking his head. He was genuinely disturbed for his friend, but Jason could not allow him to say such things. He was married to Irena; she was his wife; if anyone was to blame it was him. . . .

As the steamer *Celeste* neared Cordova, Sarah wondered for the thousandth time whether indeed she was being as impulsive as Reverend Mother had stipulated. After all, here she was thousands of miles away from England and the convent which had been her home all her life, with nothing to commend this man who was to be her employer but a letter from Father Dominic Sanchez, the Catholic priest on the island.

The solicitors in London who had interviewed her on Jason de Cordova's behalf had seemed singularly out of touch with the situation on the island, and Sarah could only assume that they did not have many dealings with her proposed employer.

But when she had read the advertisement in *The Times*, it had sounded so exciting and different that she had not thought before replying and offering her services. She was always acting impulsively, and in any case she had been sure there would be so many applications her own would not even be considered. But her application had been considered, and a letter had arrived for Reverend Mother, asking for her references. It appeared her convent upbringing was a recommendation in itself, and Sarah refrained from mentioning that she was not herself of the Catholic faith. She was afraid this would influence her case, for it seemed that this was a Catholic family requiring a governess, capable of teaching three infants elementary lessons. And, she had argued with herself, elementary lessons were not religious instruction, so why should she not be suitable anyway?

It had been too good a chance to miss. The West Indies had long been a place Sarah found utterly fascinating, and to live, even for a short while, on an island there sounded marvellous. Besides, she knew she was fast losing the will to leave the convent, and that if she did not leave soon she would never leave at all. Orphaned as a baby and adopted by the nuns at St. Teresa's, Sarah had found a home so completely understanding that many times she had been tempted to become a novice herself. But her parents had not wanted it and the nuns refused to let her decide until she was over twenty-one. They had sent her to a training college in the town after she left school, and she had become an infant teacher. Then she had returned to the convent school and taught the pupils there for the last eighteen months.

At the time she read the advertisement she had been at a crossroads. Unlike most girls of almost twenty-two, Sarah had never bothered about boys. She had never had a date, and she had never been even mildly interested in any male. The priests who visited the convent school were kind and friendly, and that was all she felt she ever needed from any man.

Only Father Donahue had seen things differently. "Sarah, my dear," he had said, "you've seen nothing of the world outside this town. Even the convent walls provide a barrier to you. It's my belief that you need to be taken from this atmosphere to a place so different that you'll discover for yourself whether you really have a vocation."

He it was who had pointed out the advertisement in *The Times*. And it was he who had persuaded Reverend Mother that Sarah should be freed to find her own destiny. Thus it was she was now only minutes from her arrival in Cordova and she felt as scared as a kitten. She was being accepted on a month's probation, and likewise, if she should find the work unsuitable, she would be provided with her return fare at the end of that period. She had flown to Barbados and this steamer was the last leg of the journey. It had all been immensely exciting and thrilling, and even now, with the azure blue waters of the Caribbean lapping the sides of the vessel, she could hardly believe she was here. But the sun was warm upon her shoulders, and the scenery was more spectacular than any technicolor film, so she had to believe it, and she hugged herself for a moment in anticipation. She was so glad Father Donahue had shown her that advertisement. He was right – she was naïve and inexperienced. And now she was to find life an adventure instead of a pilgrimage.

She leaned against the rail of the steamer as the Captain skilfully negotiated the narrows of the reef, and looked across the stretch of calm water to the ant-like activity on the quay ahead of them. This then was Cordova; her home for the next four weeks at least.

From this distance the island was like a green, fertile mound rising out of the sea, its fringing of coral beaches and creaming surf providing a lace-like fragility to the shawl of greenery. It was still comparatively early in the morning, but the glare was strong after an English winter, and Sarah drew a pair of dark glasses from her bag and placed them on her nose. Then she turned to the tall, dark-skinned Barbadian who had left his bridge and joined her at the rail.

"Almost there," he said, indicating the harbour. "Are you ready to face your new employer?"

Sarah smiled. "I'm terribly nervous," she confessed candidly. "I'm not very used to dealing with strangers, and the little I know of the family sounds quite intimidating."

"Intimidating? Jason? No, I don't think Jason is intimidating. The children ... well, who can say? They've been allowed free licence since their father was killed. There's no one to care for them."

Sarah frowned. "But surely, I understand from the solicitors that the children's mother was still alive."

"Yes, she is." The Captain touched his cap politely. "We'll be there shortly. I must have a word with my mate."

Sarah watched him go and shrugged her shoulders bewilderedly. It seemed the Captain did not wish to discuss the Cordova family, and perhaps she had been a little indiscreet asking questions. She sighed. She was not used to subterfuge of any kind. At the convent there had been no secrets and she saw no harm in obtaining the facts about the Cordova children. As she understood it, Jason de Cordova was the children's uncle and their widowed mother lived in the same house. What could be more simple than that? Shaking her head, and shaking thoughts like this from her mind, she turned again to the colourful quay alongside which the channel had been dug to take the steamers passage.

The Captain, from his bridge, watched her interest thoughtfully. In truth he considered the girl might prove rather a responsibility on Cordova. She was so fair she could not fail to cause a stir among the dark-skinned Africans and swarthy Spaniards. Although she was not strictly beautiful she had very

14

large and luminous eyes, black-lashed and blue as sapphires, and her hair was long and plaited and wound round her head in a classical style. It was silvery in colour and in her demure blue poplin dress with the white collar she looked more like a novice than a governess. She had told the Captain of her upbringing in England, and privately he had thought the convent a fitting background for her. What she would make of the intrigues and passions of Cordova, he did not dare to think.

As the *Celeste* drew alongside, a gangplank was run out to her by several of the dark-skinned boys on the quay, and Sarah experienced a thrill of apprehension as she moved forward to disembark. Her arrival in Barbados had not prepared her for this absolute absence of order, and the hustle and bustle on the quay unnerved her.

She looked above the heads of the jostling crowds on the docks to the town of El Tesoro climbing up the shallow hills above the harbour. Above the flat-roofed dwellings of the African population she could see, set among flowering shrubs and clematis-hung stucco walls, the villas of the white population of Cordova, and she felt a sense of relief. For a moment she had wondered whether she would ever see a white person again. Inwardly chastising herself for her lack of worldliness, she moved to the gangplank, and met the Captain again.

"There are no customs on Cordova," he said kindly. "Go ahead. Jason is waiting for you on the quay. He won't mistake you."

Walking down the gangplank, Sarah was aware that almost every eye on the quay had turned in her direction, and she blushed in confusion, and looked about her self-consciously, searching for a white face. Somewhere was this Jason de Cordova; but where?

As she stepped on to the hard surface of the quay, she felt some of the nervousness leave her. The sound of the steel band, playing its own welcome to the steamer, reassured her somehow. Already she could feel a kind of magnetism about the place; the pull of the islands. This was where she had wanted to live and now she had her wish. The passing thoughts of hurricanes and storms, lack of civilisation and ritual magic, all swelled her determination to stay here and make a success of her work. Later, maybe, she would return to the convent and take her vows, confident in the knowledge of having lived life to the full and found the life of seclusion more worthwhile.

Suddenly she felt a hard hand grip her arm, and a deep, attractive male voice said: "You surely can't be Miss Sarah Winter?"

Sarah swung round to face the speaker, her cheeks flushed, her breath catching in her throat when she saw his face, and the livid scar which disfigured his cheek. She saw his eyes, strange yellowish, tawny eyes, like the eyes of the tiger, harden as they recognised her sudden withdrawal, and she immediately felt a sense of contrition that even for one moment he had thought she was repelled by it. Instead, as she took in the other details of his appearance she realised that the scar did not detract from his powerful, attractive features, but rather added to them. He was tall, with broad shoulders and a lean hard body. She realized he was most probably a Spaniard, his hair, thick and black, lying close to his head. He was simply dressed in cotton trousers and a light blue shirt. Who could he be? Not her employer, that was certain! He must be someone Jason de Cordova had sent to collect her. Her eyes returned to the scar, and then she looked swiftly away.

"Yes," she said clearly, "I'm Sarah Winter."

Jason stared at her incredulously, and then he moved his shoulders helplessly. She was nothing at all like the woman he had expected. She was young, much too young, and how could she possibly be expected to handle those three wild things that were his nephew and nieces?

As he stared at her, Sarah felt half amused suddenly. Brought up as she had been, supremely conscious of the presence of both heaven and hell, she thought that this man must surely as closely resemble her imaginings of the devil himself as was humanly possible. She wondered what Sister Theresa would have made of him. She thought the gentle nuns might have found him even more overpowering than she did herself.

"Well," he said at last, "you're certainly much younger than we expected. As I recall it, your age was not questioned. The fact that you'd had experience with young children pointed to your being older."

"Does it matter?" asked Sarah, beginning to feel uncomfortable under his close scrutiny. "I am experienced, and if you've come to meet me, I suggest we go on up to the Cordova residence and ascertain their views on the matter."

Her voice was cool now and detached, and Jason admired her veneer of assurance. For that was all it was, he was certain. He could tell from her revealing eyes that she was far from relaxed. And she did not realise to whom she was speaking, that was obvious.

"Very well," he agreed easily. "Let's go!" It amused him to keep her in ignorance of his identity for the time being. She would learn soon enough.

16

The market was a mass of moving humanity, and Jason went ahead, forging a way through to the Land Rover. The laughing greetings of the West Indians were acknowledged casually, and Sarah wondered who he could be to be known so well, and to arouse such apparent respect among these people.

He helped her into the seat beside the driving seat, and then walked lithely round the vehicle to slide in beside her. Sarah found herself admiring the rippling muscles of his back and thighs as he walked, and the smoothness of his long legs as he slid in beside her. There was something wholly masculine about him that she had never encountered before in her associations with men. It embarrassed her to think this way. For so long she had considered herself immune from the desires of the flesh.

Forcing her thoughts into more innocent channels, she began to look about her with interest as the Land Rover drove up the curving main street of the town. There were shops, but few shop windows, and the goods for sale were displayed outside the stores. Indians sat in the shop doorways, smoking and drinking, and showing little concern for their progress. The flamboyant colours of material hung outside one store caught Sarah's eye, and she said impulsively: "I should have brought my sewing machine. I can see I must make myself some dresses from these gorgeous materials."

Jason looked at her briefly, and then said: "I imagine the seamstress who sews for my wife could run you up anything you required."

Sarah shook her head. "I wouldn't dream of it. Does she have a machine?"

"I'm afraid not. The Indian women prefer to do everything by hand. They produce works of art, believe me!"

"Oh, I do." Sarah shrugged. "I suppose I'll have to do likewise, I like sewing."

Jason smiled a little. "You may find your time a little limited. You haven't met your charges yet."

"That doesn't worry me. I've been used to handling a class of almost forty children, so three on their own shouldn't provide much difficulty."

Jason refrained from commenting. Already he was thinking that at the end of this trial period of one month, he would have to start all over again in finding a governess.

They were driving now between the high walls of the villas of the white families, and between the wrought iron gateways, Sarah could see the paved courtyards and fountains, the swimming pools and tennis courts, so removed from the squalid little huts down in the town. The swarming children there had ap-

17

palled her. However could they all be taught?

"So," said Jason suddenly, "what do you think?"

"About the island?" Sarah gave an involuntary gesture. "I can hardly take it all in. It's very beautiful, but the poverty disturbs me. I think if I lived here I would try to do something for these people. Ignorance is a great breeder."

Jason nodded his assent, surprised at her remarks. He had not thought she would be any different from the rest of the white population. Particularly the women; they, for the most part, acted as though they knew nothing about the squalor beneath their windows.

"You're right, of course," he said now. "But they don't welcome help. They're too used to this kind of life. You may be surprised to learn that they've very happy, in their way. And very contented, a word that's gone out of use in so-called civilised countries."

Sarah frowned. "Are you content?"

"Me?" Jason laughed, amused at her candour. "I suppose you would think I ought to be."

"Why not? In such idyllic surroundings? After all, the sun can ease a lot of heartache."

"Are you a philosopher, Miss Winter?"

Sarah laughed now, and looked at him in sudden liking. "You might say that. But I'm afraid I've always been told that talking is not acting, and I do an awful lot of talking."

As the Land Rover curved round a promontory, Sarah gasped at the precarious angle of the road, and looked down breathlessly on the harbour below them, the steamer much smaller now from this height. "My luggage!" she gasped suddenly, "I forgot all about it!"

"Abe, the harbourmaster, will have it sent up to you," said Jason easily. "There were no other passengers on the *Celeste*, so there'll be no cause for concern."

"Thank you." Sarah lay back in her seat, and in doing so looked upwards, her eyes caught by the sight of the ruined walls of a house, just visible on a high, jutting headland above them. "What's that place? That ruin?"

Jason did not look up but kept his eyes on the curving road ahead. "That was the old Cordova house," he replied quietly. "It was burned out about fifteen years ago."

"Really!" Sarah was intrigued. "That must have been some spectacle, high above the island like that."

"It was." Jason's fingers tightened on the wheel, and Sarah, glancing at him, wondered why his expression had darkened in that way. Surely it was no concern of his.

The road was curving down again now, and the sea was getting nearer. They ran down a final incline and turned between wrought iron gates, which were the entrance to the drive of the Cordova house. Sarah saw a cream, colour-washed house, over-hung with pink bougainvillea, with balconies to all the upper windows, the doors of which stood open to the clean air. Storm shutters were bolted back and a stout pair of doors with wrought iron hinges guarded the entrance. A porticoed walk stretched round the building, and its white pillars gave a Grecian touch to an otherwise Moorish-styled dwelling.

Jason stopped the Land Rover at the foot of the steps leading up to the entrance, and without waiting for any assistance Sarah clamberd out. After the drive up the dusty road, she felt travel-stained and sticky, and she wished she might have a wash and brush-up before meeting her prospective employer. The blue poplin dress which had been so crisp and fresh on the ship was now limp, and clung to her body, outlining the curves of her rounded figure. She was a tall girl, but had always been taught that any self-adulation was wrong, so consequently had no idea how attractively moulded she was. But Jason was aware of it, and knew without a doubt that Irena would find her completely unsuitable. But in this, Irena's views were immaterial. The girl was to teach Sarah's children, and if Serena liked her, and the girl herself wanted to stay, she should stay.

As Jason walked round to join her, the front doors opened and three children appeared at the top of the steps. They were all dark-haired and olive-skinned, the two girls wearing their long hair in plaits, and they were all dressed alike in red and white striped shorts and red tee-shirts. They looked remarkably clean and smart, and Jason half-smiled as he studied Sarah's reactions.

"Make the most of it," he said, dryly. "You'll rarely see them in this condition. I left orders that they should be here to meet you on my return — that's the explanation."

Sarah moved her shoulders deprecatingly. "I hope in future you'll often see them tidily turned out," she remarked. "Am I to understand that they usually run wild?"

Jason grimaced. "You might say that," he agreed smoothly. "Shall I introduce you?"

The children descended the steps slowly, eyeing Sarah cautiously. They had never had a governess before, but they knew children who did, and they were unimpressed.

The youngest, Maria, lost her composure and flung herself exuberantly at Jason, chattering furiously in Spanish, and Jason said: "No, Maria, speak English. This lady has come to

19

improve your English among other things, and I want you always to speak English in her presence, right?"

Maria made a face at Sarah, and Sarah gave Jason a startled glance. But he shook his head slightly and stood Maria on her feet. She guessed he meant that she should take it slowly with them, and with a sigh, she turned to the others. "Now," she said, taking their hands, "you are Eloise and Ricardo."

The children were silent, turning mutinous faces to Jason, and Sarah felt the first trepidation about these children. She did not know what she had expected, but used as she was to being liked instinctively by young people, she was unprepared for this antagonism. Particularly as they did not even know her yet!

They quickly released themselves from her hands and as Maria had done, flung themselves upon her companion. Watching them, she wondered again who he could be. He certainly did not act like a paid employee, and yet he dressed like one of the Africans. It was all most disturbing, and she was curious to have it explained to her.

"Come," said Jason, at last. "It's time we were going into the house. It will soon be lunch time and Miss Winter needs time to shower and freshen herself."

The children looked up at him. "Can we go now?" asked Ricardo.

"No. You may go to your rooms until lunch is ready."

The children stared at him, and Eloise began to talk in Spanish again, and although Sarah could not understand all she was saying it was obvious it was something very rude, and Jason looked angry. He resorted to Spanish at last, and told them they were spoiled and unpleasant sometimes, and they must learn to do as they were told.

Sarah understood a little Spanish, and could speak it in like manner, but she did not expect to be able to talk with the children, for they spoke too fast and in this mood would not alter their speech to assist her. She foresaw quite a battle in the next few days.

As they mounted the steps to the house, Jason said: "Would you prefer to have a shower before meeting the children's mother?"

Grateful for his understanding, Sarah nodded. "May I?" she asked eagerly. "I do feel hot and sticky now."

Jason nodded his head, and led the way into the house, into the wide marble hall which Sarah admired silently. The outside of the house had been beautiful, but this was very impressive. The wrought iron rail of the staircase wound into the upper

20

regions of the house, and the scent of flowers was everywhere. There were great vases and bowls of them placed on every available table and in every corner the gentle perfume of roses mingling with the more exotic fragrance of oleander and hibiscus. The colours, too, were startling against the mosaic of the floor and the light panelling of the walls.

Sarah's curiosity about her companion was heightened when a Negro manservant appeared through an archway behind the staircase and said: "May I show the young lady to her room, *señor*? And the *señora* is waiting to see you."

Jason's face darkened for a moment, and as he looked at Sarah, his fingers sought the line of the scar on his cheek. Then, as if becoming conscious of his action, he drew his hand away, and bowing politely, he said: "Allow me to introduce myself, *señorita*. I'm Jason de Cordova."

Sarah's face suffused with colour. She was astounded. This man then was her employer, the man who had contacted Reverend Mother; the man she had thought to be merely an employee!

A cool, amused voice broke into her reverie, and she looked up in surprise. A small but startlingly beautiful figure had walked through another archway which led to the apartments to the right of the huge hall. She was dressed in an elegant silk dress of various shades of purple which suited her dark colouring to perfection; her small dainty feet were encased in very high-heeled sandals and on her fingers and wrists and round her throat sparkled a veritable fortune in diamonds.

"My dear," said the voice, tinklingly but icily, "I can see from your expression that you thought my husband was one of his own employees!" Sarah blushed anew in confusion and embarrassment, and the woman went on: "It's quite understandable, of course. He dresses like a peasant because he is a peasant, aren't you, *querido*?"

CHAPTER TWO

SARAH did not dare to look at Jason. She had never felt so *de trop* in all her life, and she would never have believed that such hate and passion could be conveyed in one simple sentence. The woman was obviously waiting to see what reaction her remark had had, and Sarah sought about wildly in her mind for a reply. But what was there to say?

To her relief, Jason himself spoke, but not to his wife. "Romulus, take Miss Winter to her room, please. And have Constancia go to her in half an hour to bring her down to meet Señora de Cordova. Señora *Serena* de Cordova."

"Yes, *señor*." They had spoken in English and Sarah moved swiftly to follow the manservant up the stairs. She had not been introduced to the woman down there in the hall, but just now she had no desire to be so. There was a bewildered feeling in her heart and stomach, and she needed time to digest the events of the last few minutes. It had been startling enough to discover Jason de Cordova's identity, without the advent of his wife and her revelations. The children had silently disappeared at the sound of Señora de Cordova's voice, and Sarah thought she did not blame them. In truth that was what she had wanted to do. How could any woman speak to her husband like that? And in front of a stranger? It was inhuman.

Romulus looked rather compassionately at her as he led her into her room which was along the left hand passage at the top of the flight of stairs. The passage was lined with portraits of earlier members of the Cordova family, but Sarah had taken little notice of them. She was too absorbed with her thoughts, and with the feeling of apprehension which had descended on her.

After Romulus had taken his departure, she looked round her room with pleasure. Unlike the rather austere quarters she had occupied at the convent, this room was positively luxurious, with a thickly waxed floor strewn with woollen rugs which she suspected had been hand-made here on the island. The rugs were in vivid colours which complemented the light Swedish furniture and the orange and yellow curtains The adjoining bathroom which Romulus had told her was for her personal use was just as luxurious, with a deep step-in bath and shower attachment, and taps of beaten gold.

Back in her bedroom she discovered the wide french doors

22

opened on to a balcony which was at the side of the house which overlooked the stretch of lawn behind which a swimming pool glimmered greenly in the sunlight. To the right she could see the sea, blue and transparent, the line of the reef vaguely visible from this distance. Nearer, the breakers surfed in to the shore and disappeared on sands as white as Sarah's silvery hair.

She spun round, hugging herself again, unable to prevent the surge of freedom she suddenly experienced. Whatever problems she might have to cope with here, she felt sure she had done the right thing in coming. Until this moment, she realised, she had never known what it was like to be really free, free to eat when she liked and sleep when she liked and act as she liked. For although she was employed as a governess they did not own her spirit as the sisters at the convent had seemed to do, and there was no one to whom she felt she owed her existence. She would support herself, and be independent!

With great daring she stripped off her clothes and stood for a moment studying her reflection in the long wardrobe mirror. Until now, she had never considered herself attractive to men, but suddenly she realised that she was twenty-two and a woman, and that there was more to life than she had ever dreamed.

Smiling at her thoughts, she wrapped the massive orange bath-towel sarong-wise round her body, and marched into the bathroom to take a shower.

Constancia was a pleasant-faced pretty girl of obviously mixed parentage. Although she was more Spanish than African in features, her hair was as tightly curled as Romulus's, and she had a rather squat nose, but Sarah took an immediate liking to her.

Sarah had bathed and was dressed now in a loose shift of a honey-beige colour which she had made herself, and she had combed out her long hair and rewound it in the coronet of plaits. She wore only a coral lipstick for make-up and looked young and fresh and ready for anything.

"*La señorita es muy hermosa*," said Constancia admiringly, and Sarah, understanding this simple phrase, replied:

"Thank you. I feel rather nervous."

Constancia smiled. "You speak Spanish?" she asked haltingly.

"Only very little," admitted Sarah. "Do you understand English?"

Constancia's teeth were very white as she laughed. "*Si*, I understand English. But I do not speak well."

"I think you do very well," remarked Sarah, and then glancing

23

round the room to see that everywhere was tidy, she said: "I only brought a change of clothes in my bag with me. When will my suitcases arrive from the ship?"

Constancia spread wide her hands. "Eh, eh," she said, rolling her eyes. "That lazy pig, Abraham Smith, will send them when he gets round to it. Do not worry, *señorita.* If they have not arrived by ... lunch ... they will be sent for. The *señor* will not forget."

"Thank you," Sarah smiled. "Shall we go?"

She followed Constancia out of the room and along the corridor to the head of the stairs. As they went down, Sarah was relieved to see that the hall below was empty. She did not desire another encounter with her employer's wife for the moment. It was nearing lunch time and she wondered what the arrangements for meals would be. If there was to be a schoolroom perhaps she and the children would eat there. She expected she would be shown their rooms later.

She began wondering what the children's mother would be like. She hoped she would be far different from her employer's wife. That aspect of the situation had not occurred to her either, and it seemed that her only thoughts had been of whether she would like it here and not whether they would like her.

They passed along a marble-tiled corridor at the foot of the stairs leading to the opposite side of the house from that which the Señora de Cordova seemed to inhabit, and Sarah breathed a sigh of relief and began taking a more concentrated interest in her surroundings. There were several statuettes of saints which they passed, and a magnificent portrait of the Virgin and Child which caught her interest. That this was a Catholic household she was left in no doubt, and she wondered whether they were expecting her to be a Catholic and whether it would present any problems. Deciding not to worry about something which had not as yet happened, she stiffened her shoulders, and prayed that Serena de Cordova was a pleasant Spanish female of middle years, with no pretensions to intrigue whatsoever.

At the far end of the corridor, when Sarah was beginning to wonder how much farther they were going, Constancia stopped before a white door, and tapped gently.

"*Si*," called a voice, and Constancia smiled encouragingly at Sarah.

She pushed open the door, and said: *La Señorita Winter, señora,*" and ushered Sarah into the room.

As the door closed behind her, Sarah found herself in a spacious lounge, overlooking the terrace at the front of the house,

24

and beyond to the fruit trees visible in the gardens. The ceiling was high and arched, and the plain cream walls were a background for the scarlet leather armchairs and ebony furniture. The french doors stood open admitting a cool breeze, and Sarah for a moment was so absorbed in her surroundings that she did not take a great deal of notice of the woman on the low couch.

And then, transfixed, her eyes met those of Serena de Cordova, and she hardly suppressed the gasp of pure astonishment that almost escaped her. Serena de Cordova was of mixed blood, a very beautiful woman, but the complete antithesis of any of Sarah's speculations. It seemed to Sarah that for a brief instant time stood still as she stared at the mother of the three children she had met earlier, and then gathering her composure, she said:

"You must forgive me. But nobody prepared me for this!"

Serena rose to her feet. She was almost as tall as Sarah and was dressed in a green satin pyjama suit, a long cigarette holder with a cigarette smouldering at its tip between her fingers.

She studied Sarah for a moment in silence, and then she said:

"Well, at least you're honest. Didn't Jason explain?"

"He — well —" Sarah ran a tongue over her dry lips. "To be honest, I mistook him for somebody else. We didn't speak of you or the children on the trip up from the harbour."

Serena indicated an armchair and said: "Sit down, please." She drew on her cigarette. "You found Jason quite unconventional, I gather."

Her English was almost faultless and Sarah wondered how she had come to have such a good education if she had been born here on the island.

"Yes, I suppose I did."

Serena smiled. "Don't concern yourself. Jason can be as correct as any Englishman if the situation demands it. Now, tell me about yourself. Have you had much experience with young children? I should warn you, my children are quite uncontrollable by anyone except Jason, and he doesn't have the time to spend with them."

"I've already encountered the children," said Sarah, relaxing under the other woman's casual manner. "They seemed to resent my coming here. Have they had previous governesses?"

"No. You're the first. Eloise, as you'll have been informed, is eight now, and can't read or write. She's quite sharp at picking things up orally, but the written word means nothing to her."

"Have you tried to teach the children yourself?"

25

"Me?" Serena sounded flabbergasted. "Good lord, no! I'm no schoolmistresss!"

Sarah wanted to ask her what she did with herself all day, but it would have sounded impertinent. And yet, coming from a household where every member was supplied with tasks to be performed every day, Serena's life sounded quite empty and pointless. "I see," she said.

Serena lounged back on to the couch and picked herself a handful of grapes from a nearby fruit bowl.

"Jason has been spending a little time with them," she said, munching the grapes speculatively. "But they're getting too old to be left to run free all day long. Not that there's much else for them to do here."

"Were you born on the island, *señora*?" asked Sarah tentatively.

"Here? Me?" Serena laughed. "No, I come from Trinidad. My parents own an hotel there. That's how I met Antonio – he stayed at the hotel. He left the island, too, you know. Sold out to Jason years ago and went to Port of Spain to make his fortune. Needless to say he didn't succeed, and when we got married we came back here so that Antonio could work for Jason."

Sarah swallowed hard. In two minutes Serena had told her quite a lot about herself and explained her different attitudes.

"I would have liked to go back to Trinidad," went on Serena, sighing a little, "but my parents haven't room for me and three kids as well, and besides, how would I support them?"

Sarah nodded. Serena's dilemma was quite understandable. Besides, if Jason was fond of the children, it seemed unlikely that he would allow this girl to take them to another island where he would not be able to supervise their upbringing. They were his brother's children, and from what she had gathered from the solicitors in London, he was their guardian as well.

Looking at the other woman, she realised that she must be at least twenty-five, but she looked little more than a teenager. She was very slim and boyish in appearance, and her curly hair had been allowed to grow and was a mass of ebony confusion about her small face. She was elegant but unsophisticated; a mother yet a child still.

"And what do you suggest the arrangements should be?" asked Sarah, reverting to less personal matters. "When will I have charge of the children? Where will we take our meals?"

Serena drew on her cigarette and watched a smoke ring disappear in the air above her head. "Now, let me see," she said slowly. "The children and yourself, of course, will eat lunch with me here, in the adjoining dining room. They always eat

26

lunch with me, so I see no reason to change that state of affairs, do you?"

"No, *señora*," Sarah agreed.

"Good. As to the other, I think you'd better wait and let Jason give you your instructions. You're his employee, not mine. Although," her eyes grew a little taunting, "I have the say-so as to whether you stay or go."

Sarah flushed, and at once Serena leaned forward and touched her hand, like a child asking for forgiveness when it knows it has done something wrong. "Of course you'll stay," she said, leaning back against the red upholstery. "I like you. You're my own age. It will be nice to have someone other than that bitch Irena in the house. Have you met dear Irena?"

Sarah's colour deepened. "That is Señor de Cordova's wife?"

"Yes."

"I . . . er . . . we met as I arrived."

Serena grimaced. "Old cow!" she muttered, stubbing out her cigarette and leaning forward to take another from the ebony box on the table.

Sarah clasped her fingers together. She did not want to become involved in a discussion about her employer's wife. Their personal affairs were nothing to do with her. Her only concern was the children.

She was relieved when a shadow appeared in the French doorway, and they looked up to see a small, attractive Spanish girl standing there. She was dressed in a flame-coloured swirling skirt and a peasant-type off-the-shoulder blouse of white chiffon. Her dark hair was short and straight and shaped her head like a cap of black velvet.

"Serena," she said, smiling vividly, "darling how are you?"

She came forward and smoothly kissed the other girl's cheek before turning to Sarah and giving her the benefit of her gleaming smile, which Sarah privately thought was rather too effusive.

"You must be the Señorita Winter!" she exclaimed. "But you are so young! Whatever has Jason been thinking of, Serena?"

Sarah hated to be treated as though she were a child, and that was exactly the impression which this girl was creating, so she rose stiffly to her feet and said: "The *señor* seemed quite prepared to give me a trial."

The girl's laugh trilled merrily. "My dear, don't be so quick to take offence."

"This is Señorita Dolores Diaz," said Serena, intervening. "Her father and Jason are partners in the distillery. Dolores is a good friend of mine."

Sarah shook hands with the other girl, but felt strangely intuitive that this Spanish girl's assumed friendship with Serena was merely a ruse to gain access to this house. But why? Shrugging these thoughts away, Sarah allowed herself to be wafted into a seat again, while Serena rang a bell and summoned the African housemaid who appeared to bring them pre-lunch aperitifs.

Sarah, who did not smoke, watched the other two girls light cigarettes, and seated together begin to discuss the coming fiesta which was to take place on the island.

"There is even to be a bullfight this year," said Dolores proudly. "Have you ever seen a bullfight, Miss Winter?"

Sarah shook her head. "I'm afraid not. Have you?"

Dolores clasped her hands excitedly. "But of course. I have visited Spain, you understand, and in the great bullring in Madrid I saw El Cordobes."

Recognising the name of the famous young bullfighter, Sarah nodded her understanding. "I don't think I would like to see a bullfight," she said quietly. "I'm afraid I'm very English. I don't like blood sports."

"And yet you hunt the fox until it is caught and torn to pieces by the hounds," exclaimed Dolores, at once.

"Not me," said Sarah, with a half-smile. "And we do have societies that try to prevent that sort of thing."

"Pah!" Dolores said something in Spanish which Sarah felt sure was not very pleasant, and Serena, seeing the flashing eyes of her Spanish friend, said soothingly: "What does it matter, anyway? The subject bores me. Tell me, Dolores, are your family having guests for the fiesta?"

After a while, during which Sarah had been sitting quietly sipping her aperitif, Dolores again turned her attention to her. It seemed that the Spanish girl resented her for some reason, and Sarah hoped she was not going to have to do battle with Dolores Diaz every day.

"You are very young to have undertaken a post so far away from your home," she said sharply. "Do not your parents object?"

"I have no parents. I was brought up in a convent, by the nuns."

"I see." Dolores studied her insolently. "But even so, were these sisters of the faith not concerned that you should journey so far to live with people of whom you know nothing?"

"I had contact with the solicitors in London, and Reverend Mother herself corresponded with Señor de Cordova. Also,

28

Father Sanchez of the church here was a sponsor. What more could I ask?"

Dolores shrugged her slim shoulders delicately. "I am glad I do not have to work. I should not care to be tied to some job all day."

"To become a teacher one must attend a college," said Sarah carefully. "I don't suppose the *señorita* has done this."

After saying these words, she felt penitent. Had all the nuns' work been in vain? Why was she behaving like this? It could only be that this haughty Spaniard had got under her skin, and she could not help but retort. Linking her fingers behind her back, she said placatingly: "But of course your education will have been at a good public school, will it not?"

Dolores, who had been looking extremely annoyed, now looked slightly mollified, but her tones were acid, as she replied: "I had a governess from a very early age, and afterwards, as you said, I did attend a public school. But I think that travel is the greatest teacher. Why, to have history and geography unfolding before your eyes instead of in some story book is wonderful! I doubt whether you can claim, as I can, that you have travelled all over the world. You may have read a lot, *señorita,* and have had a college education, but second-hand knowledge can never be anything else than second-hand!"

Sarah swallowed hard. She would not be baited. She merely smiled, albeit a little tightly, and said: "The *señorita* is right, of course."

Dolores was obviously astounded at Sarah's acquiescence, and also a little disappointed, and as it showed in her face, Sarah again felt she had scored a victory. But again she felt rather ashamed of her feelings, and was glad when the maid returned to say that lunch was served.

"You're staying to lunch, of course," said Serena to Dolores.

"Thank you. I would be delighted," Dolores smiled prettily, and Sarah compressed her lips and followed the other two through the double doors which led into the dining room.

The dining room, although smaller than the huge lounge, was a long room with a polished mahogany dining table set with place mats and shining silver cutlery. Cut glass wine glasses were set at every place, and the sun glinted on the bone china plates and dishes. As they entered the room, the three children appeared from the direction of the garden, through open terrace doors where was glimpsed the sweep of lawn and pool. Their red shirts and shorts were stained with earth and sea water, and their once-tidy hair now looked rough and uncombed. Their faces were smudged and sticky, and they looked defiantly in Sarah's direction as though expecting some horrified reaction from her.

But in this they were disappointed, for it was not Sarah who gasped in disgust, but Dolores. "Serena! Surely these children do not expect to take lunch in that condition!"

Serena gave them a cursory glance, and turning to a tall man-servant who was attending to the food on a serving table, she said: "Max, take these horrors to Constancia. She'll deal with them."

"Oh, but no!" exclaimed Eloise, and lapsing into Spanish she launched into a tirade of anger. "*Tengo hambre!*"

Serena shrugged indifferently. "You should have thought of that before you got yourselves in this state," she replied easily.

Sarah bit her lip. No wonder the children were rebellious if they were left in the charge of servants all the time. Did not Serena have any interest in them at all? It did not sound as though she was greatly concerned.

"I'll take them," she offered. "If you'll tell me where to go."

Serena looked at her askance, and then shrugged. "All right. Max will show you then. Go along, Max. Anna can see to that."

Sarah followed Max and the three children out of the room. They did not welcome her intervention, that much was obvious from the glances which were cast in her direction, and she wondered why they resented her so much. After all, they did not even know her!

Max led the way down the corridor, to where, at a bend, a flight of stairs led upwards. "The bathroom is to your right at the top of the stairs," he said, smiling cheerfully. "The children will show you their rooms themselves."

"Thank you." Sarah viewed the three youngsters with some trepidation, and then urged them forward.

The bathroom had obviously been re-designed for their needs, for it contained three baths and three washbasins and three sets of towels. The floor was of the same mosaic as in Sarah's bathroom, but here there were no shower fitments. Two of the porcelain baths were pink and the third was blue, and Sarah thought it all quite beautiful. She shut the bathroom door and studied the three mutinous faces before her solemnly.

"Now," she said, in a firm voice, "we're going to get something straight. I didn't ask to come here, I was employed by your uncle to teach you not only simple lessons, but some social manners as well, and having met you I can see that I'm going to have quite a job." She looked at them all to make sure they were listening and went on: "If you considered the exhibition you've just made of yourselves down in the dining room would shock me, I should tell you that I've been used to teaching five-year-olds recently, and although Maria comes into that category, you certainly do not." She was addressing Eloise and Ricardo now.

Eloise shrugged. "If you think I acted like a five-year-old, I will have to think of something worse to do."

Sarah sighed. "Then tell me why. You don't know me. Why this stupidity?"

Ricardo turned his back on her and walking over to the wash-basins he began taking off his clothes. Sarah watched him for a moment, wondering whether he was going to prove he was different from the other two, when something warned her he was hardly likely to have been converted so easily. Her suspicions were proved when he stripped off the last of his clothes and stood naked before her. The two girls turned away, giggling helplessly, and Sarah felt a rising sense of frustration.

"Ricardo," she said, shaking her head, "what do you intend to do now?"

"*Nada!*" he replied clearly, and walked to the bathroom door as though intending to walk outside.

"Now wait a minute," exclaimed Sarah hotly. "Put on your clothes, Ricardo. You're not very amusing."

Ricardo shrugged and leaned insolently against the bathroom door.

Sarah looked round to find that the girls were watching her with interested eyes and wondered what her best tactics would be. She was half afraid that the girls would follow his example if she did not think of something soon. To attempt to dress him would be admitting defeat when she knew full well he was quite capable of doing so himself.

"Are you going to get dressed?" she asked brightly.

Ricardo shook his head, and Sarah managed a smile. "Very well. As you seem determined to stay that way, I shan't prevent you. However, nude males, no matter how small, do not take lunch in the dining room."

She filled one of the basins with water from the tap as she was speaking, and seeing them exchange startled glances she squeezed out a soapy face-cloth and carried it across to him. Taking him firmly by the arm, she turned his back to her and applied the face-cloth to his grimy countenance. He resisted vigorously, but Sarah was young and strong, and quite capable of handling him. After he was clean and dry, she threw the face-cloth back into the bowl.

Then, taking him by the arm, she led him out of the bath-room and into the corridor. She did not bother to ask him which was his room. She was sure he would not tell her anyway, and it was easy enough. The heap of boys' toys in one room confirmed her belief, and she pushed him inside firmly. Keeping a tight hold on him she closed the door.

She drew down the coverlet on his bed, and lifting his struggling body she put him between the sheets and drew them up to his chin. Tears were vying with his anger now, as his dark eyes met hers over the bedclothes. But she would not allow him to see that she felt any regret whatsoever, and merely said: "If you decide you're hungry at teatime, I'm sure if you put on some clothes, you might be fed!"

Ricardo grimaced, and said: "I hate you!"

Sarah raised her eyebrows. "I'm not too keen on you either," she retorted, and went out swiftly, closing the door.

Then she opened it again, only a few inches, and put her head round. "Oh, and if you do decide to get up and leave this room before teatime, I've got quite a firm hand with a slipper!"

She closed the door firmly, and leant back against it for a moment. What a beginning! She had hardly been here three hours and already one of the children hated her! Stiffening her shoulders, she walked back to the bathroom. Now for the other two!

Eloise and Maria were standing where she had left them, their faces revealing their mixture of anger and fear as she entered. Sarah sighed. This was not what she wanted. She wanted the children to like her, not fear her. But just now, with Ricardo, force had been the only solution. Was that how Jason de Cordova kept order? By brute force? She doubted it. The children seemed to adore him!

"Well," she said now, "shall we get washed and go down for our lunch? If you're not hungry, I certainly am!"

When they appeared downstairs again, minus one, Serena looked surprised. "But where is Ricardo?" she asked. "Did he not want any dinner?"

"*She* put him to bed," said Eloise, glaring at Sarah. "He's not going to be allowed to have any dinner."

Dolores Diaz looked triumphantly amused, Sarah thought. "Oh, but surely, Miss Winter, you cannot starve the children!"

"In this instance, it was necessary," replied Sarah calmly. "Please carry on with your lunch. Eloise, Maria and I can catch you up."

Maria stared at Sarah blankly. "Aren't you going to tell them what he did?" she asked, in her small, childish treble.

Sarah shook her head. "Eat your lunch."

32

Dolores could not leave it alone. "What did he do?" she persisted.

"Nothing of consequence," replied Sarah. "This scampi is delicious, *señora*."

And with that Dolores had to be content. Sarah was conscious that both Eloise and Maria exchanged glances, and she hoped they considered her action that of a friend and not an antagonist.

When lunch was over, Serena said: "If you would like to look around, please feel free to do so – outside, I mean," she added as an afterthought.

Leaving the two other women, Sarah went out through the French doors, seeking the warm air and the sun on her shoulders. Serena had given the girls permission to leave while they were drinking their coffee, and Sarah had no idea where they were now. Serena had also told her that both she and Dolores indulged in the Spanish habit of *siesta*, and consequently she was free to do as she liked until five o'clock when tea was served for the children and she would be expected to supervise them.

"We take tea, too," Serena had said, "but lunch is the only meal the children take with me. They're naturally in bed before dinner is served, and I always breakfast in my room. It's up to you whether you want to take your first meal of the day with the brats!"

Both she and Dolores had laughed at this, but Sarah thought it rather sad. Although the children were antagonistic towards her, they seemed to regard their mother with a kind of repressed admiration, and it seemed a pity that she took so little notice of them.

Leaving the formal front terrace, Sarah walked round to the rear of the building, coming upon the sweep of lawn she had seen from her bedroom window. She walked past the swimming pool which looked as though no one ever used it, and reached the copse of trees which hid the stables from the house.

She saw the African stable boy, and said: "Hello. I'm Sarah Winter. I've come to teach the children. Tell me, are there any ponies for them?"

The boy smiled his broad smile. "Me, Jacob," he said. "*No comrendo inglés, señorita!*"

Sarah linked her fingers, and in halting Spanish she asked the question again, and this time he smiled firmly and drew her round to the stable doors, over which she could see the three ponies Jason had bought for his nephew and nieces.

"Oh, good!" she exclaimed, clasping her hands. Recently she had learned to ride at a stables near the convent, and perhaps the horses would provide a link between herself and her charges.

She was allowed into the stall and fed the ponies lumps of sugar which Jacob provided for her. She loved the feel of their soft noses nuzzling against her hand, and said so to Jacob, who nodded his approval.

He showed her the two other horses in the stable, and Sarah guessed without being told which was Jason de Cordova's. Like him, Apollo was dark and powerful and handsome, for although Jason's cheek was disfigured by that stark scar, he was nevertheless a very attractive man. She was surprised at her thoughts about her employer. Coming up from the harbour, she had thought him an employee, of the Cordova family, like herself. To find he was himself the head of that family, and also a married man, had been disconcerting; and she could not understand her interest, for hitherto men had meant nothing to her other than separate beings with whom she could discuss her interest in Catholicism. At college she had encountered young men of her own age, but had refused all overtures by them to become closer acquainted. She had had no inclination to delve into any association with a member of the opposite sex.

But Jason de Cordova had been different somehow. She could not understand the strange feeling she experienced when she thought about him, and felt ridiculously aware that in matters of this sort she was very naïve. Altogether, so far, this day had provided her with rather too many surprises to be thoroughly accepted at one go, and she assumed Jason de Cordova had been just another of those surprises. After all, in truth, she had expected an elderly Spaniard, strong in the hauteur and aloofness of generations.

Leaving the stables, Sarah found herself at the top of an incline which led down to the white sand of the beach. The temptation was too great to miss, and with a feeling of anticipation she ran childishly down on to the sands. Releasing her feet from her sandals, she ran impulsively to the water's edge, allowing the creaming water to curl about her ankles. It was incredibly warm, and she curled her toes appreciatively. The air was wonderful, and she felt it was great to be alive. This was worth anything she might have to face here – this feeling of complete independence!

When she returned to the house, carrying her sandals in her hand, her face flushed from the sun, she entered the house by the rear terrace, where the glass doors opened into the corridor that led through to the front hall. Hoping she would not encounter anyone in such an untidy state, she walked swiftly through to the staircase, and was about to climb it when a voice which she recognised immediately said: "Señorita Winter, I would like a word with you."

Swallowing hard, Sarah turned to face her employer's wife, Irena. "Yes, *señora*," she said politely.

"Come in here." The woman indicated a small ante-room which opened from the hall.

Sarah hesitated for only a moment, before preceding the woman into the room. She felt nervous and apprehensive, and hoped this would not be a long interview. She took in little of her surroundings. She was too concerned with the woman before her.

Now Señora de Cordova was wearing a long, quilted satin housecoat in a deep shade of green, which gave her olive complexion rather a sallow appearance, but she was still startlingly lovely, and Sarah wondered why she treated her husband as she did. There was something faintly repulsive about the fanatical gleam in her eyes, and Sarah hoped there was not going to be a scene. She could feel herself growing hotter as the *señora*'s eyes raked her appraisingly, taking in every detail of her crumpled dress, windswept hair and bare feet. Sarah felt enormous beside the delicate fragility of the Spanish woman, who could not have been more than five feet in height even in her high heels.

"Now," said Irena, her eyes cold, "just where have you been?"

Sarah twisted the strap of the sandal in her hand. "On the beach, *señora*."

"I thought as much. And who gave you permission to go on the beach?"

"The Señora Serena told me I might explore. I decided of my own accord to go down to the beach." Sarah's voice was cool and clear.

"Oh, you did! Well, the beach is private. It's not to be used by so-called governesses!" Her gaze swept Sarah contemptuously. "And while you're in this house, you will refrain from going around looking like a gipsy."

Sarah compressed her lips. She did not know what to say in reply. Her position here as yet was so nebulous, she did not feel entitled to retaliate.

"Is that all, *señora*?" she asked politely, longing to escape from the confines of the room, and the aura of cold hauteur which surrounded this woman, along with something else, something more sinister. Irena was quite a frightening person, and to a girl who had rarely come into contact with frigidity, she

35

was doubly so. And yet Sarah did not feel scared so much as repelled.

"Yes, that is all, for now." Irena stood aside to allow Sarah to leave the room. "But remember what I have said, *señorita*."

"Yes, *señora*," said Sarah, with relief, and escaped before she could say anything else.

She crossed the hall and mounted the stairs as though the devil himself were at her heels, and once she had reached the sanctity of her room she sank down on to the bed, her legs giving way beneath her. What a day!

Lying back, she stared at the ceiling. She suddenly felt incredibly tired and unwillingly her lids drooped.

When she opened her eyes the room was dark and for a moment she thought she was back in her small room at the convent. Then the sweet scents from the garden, coming through the open windows, reminded her of her situation, and she sat up with a start, reaching for the switch of the bedside lamp.

A glance at her watch confirmed her worst fears. It was almost nine o'clock. She scrambled off the bed, smoothed her creased dress, and noticed irrelevantly that her cases had arrived from the *Celeste* and had been carefully unpacked for her and the clothes put away. They must have been dealt with during her walk that afternoon, but she had not noticed them earlier.

She was about to open the door and make her way downstairs in an attempt to discover what was going on, when Constancia herself opened the door and smiled her pleasant smile.

"Ah, the *señorita* is awake! You are hungry, yes? I will bring you a tray. What would you like? There is chicken, or salmon, or shellfish. You tell me what you would like and I will fetch it –"

Sarah lifted her shoulders helplessly. "But, Constancia, I've been asleep for over four hours. I was supposed to supervise the children's tea at five o'clock. Whatever will Señora Serena think of me?"

Constancia moved her hands in a soothing gesture. "Max supervised the children's tea, as he had done for many months now. And the *señor* said you were not to be disturbed."

"The *señor*? Oh!" Sarah pressed the palms of her hands to her hot cheeks. "Did the *señor* expect to see me?"

Constancia nodded, and then as Sarah began looking agitated, she said in reply: "At six o'clock, before dinner, he asked me to come and fetch you. When I found you were asleep I told the *señor*, and he gave his instructions. It is natural that you were tired. You have had a long journey and the weather here can be tiring if you are not used to it."

"Did the *señor* say that?"

"*Sí.* Do not worry, *señorita.* The *señor* is not a slave-driver."

Sarah smiled and allowed her arms to fall to her sides. "Do you think he'll want to see me now?"

"No, of course not, *señorita.* Besides, he is not at home. He left after dinner to visit with the Diaz family. He took the Señorita Dolores home."

"I see." Sarah felt that strange feeling stirring in her stomach again. She did not know what it was, but it was not pleasant; it was disturbing.

"He told me to tell you that he would see you in his study tomorrow morning at nine o'clock sharp." Constancia smiled wider. "You will not sleep in tomorrow, *señorita.* I will see that you have plenty of time to prepare yourself."

Sarah had to smile in return "And will you show me where his study is, Constancia? I have no idea where to go. And what time do the children have breakfast?"

Constancia shrugged. "Sometimes seven, sometimes eight – why? Surely you do not intend to breakfast with them? Everyone breakfasts in their rooms, except the *señor,* of course."

"That's exactly what I do intend," said Sarah firmly. "After all, I'm not a guest, Constancia. I'm here to work." She bent her head. "But will you please call me about six-thirty, please, as I doubt whether I shall wake of my own accord."

"Certainly," Constancia nodded. "That is the time I begin my work. I will call you then." She turned to go. "And now you will leave it to me and I will provide you with a delicious supper, *si*?"

"Very well." Sarah allowed herself to relax, and with a flourish of her full skirt, Constancia left to get the meal.

Sarah wandered over to her balcony and leaned against the rail listening to the steady lap of the waves. It was a wonderful night. The sky overhead was an arch of dark blue velvet inset with diamonds, while a sickle of a moon floated behind wispy clouds. Never in England had she felt this aching longing to be out in the night, doing something exciting. Faintly, she could hear the sounds of music and voices, far away, and she thought it must be a party going on at one of the other villas. The music was the throbbing beat of the calypso, and Sarah felt she wanted to move in time to its compelling rhythm.

She thought about Dolores Diaz, and wondered whether it was from her home the sounds were coming. Was she there, dancing with Jason de Cordova? Was that why she was so friendly with Serena, to gain access to this house to see the *señora*? It did not seem unreasonable. The *señor* and his wife did not seem on the best of terms with one another. Could it be that he was seeking consolation with another woman? The thought was repulsive. She had liked Jason de Cordova, and she did not like to think of him with Dolores Diaz.

Constancia returned to interrupt her reverie and she was glad. Whatver was going on in the personal lives of the occupants of this house was none of her business, and the sooner she realised it the better.

CHAPTER THREE

SARAH dressed the next morning in a lemon cotton dress and the slip-on sandals of the day before. Her hair as usual was bound round her head in the plaited coronet. She wore no make-up, but her time spent in the sun the previous day had not gone unwasted, and her skin was very lightly tanned. She looked much younger than her twenty-two years, although she was unaware of it, and as she went down to breakfast there was a spring in her step.

There was no one around when she reached the dining room, but Max soon appeared and asked her what she would like. She decided on fresh fruit, rolls, and several cups of strong, continental-flavoured coffee.

At about seven-thirty, when she was finishing her third cup of coffee, Ricardo appeared, alone. He had washed and combed his hair, and was wearing blue denim jeans and a white tee-shirt. He looked taken aback when he saw Sarah, and she said, smiling: "Good morning, Ricardo."

Ricardo hesitated for a moment, and then he said: "*Buenos dias, señorita.*" He seated himself opposite her, and when Max appeared he ordered rolls and butter and some fruit juice.

After Max had gone, Sarah poured herself another cup of coffee, and resting her chin on her hands, elbows on the table, she looked across at Ricardo. He looked up at her, and then involuntarily he smiled, and said: "I got dressed at tea time, but you weren't here."

Sarah sighed. "I know. I fell asleep."

"You went on the beach yesterday afternoon," he said. "I saw you from my bedroom window. You went in the water."

"Yes, do you? Can you swim?"

"Yes, I can swim, but we are not allowed to swim in the sea without supervision." Ricardo pulled a face. "We are considered too young to take risks."

Sarah frowned. "And the pool? Do you use that?"

Ricardo bent his head. "We are not allowed to use the pool. The Señora Irena can see it from her windows and she doesn't like to see us there."

"Indeed!" Sarah felt indignant. What was the use of a pool if no one was allowed to swim in it? "And why do you call her the Señora Irena?" she was puzzled. "She is your aunt. isn't she?"

"Yes, she is our aunt." Ricardo said nothing further, for at that moment the two girls came bounding into the room, stopping abruptly at the sight of Sarah.

"Good morning, girls," said Sarah, but the two girls did not answer. They merely gave Ricardo a killing glance and seated themselves at the table.

Sarah bit her lip. "I said good morning," she remarked easily. "I would like to hear your answers."

Eloise looked indifferent, and Maria, who seemed to follow her elder sister's lead, did likewise.

Sarah sighed, and looked at Ricardo, who shrugged almost imperceptibly, and growled: "Answer her, Elly."

Eloise stared at him. "*Traidor!*" she spat at him angrily.

"Eloise," said Sarah wearily, "please. You will soon be a young lady. Kindly try to act like one."

Eloise looked at her. "Why should we care what *you* think of us?" she cried furiously. "Nobody cares about us, and we care about nobody!"

Sarah felt a kind of compassion. The children were entirely too conscious of their background, and Irena was probably to blame, if yesterday's episode in the ante-room was anything to go by.

"You'll just be another one like *her*," Eloise hissed, at Sarah. "She hates us, you know – really hates us! She spat at us once!"

Sarah was shocked now and showed it, but gathering her scattered wits she managed to say: "To me you are just three children whom I have come to teach. Why, back home in England I taught lots of girls and boys. I can assure you I won't spit at you, so can't we be friends?"

Eloise looked sceptical still, and Sarah turned to Maria. "Maria, can you ride? I can. I thought we might take the horses out after breakfast if your uncle gives his permission. Would you like that?"

Ricardo gave a whoop. "Can we, really?" he exclaimed. "We never get to take the ponies out unless Uncle Jason is with us. Will you really take us?"

"If your uncle has no objections," agreed Sarah thankfully, aware that two of the children at least were weakening towards her. Eloise still looked unsure of herself, but Sarah felt that given time the other two would bring her round.

Thus it was that she was feeling quite a lot more sure of herself as Constancia led the way along the opposite corridor from the hall to Jason de Cordova's study. A glance at her watch showed her it was still two minutes to nine as Constancia knocked at the door, and they heard the *señor*'s voice call: "Come."

Constancia indicated that Sarah should go in, and then walked firmly away down the corridor. Sarah stiffened her shoulders, and pressed down the handle of the door and allowed it to swing inwards.

As she closed the door, she found herself in a book-lined room, panelled in dark wood, with a restfully coloured tawny carpet on the floor and heavy drapes of a beige colour at the long windows. Set square in the centre of the room was a heavy ebony desk with a black leather armchair behind it. In front of the desk were placed a couple of easy chairs, also in black leather; and several filing cabinets and a telephone indicated that this was a room where work was done and not merely a den. The desk was littered with papers, and a typewriter stood on a side table beside a comprehensive array of bottles containing various wines and spirits.

A man was standing by the open French doors, his back to her, and although he was tall and dark, Sarah thought for a moment she had been mistaken in thinking that it was Jason de Cordova. But as he turned to face her, and her eyes were drawn irresistibly to the blatant scar on his cheek, she saw indeed that it was her employer. But this man looked nothing like the Jason of yesterday. He was casually but immaculately dressed in a suit of light fawn silk, and his cream shirt contrasted favourably with the tan of his skin. A dark red tie was slotted about his neck, and he looked thoroughly businesslike this morning. His rather sinister attraction was enhanced by his appearance, and Sarah felt as though she was staring quite helplessly at him. Gone was the friendly stranger of yesterday, and in his place was a man who frightened her a little by his detached manner.

"Ah, Miss Winter," he said, moving to the desk. "Won't you sit down, please?"

Sarah subsided on to an armchair, feeling her earlier fears materialising again. She had thought her success with the children this morning had removed all her tension, but back it came flooding over her at the sight of this man, so cool and aloof.

"I ... er ... I'm sorry I feel asleep last evening," she ventured awkwardly. "I understand you wanted to speak to me."

"This morning is just as convenient," he replied easily. "Have you met the children again?"

Sarah had to smile. "Indeed I have," she said impulsively. "Several times."

"I see. And what do you think? Can you handle them?"

"I'm sure I can," she said, without conceit. "I think they're lonely, that's all."

41

Jason studied her a moment and then said: "Lonely? I should never have believed it. What makes you say that?"

"Lots of things!" She sighed. "Perhaps I'll be able to explain better when I've had more time with them. Eloise is going to be the most difficult, but I'm confident that given time I'll be able to change her."

Jason looked a little amused now. "And you've discovered all these things in twenty-four hours," he said, with some sarcasm.

"Yes." Sarah looked down at her hands and studied the ovals of her finger nails, not wanting to look at his face, too conscious of her own vulnerability. She had never been able to hide her feelings and she did not want to see the mockery in his eyes and feel the nervous tension that it would bring.

As though aware of her feelings, Jason said: "Would you like a cigarette?"

Sarah looked up. It was on the tip of her tongue to explain that she did not smoke, but then she decided against it. Why not, after all? Perhaps a cigarette would rid her of some of this nervousness.

"Thank you," she said, and accepted one from the box he held out to her.

He lit hers and one for himself from a gold table lighter and with some trepidation Sarah drew on the cigarette. It did not make her cough as she had been half afraid it would, but instead the room swam round dizzily. Pressing a startled hand to her throat, she sat up straight, and prayed for the feeling to pass. She had heard from other girls that a first cigarette sometimes caused this kind of reaction, but she had not believed them.

Jason looked at her strangely. "Are you all right?"

The room steadied, and Sarah managed a half-smile. "Of course. What suggestions have you regarding the children's lessons, *señor*?"

Jason seated himself behind his desk, leaning back in his chair looking at her, and with great daring, she thought, she drew again on the cigarette.

"You were not surprised to learn that Serena was not wholly Spanish, then," Jason was saying, as the room swam even more giddily, and Sarah gripped the arm of her chair painfully, feeling the colour receding from her face. Leaning forward, she managed to hit the ashtray on the desk with the cigarette, and then she lay back weakly, fighting for composure. She was aware that Jason had risen from his seat and crossed to the tray of drinks on the side table. He returned with a glass full of amber liquid, and putting it in to her hand, he said quietly:

"Drink this and you'll feel better."

Gratefully, Sarah did as he asked, and immediately she felt the room begin to steady and her head stopped spinning.

"Now," he said, on his haunches beside her, "what's wrong?"

His nearness disconcerted her. There was in his eyes the kind of understanding that was quite overwhelming, and she had the feeling that he was again the man she had met on the quay the previous day. At close quarters the scar was an ugly sight, and as though conscious of her scrutiny, he ran his finger lightly along its length. He rose to his feet, and said: "I'm sorry if this upsets you. I suggest you try to ignore it." His voice was cool again.

Sarah rose too. Even as tall as she was, he was much taller, but she felt at less of a disadvantage standing. "It doesn't upset me," he said, looking at him candidly. "It fascinates me!" Then she flushed as she realised what her impulsive tongue had said now, but was relieved when he did not appear to consider her remark personal.

"So," he said, looking down at her. "You will now tell me what was wrong with you."

Sarah sighed. "I'm not used to smoking. I'm afraid it was the cigarette; it made me dizzy."

Jason smiled. "Was that all?" he asked, amused.

"Yes, why? Did you think you had an ailing governess on your hands?" Sarah laughed, albeit a little nervously.

Jason shook his head. "You look very well to me," he remarked, his eyes surveying her thoroughly, making her acutely conscious of the shortness of her skirt.

Sarah subsided again, clasping her hands together. "Sh – shall we discuss the timetable as we were going to do before I acted so foolishly?"

Jason shrugged, and moved back round the desk. "You tell me what you suggest," he said slowly, "and I'll tell you what I think."

For several minutes they discussed the children. Jason told Sarah that he had had a room cleared on the first floor and three desks installed for the children and one for herself. He had also provided exercise books and textbooks and plenty of paper and pencils.

"If there's anything else you require, you just have to ask," he continued. "At what time of the day do you intend to work? Mornings, I think, would be the most convenient. The afternoons could then be your own until tea time, and of course after the children are in bed in the evenings, you're free to do as you wish."

"Thank you." Sarah bit her lip. "*Señor!* Would it be all right if the children and I rode sometimes?"

Jason frowned. "You ride?" he asked.

"Yes. And I spoke to Jacob yesterday and he told me that the ponies were for the children's use and that there was another horse which I could use. Not yours, of course."

Jason half-smiled. "Why? Do you think you couldn't handle Apollo?"

Sarah shrugged. "I think I could," she retorted impulsively.

"Indeed? Then you must be a very good horsewoman. Apollo is a spirited devil at best. At worst he can act like a creature possessed. I shouldn't care to think of you riding him alone. But perhaps one day I'll find the time to ride with you, and the children, of course, and I may put you to the test."

"Then we may use the horses when we like?"

"You may. Providing you ride on the beach. You can come to little harm there."

Sarah looked taken aback, but she did not demur. Jason studied her in his intensive way for a moment, and then he said: "Before you contracted the vapours, I asked you whether you were not surprised to learn of Serena's nationality," he said slowly.

Sarah flushed. "I was surprised, naturally," she said, making a helpless gesture. "But it doesn't make any difference to me, if that's what you mean."

Jason leaned forward, resting his arms on the desk. "Yes, that's exactly what I meant." He relaxed again and lay back in his chair. "Is there anything else you want to know?"

Sarah bent her head self-consciously. "There is something," she said quietly. "Ricardo tells me the children are not allowed to use the pool – is that right?"

Jason's expression darkened. "That's correct. Why?"

Sarah looked up. "I was going to ask you that question."

"Were you indeed?" He rose to his feet, and moved round the desk restlessly. "Did Ricardo give you any reason?"

"Yes. He said it was because they could be seen from Señora de Cordova's windows."

Jason's expression was unreadable. Sarah was only aware that he was annoyed about something, and she could only assume it was because of her question. "And if I tell you that this is so, what then?" he asked, from behind her chair.

Sarah felt a tingle running up her spine. She wanted to turn round to rid herself of the feeling that he was studying her intensely. But she could not do that. She was forced to sit upright in her chair, and pray for him to return to his side of the desk.

"W... well," she said awkwardly, "all I can say is that it

seems a waste of a beautiful pool. In my experience, beaches are for playing on, and the sea, for children at any rate, is for paddling in. The young children of my acquaintance swim in the swimming baths. At home there are public baths in most towns. Few children have the luxury of a pool in their back garden." She swallowed hard. "These children, your nephew and nieces, seem to have neither. They tell me they may not swim in the sea without being supervised. I can understand this, but they could have such fun in the pool if you would let them . . ." She halted, and bent her head. "Of course, that's only my opinion."

"You've made your point," he conceded, moving across to the open windows. This side of the house faced the beach and the sea, and Sarah followed his gaze out to the waving palms and coral sands beyond the gentle cliffs.

She looked at him as he stared out to sea for a brief moment, wondering what he was thinking. She was sure he must consider her an interfering busybody. After all, that pool must have been there for years, and she really had no right to question its deployment.

But he turned back to face her, leaning against the frame of the window. He looked a little amused now, she thought, and she rose swiftly to her feet. "Is that all, then?" she asked.

Jason shrugged his shoulders. "What about the pool? Do you want to use it? The children as well, of course."

Sarah stared at him, her eyes bright and dancing. "Are you serious? May we?"

"I think you might. After all, what's the use of having a governess if she can't be allowed the facilities provided for every English child?" His tone was a little sardonic, but Sarah could have hugged him. She was so pleased and excited. How delighted the youngsters would be!

"Thank you," she exclaimed, her voice revealing her inner vivacity. She turned to the door, but moving towards it she remembered her interview with Irena the previous day, and a shiver ran down her spine at the thought. There was something utterly menacing about her presence and when she found out about the swimming pool she would not be pleased.

Turning back, she said: "*Señor*, may I ask you something else?"

Jason straightened up. "By all means. What is it?"

Sarah frowned. "Am I allowed to use the beach – I mean, am I allowed to swim in the sea?"

Jason's fingers sought the jagged disfiguration on his cheek. "Why do you ask?" he questioned her softly. "Surely that requires no answer. You may use the beach whenever you wish, naturally."

"I may?" Sarah pressed a hand to her throat. "Thank you, *señor*."

She would have opened the door, but he said: "Wait," and moved across to her side, looking down on her intently, his tawny eyes guarded. "Has Irena – my wife been speaking to you?"

Sarah's hot cheeks provided his answer, and he ran a restless hand round the back of his neck. His nearness was doing strange things to Sarah. She had the strongest desire to get as far away from him as possible. And she knew she ought not to feel this way, just being close to him like this. But she had never experienced feelings of this kind; never been aware of a man, not only as a friend or associate, like the priests who visited the convent, but as a controlled yet primitive being, capable of gentleness and violence, love and hate. She was aware of everything about Jason de Cordova; the width of his shoulders, the lean strength of his hard body, only lightly disguised by the fine material of his suit, the indefinably male smell about him. The desire to touch him grew so overwhelming that with a kind of panic-stricken movement she opened the door, and with a brief: "Good-bye, *señor*!" she found herself thankfully out in the corridor.

She was breathing quickly, as though she had just completed a marathon race, and heaving a sigh of relief she turned and ran swiftly down the corridor to Serena de Cordova's apartments. She half-closed her eyes as she ran, seeking for the composure which had completely deserted her. Oh, God, she thought tremblingly, Father Donahue was so right! How could she possibly consider becoming a novice when even the thought of one man's body turned her bones to water and sent her senses reeling?

The prospect of facing her three charges brought her finally to her senses. She had told them to wait for her in the dining room, and she would join them as quickly as she could. But when she reached the dining room it was deserted, apart from Max who was arranging some flowers on the window seat.

"Max!" exclaimed Sarah, in surprise. "Where are the children?"

Max turned to her shrugging. "They disappeared soon after you went to see the *señor*," he replied, shaking his head. "They very disobedient, yes?"

"Very," said Sarah, sighing heavily. She might have known that left to herself, Eloise would easily persuade the other two that waiting here for a governess was downright stupid!

46

She had been so sure of herself, and now she was back to square one again, or almost. Hunching her shoulders, she sat down on one of the dining chairs and looked wearily at Max, who had resumed his arranging.

"Do you have any idea where they might be?" she asked hopefully. "What do they usually do all day?"

Max spread wide his hands. "Sometimes they go down to the plantation. They got friends down there. Nothing for them to do here."

"Well, I plan to change all that," retorted Sarah, getting to her feet firmly. "Can you show me where to go, and I'll go and find them."

Max looked astounded and shook his head. "Cane fields no place for a white woman," he said heavily. "The *señor* would not like it."

"The *señor* need never know," replied Sarah briskly. Just at this moment she needed to do something to take her mind off other things. "If you don't tell me, I shall go anyway, so you might as well give in."

Max grumbled a bit. "I don't want to take no responsibility for you going down there," he muttered gloomily.

"Look," exclaimed Sarah, "I don't intend to spend the morning kicking my heels round here doing nothing. I assure you, if the *señor* finds out, your name won't be mentioned. I'll take full responsibility. Now, shall we go?"

Max grunted and gave in, and Sarah breathed a sigh of relief. It would be pleasant to get out of the house anyway. It was a wonderful morning, and the trip should prove interesting.

The offices of the Cordova Corporation overlooked the quayside at El Tesoro. The lower floor was used as a storage warehouse, but the upper part of the building had been extensively modernised in recent years and provided a light and airy block for the employees of the Corporation. Most of the families of the white population of Cordova were represented here in some capacity or another, from office typists to Manuel Diaz, who ran this side of the business for Jason.

Manuel's family had come to the island shortly after the first Cordovas settled here three hundred years ago, and Jason and Manuel were second cousins. Most of the Spaniards were related in some way, distant or otherwise, and marriages were still arranged as they had been back in the old country. The women did not demand emancipation, and the rather confined life of the island was almost feudal in its isolation. Even the younger set seemed content to remain in subjugation to their parents' wishes, although their pursuits were more daring than those of their parents and grandparents. Skin-diving and yachting were favourite occupations, and most days during the college vacations there were picnics and parties and barbecues.

Jason, now, mounted the staircase leading to the office floors two stairs at a time. He was making one of his rare visits to Manuel here. Offices were not to Jason's liking; he preferred the unconfined acres of the cane fields, the creaming curve of beach and shoreline, the restless sweep of the surging water, foaming its wake behind his yacht.

Manuel had asked him to call in the various evening when Jason had taken Dolores home. He knew it was something to do with the crop of cane which was at present maturing in the fields. Soon would come the time for harvesting, and the sound of machetes would be heard from dawn to dusk. The tractor-driven wagons would convey the cut cane down to the factory and the process of the manufacture of the raw product into granulated sugar, and the molasses into rum, would begin. Although Cordova was a small island and the production of sugar was small in comparison to the larger islands, the factory was quite a modern one and the methods were not so primitive as they had been in the days when Jason's father had owned the plantation. The rum they produced in such small quantities was considered to be very potent, and Jason was aware that had he had the facilities and space for greater production Cordova rum would be well-known all over the world instead of only in a limited area. But in many ways he was glad he did not have the kind of organisation that required constant attention to detail; he liked the freedom he could enjoy; he loved the island and its surrounding atolls and had he been enmeshed in the demands of a big concern he would not have been able to do as he pleased. As it was, he was his own master. When the sugar cane had all been gathered in there would be fiestas and carnivals, and the colourful pageants common to the West Indies. The people would eat, drink and be merry, and the sound of the ritual drums would reverberate round the hills above the harbour, primitive and intoxicatingly rhythmic.

Smiling at his thoughts, he entered Manuel's office directly, and without ceremony, not consulting the secretary who sat in an outer office ready to advise visitors whether Señor Diaz was free. Manuel Diaz looked up and smiled a greeting, immediately aware of the identity of his visitor by his lack of formality. Only Jason entered his office without first knocking.

Manuel was a man in his early forties, only a few years older than Jason himself, and was a widower with one daughter,

Dolores. The Diaz' lived in a large sprawling hacienda-type dwelling in the hills above El Tesoro, and were considered the leading socialites of the island, if there were such things in such a small community.

Jason himself was quite remote from the social life led by his contemporaries, and the Cordovas rarely accepted the many invitations sent their way. Nor did they entertain; it was many years since Jason had presided at the head of his own table for a dinner party.

Jason's height and bulk seemed to minimise the limited proportions of the office, and Manuel rose to his feet indicating that Jason should be seated at the opposite side of the desk. Jason relaxed into a low leather armchair, and accepted the cool lager that Manuel produced from a wall refrigerator.

"I'm glad you have come in early," said Manuel, reseating himself, a glass of lager in his own hands. "I want to leave early myself; I think today is going to be a good day for *La Joya*."

La Joya was Manuel's yacht, a thirty-foot ketch, of which he thought almost as much as of his daughter. Yachting was Manuel's favourite pastime, when he was not in the office, and Jason smiled now in understanding. He, too, found the sea a demanding mistress.

"Tell me," went on Manuel, "did you have the interview with the new governess this morning? Was she embarrassed at her indiscretion of last evening? Falling asleep on the job on her first day!" He laughed.

Jason shrugged his broad shoulders. "Yes, I interviewed her. She's quite self-possessed. She seems to think she can handle the children. The chances are that within a week she'll be tearing out her hair!" He smiled. "Perhaps that's doing her less than justice. She's young; maybe the children will react to her youth. But Ricardo and Eloise ..." He sighed. "They're very self-willed."

"*Si*, that is true," Manuel nodded. "Dolores tells me they tried to shock your governess at lunch yesterday. They appeared covered in dirt, and waited for her expostulations. It seems she took them to be washed and cleaned up and young Ricardo found himself in bed. Dolores did not think she scored a great success with them. Did she tell you?"

Jason shook his head. "No." He frowned. "But I think if she put young Ricardo to bed she had the right idea."

"You do?" Manuel looked surprised. "But surely a governess should not need to resort to those methods. It seems to me she does not exert much discipline if this is the case."

"Oh, come now, Manuel," exclaimed Jason, without rancour. "You know those children are not like normal children. They've been allowed too much freedom for too long. Naturally, they won't accept discipline lying down. It's going to take a great deal of courage and patience to civilize those rips."

Manuel shrugged. "I suppose you are right. However, I cannot but think that had Antonio still been alive, they would have been more manageable."

"Why? Antonio had little time for them. He was away a lot. And Serena was far too young in the first place ever to have children. She was only seventeen when Eloise was born. What could a seventeen-year-old girl know of babies?" He shook his head. "Antonio was a fool to permit such a thing."

Manuel accepted the cigarette his friend held out to him, and after they were both smoking, he continued: "Antonio was young and foolish, Jason. He was in love." He sighed. "You were in love once, Jason. Have you forgotten?"

Jason's fingers sought the scar. "No, Manuel, I have not forgotten."

Manuel compressed his lips. It was unfortunate he had spoken in that manner. There were too many memories evoked by Jason's youth, memories that were tortuous and displeasing.

Changing the subject, he leaned forward to discuss the cane crop. There were papers which he wanted Jason to sign, and it was easy to ease the tension in the air. He was on safer ground now, here there were no shadows of the past to cause painful remembrance.

But Jason, drinking the lager and listening to Manuel's pleasant voice, could not forget so easily, although it appeared that he had. There were too many things that had left their mark upon him, and the scar was only one of them. He drew his pen out of his pocket to sign Manuel's agreements, and determinedly shook the soul-destroying thoughts from his mind.

When he left the office she drove along the quay and had a few words with Abe Smith. Then he turned the Land Rover in the direction of the plantation, and loosening his tie and the top button of his shirt, he relaxed. Here, away from his house, and Irena, he was at peace with himself, almost content.

At that word he recalled the conversation he had had with Sarah Winter on their way from the harbour. She had thought he ought to be content, but he wondered what she thought now after meeting Irena and being subjected to her malicious tongue.

Thinking of Sarah reminded him that he had yet to tell Irena about the swimming pool. But why shouldn't the children use it, after all? It was ridiculous having a pool and not using it. All the other families who were lucky enough to possess one used theirs, so why not he? But it was going to provide Irena with yet another subject to belabour him whenever they had one of their frequent clashes of words.

The spears of cane moved rhythmically in the breeze as he drove along the rim of the plantation. Soon the long plumes of grey flowers which appeared at the top of the sugar-cane stalk would begin to appear, indicating that the time for cutting had come.

A distant rumble of thunder caused him to glance upwards in surprise. It had not looked like rain earlier when he had been talking to Manuel, and he half-smiled as he recalled his partner's desire to go yachting. He would be hardly likely to go now. With the prospect of a downpour blowing up, Manuel would not risk getting wet.

He glanced at his watch. It was gone eleven o'clock, but if he returned to the house Irena would demand his attention at once, and the problem of the pool would have to be dealt with. With a resigned feeling he decided to forgo that argument for a few minutes at least, and turning the vehicle, he drove down the track between the tall cane stalks. As he drove along, he glanced with an expert eye along the rows of the crop, noting the carefully maintained irrigation channels, and the absence of weeds about the stems.

Almost at the end of the track, he suddenly caught a glimpse of a lemon dress, and the unmistakable sight of a fair-skinned girl running down the length of one of the rows of cane. His foot found the brake and the Land Rover halted abruptly, causing him to swerve slightly. He slid out from behind the wheel and looked back along the track. As he had expected, Sarah appeared from out of the row not far behind him, and stared in astonishment as she recognised him. Her face was flushed from running, and tiny beads of perspiration stood out on her forehead. Her legs were scratched in places and she carried the strapless sandals in her hand.

"*Madre mia!*" he exclaimed, striding towards her. "What's the meaning of this?"

Sarah heaved a sigh, and gave a helpless movement of her shoulders. She looked utterly weary and felt hot and tired and heartily sick of trying to locate the whereabouts of her three charges.

Jason stared down at her, and then, as though becoming conscious of her worn-out condition, he said: "Come; get in the vehicle. Then you can tell me."

51

Sarah trudged to the Land Rover, and climbed in thankfully. Although she had yet to face Jason's anger, anything was better than the sun burning down on her shoulders and neck, and the disturbing rumbles of thunder that had sent her running back to the house before she was caught in the rain. Hot as she was, she was sure she would have felt chilled by the wet, and she did not want to extinguish her chances of success with the children by retiring to her bed the day after her arrival with a severe cold.

Jason slid into the seat beside her, and turning sideways said:

"I imagine you are here because the children brought you. Am I right?"

"Indirectly," said Sarah, running a hand round the back of her neck, feeling strands of hair which had loosened themselves from the plaits during her hasty retreat. "I came looking for them."

"What!" Jason was astounded. "Who let you do such a thing?"

Sarah straightened her shoulders. "Nobody *let* me," she said. "I wanted to find them."

Jason lit a cigarette, his hands providing Sarah with something to watch, instead of the middle distance into which she had been staring. They were hard, brown, strong hands, and she wondered idly what it would feel like to have those hands touch her, caress her . . .

She went unbearably red, and turned away from him in confusion. She must be slightly deranged, she thought in agony. Whatever was happening to her? It was madness!

Jason watched her curiously through the veil of smoke he exhaled from his cigarette. He did not know whether to be angry or sympathetic with her. It must have taken some nerve to come down to the cane fields looking for three children alone, among a crowd of strange West Indians. And yet it was a foolhardy thing to do. There was no shortage of stimulants on the island, and just now, in the calm before the upheaval of the harvesting, many of the black West Indians spent their time in drinking. A white woman might not be safe in their villages, even if she was well known. And Sarah was certainly not that, yet. Resting one arm along the back of her seat, he said: "Did you encounter many of the workers?"

"Some." Sarah was non-committal.

"But you were not molested?"

"No, of course not. If I look dishevelled, it's because I've been running, trying to get back to the house before it rained."

"You do look dishevelled," remarked Jason coolly. "But I'm

glad to learn you were not approached in any way."

"Whatever do you mean?" Sarah turned to look at him, her eyes wide and surprised.

Jason frowned. "Surely I don't have to explain in detail," he replied, in his cool voice. "There are some unpredictable types down here."

"Oh, really!" Sarah was scornful. "I'm sure I'm quite capable of taking care of myself, thank you."

Jason's eyes narrowed. "Never think that," he retorted coldly. "Never for one moment! You're a woman; you're vulnerable. And I would be grateful, in future, if you would confine your activities to the villa grounds unless you are accompanied –"

"– by a responsible adult," finished Sarah bluntly.

"If you like, yes." Jason swung round in his seat. "You will bathe those scratches as soon as we get home." He flicked a hand in the direction of her bare legs. "And don't run about barefoot; you may see the natives doing it, but you might step on something unpleasant."

"Thank you for your confidence." Sarah could not veil the annoyance she was feeling, and sighed deeply.

Jason turned the Land Rover and drove back along the track from whence he had come, and soon they were on the road again leading to the villa. There was silence as they drove along, and Sarah felt very guilty at her defiance.

"I . . . I'm sorry if I was rude, *señor*," she said suddenly.

Jason looked astonished. He gave her a swift glance. "That's quite all right," he remarked dispassionately.

"No, it's not." Sarah rubbed her legs restlessly. "I really mean it. You think I'm only saying it because I'm your employee."

"And aren't you?"

"No, honestly I'm not." She smiled a little. "But I wish I'd found those three monsters."

"Monsters!" Jason smiled now. "I thought you were confident you could handle them."

"I am. But Eloise is going to be the most difficult."

"Well, don't try to find them in the cane fields again," he warned, half-solemnly now. "They're at home down there. And you would never find them unless they decided you should. They were probably watching your progress with some amusement."

"Oh!" This possibility had not occurred to Sarah. "I never thought of that!"

"No, I don't suppose you did." Jason was sardonic.

"But won't they get wet?" It was beginning to rain now, and

53

the drops splattered against the windscreen.

"Very likely. However, they've been wet before without taking any harm. If you think I intend searching for them you're mistaken. However, I'll speak to them when they come home, and I guarantee they won't disappear tomorrow morning."

"Oh, no! Thank you," she added belatedly. "But I would prefer you not to speak to them on my behalf. That would give them entirely the wrong impression. No, I'll deal with them when they return."

Jason gave her an amused but tolerant glance. He did not rate her chances of success very highly just then.

When they reached the villa Sarah went straight to her bedroom to repair the ravages of the morning, and Jason walked slowly along the corridor to his own lounge. He lit a cigarette as he walked, and drew on it deeply. He knew Irena would likely be in the lounge discussing the day's menus with Ignatia the cook, and he had decided he might as well clear the subject of the pool at once.

As he had expected, Irena was in the lounge, drinking coffee from a delicately cut bone china coffee cup, and eating dainty bourbon biscuits from a dish. She was alone, and glanced up indifferently when Jason came in.

"You're back early," she remarked coldly. "Why are you here?"

Jason closed the door and leaned back against it. "I've given the children permission to use the pool," he said, without preamble.

As he expected there was an immediate reaction. Irena's coffee cup clattered into its saucer, and she rose abruptly to her feet.

"I refuse to have those savages bathing in my pool," she cried furiously. "So whatever you've said, you'll have to unsay it. I will not permit it!"

"You have no choice," returned Jason quietly. "This is my house, and the pool is my responsibility. There's nothing you can do."

"You beast!" she exclaimed, her face convulsed with anger. "You can't do this to me! Haven't you done enough already, without allowing me any choice in the matter? Oh, God, how I hate you!"

Jason bent his head wearily. "Irena, Irena!" he muttered, his voice almost inaudible. "I've tried to do what you wanted me to do whenever it was possible, but in this I'm adamant. Why should the children be deprived of a pool when that one stands there every day unused?"

"You've tried to do what I've said? Hah!" Irena was incensed.

"You've always gone against my wishes; you brought that woman and her brats here; you employed a governess without my knowledge or consent; and now you intend giving them the use of the pool so that every day I must be reminded of their existence!"

"Irena! Are you quite inhuman? Serena was alone and insolvent. How could I let her live alone with three children to support? She'd been used to company."

"The company of men!" snorted Irena. "Don't think I can't see why you brought that witch here! Don't think I don't know what goes on under my very nose! And Antonio not dead two years yet! It's nauseating!"

"I agree," muttered Jason, trying to control his own temper, "But not in the way you think. Do you honestly imagine I'm interested in Serena? It's ludicrous!"

"Why? You're a man, aren't you? And as you don't satisfy your appetites with me, you must satisfy them somewhere, *querido*!"

Jason's fingers moved lingeringly over his scar, and he wondered how much more of this he could stand.

But Irena was not yet finished. "Of course," she flashed at him, "there's Dolores. I'd almost forgotten her. And now there's the new governess. Does she appeal to you, peasant boy?"

But Jason had gone. He did not trust himself to stay in the same room as his wife. The desire to strike her at times like this was almost overpowering.

He strode swiftly away to his study and closing the door he locked it and pocketed the key. Then he closed the terrace doors against the downpour of rain outside and seating himself at his desk, he buried his face in his hands.

He was surprised to find he was trembling, and he cursed himself for being so emotional. But it was impossible to have a normal conversation with Irena. She always turned the discussion to his personal life, continually, and without any need for proof, denouncing him as a sensual peasant. The arrant fabrication of her lies did little to assuage the mental torment she aroused in him, or the self-recriminatory feeling this produced. He could feel a throbbing beginning behind the scar on his cheek, and he massaged his temples in an attempt to ease the pulsing. Was it always to be like this? he thought, in agony. Was he always to suffer for one mistake? The mistake of marrying Irena!

CHAPTER FOUR

As it turned out, Sarah did not see the children any more that day. At lunch time there was no sign of them, and during the afternoon, which she spent mainly in her room, Constancia informed her that the Señora Serena had decided to make one of her infrequent visits to see some friends at the other side of the island and had taken the children with her. Sarah was therefore left to her own devices, and with a steady drizzle outside the windows there seemed little to do.

Serena had returned at dinner time, although the children had been put to bed. Sarah wondered whose duty this was, and asked Serena as they were eating a delicious dish of crab and green salad and mayonnaise.

"Oh, I think Anna takes care of them," remarked Serena blithely. "Or Constancia. I'm not sure."

"But surely they have a routine?" exclaimed Sarah, in surprise. "Surely someone is responsible for their bathing and clothes and so on."

Serena wiped her mouth, and took a sip of her wine before replying. Then she shrugged. "There are plenty of servants here to deal with that sort of thing. When I lived with Antonio we could only afford a maid and I had to wash the children and see that their clothes were kept in reasonable order. But when we came to live here, all that changed. There are servants here for everything!" She spread wide her hands. "Some cook, some sew, some clean! It's fantastic. Servants are cheap, I know, but when you have none, you appreciate what they might be doing for you. I couldn't wait to hand over all my chores to someone else. I'm not domestically minded, thank goodness!"

"But they're *your* children," exclaimed Sarah helplessly.

"Yes, they are, Miss Winter. And I think you forget yourself."

Serena was very much on her dignity now, and Sarah flushed in embarrassment. Her innocent remark had not been meant to sound like a reproof. It was not for her to question Serena's actions even if she did not agree with them.

"I'm sorry if I said anything to annoy you," she said, a little awkwardly. "Being an orphan myself, I can't help feeling that if I had children of my own I would do my utmost to look after them myself. It would be a pleasure for me, I think."

Serena raised her dark eyebrows, and shrugged her slender shoulders. She was looking quite lovely this evening in an amber-coloured suit of heavy linen, cut low at the breast and clinging to her body like a second skin.

"But you have no children, Miss Winter," she reminded her coldly. "And I don't care to listen to advice from you, however well meant."

Sarah sighed. Serena was not to be placated so easily. She was touchily resentful of any criticism, it seemed, and who could blame her if she came into contact with the Señora Irena very often.

The rest of the meal passed in uneasy silence, and Sarah was relieved when it was over and she could escape from the room. Serena seemed in no mood for conversation with her governess, and Sarah thought perhaps she grew very bored living a life of seclusion as she did. It was a pity she could not return to Trinidad, if only for a visit. The change of environment would do her good.

Feeling restless herself, and unwilling to return to the isolation of her room, Sarah stepped out of the open front doors on to the terrace. Leaning against the rail she breathed deeply, savouring the scents of the night, all the more poignant now since the rain had stopped, leaving everywhere fresh and sweet. The gentle sound of the cicadas was soothing, and combined with the constant splashing of the water from the shore, provided a drugging tranquilliser for the tense nerves in her head. It was so peaceful that for a time she forgot the problems she would have to face in the morning, and relaxed completely.

The purr of a car engine as it accelerated down the incline to the villa disturbed the rhythm of the night. Headlights swept the terrace momentarily as the vehicle turned between the drive gates and ran up towards the house. Sarah drew back hastily, to the shadow of the overhanging balcony, and feeling the edge of a rattan lounger behind her, she sank down into it, hoping to go unnoticed by whoever was visiting her employer.

The car halted at the foot of the terrace steps, and a man detached himself from it and mounted the steps to the front doors. From the light which flooded from the open doors Sarah could see the visitor was a slim elegant man, in evening dress, a white tuxedo complementing the swarthy cast of his skin. His dark hair was flecked with grey, and he was not much taller than herself, but he had a distinguished appearance, and moved easily.

"*Buenos tardes*, Serena," he said lightly. "*Como esta usted?*"

Sarah's fingers tightened on the arms of the lounger for a moment and then she rose swiftly to her feet and stepped out into the light. "*Lo siento mucho, señor*," she murmured apologetically. "*No estoy Serena.*"

57

"*Qué!*" The man looked amazed. Then in English, he said: "Are you the governess, *señorita?*"

"*Sí, señor.*"

Although he was obviously surprised, the man covered his astonishment very well, and giving a slight smile, he said: "Neither Jason nor my daughter prepared me for this. My apologies, *señorita,* if I seem a trifle dazed. I did not expect you to be so young, or so charming."

Sarah moved awkwardly. She did not, as yet, know how to accept such compliments gracefully, and could not help but feel that the visitor was merely being polite as only Spaniards can be polite. "You are the Señor Diaz, then?" she said slowly.

"Yes, *señorita,* I am Manuel Diaz. And your name? It is Winter, *sí?*"

"Yes, *señor.*"

Manuel nodded in satisfaction. "I am delighted to make your acquaintance, Miss Winter. And how do you like our small paradise?"

Sarah relaxed. "I like it very well," she replied. "But as yet I've seen little of the people, or the island, for that matter. I've been concerned with the children, and of course this afternoon it rained," she grimaced smilingly.

"Yes, it did." Manuel looked rueful. "I wanted to sail in my yacht, but the weather would not permit it. I, too, was a victim of the wet. But tomorrow if it is fine, I shall have my sail." He smiled at her. "Do you sail, Miss Winter?"

"I'm afraid not."

"Then that must be remedied while you are here. The young people of the island all sail and swim and skin dive; you must learn all these things."

"I'm here to work," she reminded him gently.

"Ah, but not all the time. I am sure both Jason and Serena would agree with me. You cannot work all the time."

"Well, I admit I would like to see more of the island," said Sarah thoughtfully. "I would like to see how the West Indians live, and how they spend their time. I would like to help the children if I could."

"You cannot be serious, *señorita?*"

"Why not?"

"Well, because ... because ..." He sighed. "Such things cannot be of any interest to you."

"Why not?" demanded Sarah heatedly, and then clapped a hand to her mouth. "Excuse me, *señor.* I did not mean to be rude, but really, I think too little interest is taken in these people."

Manuel leaned against the verandah rail, astounded but intrigued. She was so fair and cool and young, this English girl, it was unbelievable how much fire lay just beneath the surface. His latin blood was stirred by her enthusiasm. If she could become so animated over such a little thing what would she be like if she were emotionally stirred in a very different way; if she ever fell in love! The idea was breathtaking! He smiled a little.

"So! We have a rebel in our camp. I must tell Jason."

Sarah shook her head. "I don't think it is anyone's concern but my own, señor. You must excuse me now. Your host will be waiting for you and I've wasted your time for too long already. Forgive me."

"Not at all!" exclaimed Manuel. "You have fired my interest."

"You are mocking me, señor," said Sarah coolly. "Excuse me," and without taking heed of his attempt at apology, she hastened indoors and up the stairs to her room.

Left alone, Manuel lit a cigarette slowly, and inhaled deeply. So that was Jason's new acquisition. Dolores had not liked her! Her description had been scathing and had done Sarah Winter much less than justice. The only solution was that Dolores had resented her and her sparkling youth and that so fair complexion.

Manuel raised his eyebrows. It was a long time since he had met a woman who even remotely stirred his lethargic senses. At forty-four he had thought himself immune from the desires of his youth, but in a matter of seconds this girl had changed all that. He found he was looking forward eagerly to their next meeting, and even contemplating inventing a reason for visiting the Cordova residence more often so that he might have a chance to talk to her.

He entered the villa to find Jason strolling along the corridor to meet him.

"I heard your car several minutes ago," said Jason easily. "Have you been talking to Serena?"

"No, to your new governess," replied Manuel, smiling. "I think both you and Dolores have deceived me about her."

"In what way?" Jason frowned.

"In every way. You told me she was young, yes, but not as attractive as she is. That hair! Those eyes! She is delicious, this little English girl. Do you not think so?"

"I haven't thought about it," remarked Jason, dryly, but conscious of a faint apprehension on Sarah's behalf. "What did you say to her?"

Manuel shrugged. "She told me she is interested in finding

out all she can about the West Indians. Did you know that?"

Jason shook his head. "No. For what reason? Did she tell you?"

"She is interested in the people. She says she wants to try and help the children."

"Indeed?" Jason bent his head. "Then I think I'd better have a serious talk with her. I found her wandering down among the cane stalks this morning after I left you. She's very innocent; I don't think she realises the dangers she might be courting." He sighed. "Do you think she's going to become a liability?"

"On the contrary!" Manuel laughed. "She is delightful, and a refreshing change from the monotony of everyday existence. I love my life here, Jason my friend, but I cannot help but see how this bright creature might lighten my days enormously."

"This morning you seemed willing to dismiss her chances of success with Serena's children as being negligible," remarked Jason now. "Tonight you're talking of her staying here indefinitely."

"I had not met her this morning," said Manuel, drawing on his cigarette. "Now that I have, I do not wish you to dismiss her whatever the circumstances."

Jason stared at him. "Good lord, Manuel," he exclaimed, "I can't believe you find her so attractive after such a brief conversation."

Manuel walked ahead of his friend down the corridor to Jason's study. "Can't you?" he murmured, as they walked. "I'm a man, Jason, and it is a long time since any woman interested me more than desultorily."

Jason hesitated for a moment, and then followed Manuel. But he did not say anything more. He was remembering Abe's words the morning before Sarah's arrival, when he had asked whether the new governess would be another woman to cause trouble. At the time Abe's words had seemed remote and unnecessary. Now Jason was not so sure. Although he liked his friend immensely, he did not consider Manuel's declared interest in Sarah as desirable. Sarah was young and innocent and candid, and he did not want to see her change. Manuel's interest was not likely to be more than fleeting, and she could perhaps be hurt.

The next morning Sarah was down early for breakfast. She had dressed in green cotton jeans and a white sleeveless sweater, and looked little like the governess she was intended to be. When the children arrived, all together this time, they looked as mutinous as ever. Even Ricardo indifferently returned her greeting, and she waited impatiently for them to finish their breakfast before beginning her attack. They ate slowly, as though aware of her impatience, but finally the last scrap of roll was swallowed, and the fresh orange juice was drained from the glasses.

Then Sarah rose to her feet. "Look," she said quietly, "if you expect me to be angry with you, you're mistaken. I don't intend to make myself an object for your amusement by raving at you. Instead, I'll say this: today we are going to begin the day by riding on the beach. I have your uncle's permission to use the horses, and afterwards we'll take a swim in the pool. I also have your uncle's permission for that." She ignored the bewildered expressions on their faces and went on: "Afterwards, we're going to go to the schoolroom and see just how far your general knowledge has progressed." She smoothed her hands down the sides of her jeans. "Now, if any of you don't want to take part in the lessons when they arrive, that will be perfectly all right, except that that person will not go riding or swimming with the rest of us. Right?" She looked at them expectantly.

She was praying that her approach had been the right one. If the children failed to respond now, she did not know what she was going to do next, short of spanking them.

But Ricardo, obviously, was completely won over, for he shouted: "And we can use the pool? Yippee!"

Maria glanced at her sister and then at her brother, and said: "That goes for me, too. You're not a bit like *her*, are you? And she's going to be so cross! Aren't you scared? Oh, I do think you're brave!"

Sarah swallowed hard and wondered if she was. Truth to tell, in her keenness to win the children's respect she had forgotten Irena de Cordova, but now Maria had aroused all her misgivings and she began to wonder just what the outcome of this defiance would be.

Eloise was the only one who did not seem overly impressed, although even her eyes had lit up at Sarah's mention of them using the pool. "I bet it won't last," she said finally. "I bet that woman turns us out again. She hates us, and she'll hate you, too, if you cross her." Sarah was about to remonstrate with her when she continued: "Besides, she'll probably try to prevent you staying here because of Uncle Jason. She doesn't want him herself, but that doesn't stop her being possessive about him. She hates anyone who goes near him. Do you know she made that awful scar on his cheek? With a pair of scissors!"

"Eloise!" Sarah was horrified. The child's words were dramatic and probably rehearsed, but their meaning was too convincing for them to be untrue. She felt nauseated. "You mustn't speak of such things," she managed. "It's not our concern, and you ought not to gossip in this manner." She swallowed hard. "Now, what are you going to do?"

"I'll come with you," Eloise shrugged indifferently. "I want to see what happens when *she* meets you. I bet you'll be just like the rest, another mouse for her to pounce on!" Her voice was scornful. "Everyone is afraid of her."

"Eloise, are you going to stop talking like that?" asked Sarah angrily. "If you think it's clever to try and shock people, you might stop and reflect on the fact that your aunt received no kind gestures from you three, so why should she attempt to be friendly with you?"

"You must be joking!" exclaimed Ricardo suddenly. "Honestly, Miss Winter, she hates us! All of us. And she hates Uncle Jason. But I'm not sure why, or why she slashed his face. But she did!"

Sarah turned away from them for a moment. Their statements were not reckless gossip. What they said was true. Probably they had listened to conversations not intended for their ears; she could not imagine anyone actually telling them what had happened. Possibly the servants talked, and of course Serena did not guard her tongue. She turned back to the children, and met Eloise's eyes.

"Very well," she said. "It's not our affair. I don't wish to hear any more about it. It's time we forgot all about it. Let's go down to the stables. I told Jacob to have the horses saddled ready for us."

The morning air was like wine after the tension in the house. Sarah laughed and wondered how she had ever thought she knew all about life living in a convent. It was not the simple affair she had imagined it to be. All thoughts of returning to the convent were becoming vague and unreal, even in so short a time. The nuns were to be greatly admired; they were dedicated to their work in the church, but they never experienced the thrill of being young and free and fully *alive* in a place that teemed with love and hate and passion, both good and bad. As the breeze rippled across her face and cooled the soft flesh of her bare arms she shivered involuntarily, for she knew that whatever happened now she had been meant to come here and meet these people, and find her destiny.

She glanced round at the children riding behind her. Ricardo and Eloise were allowing their ponies to splash about happily at the water's edge, while Maria followed her closely, her eyes sparkling with excitement.

"Isn't it glorious!" she squealed, in Spanish, and then at

Sarah's reproving look, she said: "Can we do this every morning, Miss Winter?" in quite faultless English, smiling merrily.

Sarah smiled at her. Maria was quite enchanting when she smiled, with a definite look of her uncle.

After making sure the children were quite at home in the saddle, Sarah cantered on, lying close against the mare's head and allowing the animal to take its own course. Melanie was as sure-footed as a mountain goat and Sarah had no fears for her safety, but it gave her quite a start when a voice, quite close by, said: "Don't you think you ought to set a better example, Miss Winter?" in a mocking tone.

Sarah sat bolt upright, soothing the mare as she did so, and looked into Jason de Cordova's dark face. He was astride Apollo and looked quite magnificent, like a statue in bronze. He had ridden out from the shade of a group of palms and she had been completely unaware of his presence.

"I'm sorry, *señor*," she said, a little stiffly. "I wasn't thinking. It won't happen again."

Jason sighed. "Relax, *señorita*, do not be so serious. I was merely joking with you. I do not think Eloise, Ricardo and Maria would come to any harm riding as you were doing. But I am glad I have met you. I wanted to speak to you."

Sarah felt a tingle run up her spine. Dressed this morning in tight cotton trousers and an open-necked shirt of a light woollen material, Jason looked very masculine and dangerous to her peace of mind. The open shirt displayed the beginnings of the mat of dark hairs on his chest, and the tan of his skin showed that his body was often exposed to the sun. After Eloise's revelations, the scar on his face seemed doubly startling, and Sarah's stomach turned over when she thought of Irena's action. To imagine her attacking him with scissors was a horrifying thought, and some of her feelings must have shown in her expressive face, for Jason said, a little coldly: "However you protest, Miss Winter, my scar seems to repulse you. I'll endeavour to keep it out of your sight."

"No, please." Sarah was contrite. "You're wrong. I wasn't thinking anything like that. Believe me!" For contrary to his assumption, she wanted, with a desire so strong as to be almost painful, to run her fingers along his cheek and smooth the line of bitterness from his brow.

But just at that moment the three children converged on them, excitedly chattering and completely monopolising Jason's attention. Their shrill voices shattered the stillness that had been all around them, and in a way Sarah felt relieved.

"Isn't this marvellous, Uncle Jason?"

63

"Can we really use the pool, too?"

"Won't we get into trouble with Aunt Irena?"

"Can we ride every morning?"

"Miss Winter says we can!"

"Am I riding better, Uncle Jason?"

"Are you going to ride with us?"

"Oh, do come! Please!"

"Yes, come with us, Uncle Jason."

"Bueno, bueno!" Jason held up his hand "Calm yourselves. I'm very glad to see you are all feeling so happy. The riding pleases you, I see."

"It's wonderful!" exclaimed Ricardo. "And afterwards we're going to swim in the pool to cool off before lessons begin. Isn't it marvellous?"

Jason gave Sarah a wry smile. "If Miss Winter says it's so, it's so," he said lightly. "But you must all work hard afterwards, or no play."

"Well, I will," said Maria, laughing. "I wouldn't miss this tomorrow for anything. And Miss Winter isn't at all like ... like ..." Her voice trailed away, and then she added: "Like we thought!"

"Indeed." Jason bent his head. "Then see that there's no more disobedience."

"Por supuesto!" said Eloise haughtily, and Jason frowned. "English," he reproved softly. "Do not forget."

"Very well, Uncle Jason," Eloise grimaced.

"And are you going to ride with us?" asked Maria eagerly.

Jason shook his head. "Not today, little one. I have not time for such things. But another morning, perhaps. And now I want to speak to Miss Winter for a moment alone. So you three ride on and Miss Winter will catch up with you shortly."

The children wheeled their horses obligingly, and rode off shouting to each other. They made for the water's edge, and waited just out of hearing distance.

"Definitely an improvement," remarked Jason when they had gone, a mocking expression on his face. "Bribery works wonders!"

"I could see no other way," replied Sarah, sighing. "It's a kind of blackmail, I suppose, only instead of demanding money, I demand work."

"I think we're all enmeshed in some form of blackmail," said Jason enigmatically, and Sarah wondered what his particular involvement was.

Jason dismounted from his horse. "And now, we talk. Get down."

64

Sarah shivered. "Couldn't I stay where I am?" she asked. "I would rather."

To her surprise, Jason merely lifted her out of the saddle and put her down on the sand beside him, his eyes surveying her slender legs in her jeans. "I prefer to have you down here," he said, smiling lazily. "I should feel at a disadvantage otherwise."

Convinced he was still mocking her, Sarah flushed. She was quite sure he would never feel at a disadvantage.

He lit a cigarette before beginning to speak, and Sarah turned her eyes from him to the shoreline. She felt sure she would never get used to the clear transparency of the water, or the many colours of the coral which could be distinguished beneath its surface.

"Do you go skin-diving?" she asked suddenly, unaware for a moment to whom she was speaking.

Jason drew on his cigarette. "Yes, sometimes," he said slowly. "Why? Are you interested in the sport?"

"Me?" exclaimed Sarah ungrammatically. "Oh, yes! It sounds exciting! I expect the coral reef is quite a spectacle."

"You're right, it is. But coral can be dangerous, too. Cuts from it can be poisonous." Changing the subject, he went on: "Now, Manuel tells me you are interested in the island people. That you would like to meet them."

"Yes. Why? Is something wrong?"

"Not exactly. However, I would advise you not to try to visit the villages alone. You might find yourself in rather a predicament if you're unable to speak the language, and as a white girl . . ."

Sarah sighed. "Does this mean you're warning me off?"

"Don't be so prickly. No, I'm not warning you off. But when you do decide you want to explore, let me know, and I'll take you."

Sarah raised her eyebrows. "I can drive, you know," she replied, rather haughtily. "If you would permit me . . ."

"Indeed? Now that's very interesting. It opens up more possibilities, you might say. For you, and the children."

"In what way?"

"There's a lagoon inland. It's a perfect swimming pool, warm and deep, but with no dangerous currents – an ideal spot for picnics. You and the children could spend hours there, if you like swimming, of course."

"I love it!" exclaimed Sarah. "It sounds marvellous. But I don't know where it is."

"I'll show you where it is. Maybe tomorrow, or the following day. It depends a lot on the situation. But I gather you find your work gratifying."

"Oh, yes. You've been very kind. I'm grateful to you." She flushed.

"Don't be too grateful," he remarked sardonically. "Those terrors are quiet at the moment, but there is no guarantee that the novelty won't wear off."

"Well, I hope that by when the time comes, the children will like me for myself, and not because of the things I can do for them."

"I'm sure they will," he returned lazily. "I see no reason why not. As to the other matter – of the driving, I mean – if you can drive, I'll put a car at your disposal, and soon I'll introduce you to some of the other white families here. It will be better if in the evenings you can go out a little. We never entertain at the villa, and it's only right that you should meet some young people of your own age."

"I'm afraid I've never found a great deal in common with people of my own age," she said candidly.

Jason frowned, thinking of Manuel, and wondering whether she was attracted by him as he seemed to be by her. "Nevertheless," he said slowly, "I think you may find these young Spaniards quite interesting. People of another race may strike you quite differently."

Sarah looked up at him, her eyes wide and troubled. "Is it necessary that I should so socially-minded?"

Jason was taken aback. "No, I don't suppose so. I promise you you won't find it boring, though."

"I don't find my life boring at the moment," she replied, reaching for Melanie's bridle. "Is that all?"

Jason dropped his cigarette into the sand and put his hands on his hips, shrugging his broad shoulders. Standing there he resembled, in Sarah's eyes, the buccaneers of old, complete to the scar on his cheek. She thought a patch over one eye would not look out of place. Smiling at her thoughts, she swung herself into the saddle, and Jason said: "Do I amuse you now?"

"No. I amuse myself," she said awkwardly.

"Why were you smiling?" he asked curiously, his hand on the pommel, preventing her from riding away.

She looked down into his tawny eyes, and replied truthfully: "I thought you reminded me of a pirate."

Jason released the pommel, and stared at her for a moment, and then he laughed. "My dear Miss Winter, are you actually indulging your imagination. I would never have believed it of you!" His tone was sardonic.

"It helps sometimes," Sarah retorted, and digging her heels into the mare's sides, she rode quickly off across the damp sand. As she went she wondered why it was that she could never have a complete conversation with Jason without becoming suffocatingly conscious of her own femininity. That she was attracted to him she could not deny, but that meant nothing, she told herself seriously. Lots of men were attractive, and lots of women found men attractive without ever becoming seriously involved with them. Why was it she felt this overwhelming sense of pleasure in his presence, even when he did mock her as he had done just now? And why did the children's words about his scar distress her so? She ought not to be concerned. She was here to do a job and nothing else. The personal affairs of her employers ought not to interest her at all.

But Irena had involved her right from the beginning, and she could not help the surge of indignation she felt remembering that first meeting with her employer's wife. She supposed that had crystallised her first reactions to Jason. She had felt embarrassed for him as well as for herself, and had envied his cool ignorance of Irena's words. But how had he really felt? Did he still love a woman who treated him like that? Surely he must submit to her moods. And yet, Sarah decided, he could not be as submissive as Irena would like. He had said the children could swim in the pool; he had said that she, Sarah, could use the beach. He was master in his own home. But for some reason, unknown to anyone but himself, he allowed Irena to continue to live there and act as she did. It was very strange. If Irena was responsible for the scar on his cheek, surely all his feelings for her would have been severed at that point!

She shook her head in perplexity. Here she was, pondering again. It would have to stop. She had never considered herself a curious person until now, but suddenly she could not seem to stop turning the Cordova's problems over in her mind.

They arrived back at the villa soon after nine, and the children ran eagerly to change for their swim. Sarah changed more leisurely, putting on a yellow one-piece bathing suit, that was quite old-fashioned in design and did not reveal the skin of her body to the sun's rays. She hoped if Irena saw them she would consider her suitably dressed.

The pool was quite cold. The water was continually being changed, and was pumped up from the sea below the villa. The children appeared, all dressed in red bathing suits, and waited impatiently for Sarah's permission to jump in. Sarah shed her towelling wrap, and pulling a white bathing cap on to her head with some difficulty over the coronet of hair, she dived in off the side. It was a long time since she had swum at all, and the nervousness she felt about her appearance was doubled by the prospect of Irena's possible intervention.

However, she surfaced without mishap, and shouted: "It's beautiful! Come on, you three, jump in!"

Both Eloise and Ricardo could swim like fishes and followed her example, but Maria was more careful, and slid in slowly. Ricardo had brought a bright blue rubber ball with him, a huge thing, that bobbed about merrily on the water and provided them with a ready-made game. Even Maria could swim a little bit and they splashed and played excitedly for almost an hour.

Then Sarah climbed out regretfully, and stripping off her cap, she shouted: "Game's over! Let's see who can be dressed and ready for work first."

If she had expected opposition she was pleasantly disappointed. All the children climbed out at her words, and although they looked back longingly at the water, they merely shrugged, and made their way indoors to dry and dress.

Sarah retrieved the ball which Ricardo had left bobbing about in the pool, and was about to enter the villa when Irena de Cordova emerged from the entrance to bar her way. Sarah's stomach plunged, and she wrapped the white towelling coat she was wearing closer about her.

"*Buenos dias, señora*," she said, hoping Irena was not going to cause a scene out here, or anywhere, for that matter.

"*Señorita.*" Irena inclined her head. "You've been swimming, I see."

"Yes, *señora*. The water is delightful. You ought to try it some time."

As Sarah said the words she thought how ludicrous they sounded. She could not picture Irena, so elegant and sophisticated, in a swim suit, splashing about in water and upsetting that perfectly coiffured head.

"No, thank you," she replied coldly. "I'm not a water baby. My parents would never allow such a thing. In my country, the women of my class do not run around like . . . that !" She waved a hand in Sarah's direction.

"Your country?" Sarah frowned. "But surely this is your country. This island!"

Irena stared at her horrified. "You are not serious, *señorita*. You thought I belonged to one of these island families!"

"Yes, *señora*." Sarah swallowed hard. She could see nothing to get so steamed up about.

"My family is one of the most affluent families in Spain!" exclaimed Irena haughtily. "My grandfather was a duke!"

Sarah digested this, and wondered whether that was all Irena was going to say. She did not know quite how to reply, so she said nothing.

"Have you nothing to say, *señorita*?"

Sarah twisted the ball in her hands. "I don't think there's anything to say, *señora*," she said politely. "And now, if you'll excuse . ."

Irena moved closer to her. "You think you've won, don't you, Señorita Winter?" she hissed, in a voice so full of venom that Sarah drew back in disgust.

"I don't know what you're talking about, *señora*," she said, with a vain attempt at ignorance.

"Yes, you do; I mean this pool, of course. You think you can twist Jason round your little finger, simply because he has agreed to let you use the pool, even though I have forbidden it."

"I don't think any such thing, *señora*," replied Sarah quietly. "The *señor* only agreed to let the children use the pool because they're being deprived of something that's not even used by you, or anyone else."

"Those brats are not children, they're animals. Less than animals. They have mixed blood!"

"Human beings are human beings, irrespective of ancestry," replied Sarah, some of her own anger aroused now by Irena's blind prejudice.

"You think so? You think that witchcraft is practised by human beings?"

"I know nothing about witchcraft," replied Sarah carefully.

"But you know that it rules the islands – *voodoo*, *obeah*, whatever you care to call it!"

"That has nothing to do with the children." Sarah felt impatient. "They're not witches! They're children, just children!"

"You think so?" Irena said again. "What would you say if I told you that my husband is part of the curse that was put on me when I first visited here nearly seventeen years ago?"

Sarah stared at her. She was rapidly coming to the conclusion that Irena was mad, quite mad! "*Señora*! I must go. The children are waiting."

"You think I'm mad, don't you?"

Sarah cast about in her mind for something to say. "No, *señora*," she began awkwardly.

"Yes, you do. I can see it in your face. But I'm not, be assured of that."

Sarah edged towards the entrance.

"Those children are manifestations of evil. They're the living proof of the power of *obeah*!"

Sarah pressed a hand to her stomach. She felt quite sick. She had never encountered such fanaticism before. She wanted to escape from Irena's words and her glittering eyes. She wanted to go to her room and lock the door, and not come out until Irena had gone for good!

"Excuse me!" she gulped, and with a swift, lithe movement, she slid through the glass doors into the hall and up the stairs as fast as her legs would carry her. Reaching her room, she locked the door and leaned back against it breathing heavily. Oh, God! she thought wildly. There's a mad woman in the house! Doesn't anyone know? Doesn't anyone care? She slumped suddenly, and flopped down on the bed, feeling worn out. She was shaking, she realised.

Then with a strength of mind she had not known she possessed until now, she stood up and flung off the towelling wrapper. She was behaving like a stupid child! Just because she had had a sheltered upbringing, that was no reason for her to behave as though she was on the point of being attacked. Nobody hated *her*; Irena was simply a harmless hysteric, who was living a life obsessed by the fear of her own shadow, imagining herself persecuted by a people she obviously hated. But why? Where was the sense in it? Why had she brought Jason into it? What possible connection could he have with her ravings?

She walked into the bathroom, swiftly showered, and then dressed in a slim-fitting sheath of ice-green poplin, with a scooped-out neckline and a scalloped hemline. Not having time to comb her hair, she had to make do with simply combing out the ends at the nape of her neck, and tucking the wisps away with hairpins. She added a coral lipstick to her lips, and then sighed. She certainly felt more relaxed now, and she did not look as though she had just had an encounter with Irena, but she thought it would take her quite some time to forget her words and their meaning . .

CHAPTER FIVE

JASON walked along the jetty towards his yacht, answering greetings from passing fishermen, on their way to the market with their catch. His yacht, *La Sombre Negra*, was moored next to the ketch belonging to Roderigo Valente, who was the son of Manuel Diaz' older sister, and who was standing at that moment examining his mooring rope. "*Buenos dias*, Jason," he said, in greeting. "Going out?"

Jason halted, and raising one foot to the low parapet he stood watching Roderigo for a moment. "No," he replied, sighing. "No crew. Why? Do you want to come?"

"If you like." Roderigo grinned. "But where is Dolores? Surely she would not turn down the chance of a sail?"

Jason smiled lazily. "Are you trying to say something?" he asked, shrugging his shoulders, flexing his muscles.

"Not me!" exclaimed Roderigo cheekily, youthfully careless of any feelings he might be disturbing. "They say your new governess is quite something. Is she going to be kept imprisoned at the villa, or are we going to have the chance to meet her socially?"

Jason drew out his cigarettes, and after offering Roderigo the case he said: "Now I wonder who's been talking about Miss Winter."

"Need to ask? Tio Manuel, of course," Roderigo laughed. "I actually think he is smitten."

Jason straightened up. "You think so, eh?" He sighed. "He's perhaps a little old for that sort of thing."

Roderigo chuckled. "Don't you believe it. He was on his way to our villa when he called on you last evening, and he was quite voluble in his praise of the girl. Tell me, seriously, what is she like?"

Jason drew on his cigarette before replying. "She's charming. She's young. And she's also very concerned with the underprivileged people on the island. She's quite unusual in that respect."

"Especially here," agreed Roderigo, sighing. "I would like to meet her myself. I take it you have no objections to me. After all, I am slightly younger than Tio Manuel."

Jason smiled, albeit a little tightly, wondering why he felt so overwhelmingly protective towards the girl. Although Roderigo was younger he had quite a name for being interested in the

71

opposite sex, and had been sent down from his university for just such a reason. He had denied the whole thing, of course, and it had been generally accepted amongst the family that he had had a raw deal, but now Jason was not so sure. In his way he was just as objectionable as Manuel.

"I think an invitation to one of your parties would not be dismissed," said Jason slowly. "It would enable her to be introduced to the younger set and also give her a chance to escape from the confines of the villa."

"Good." Roderigo was pleased. "Tomorrow evening my mother is giving a barbecue on Honey Grove Beach."

"Ideal," agreed Jason dryly. "I gather I'm invited too?"

"But of course, Jason." Roderigo frowned a little. "But you surprise me. I thought you no longer mixed with us socially. It is so long since you actually accepted an invitation to such an affair."

Jason ran a hand through his thick hair. "You would have me send this girl alone to an affair at which she knows no one." He shook his head. "I think not."

"She knows, Manuel, and Dolores, of course."

"I don't think she would go, without me," said Jason, and then realising how smug that sounded he laughed. "She's not socially-minded. Only this morning we had an argument on this very subect."

"*She* argues with *you!*" Roderigo raised his dark eyebrows. "You surprise me. It seems Manuel was right – she is different."

"Yes." Jason shrugged again. "*Bien*, I must go."

Roderigo nodded. "Very well. So we may expect you at the barbecue. About eight?"

"You may. But whether I come along or not I can't say."

"Do not disappoint us, I beg of you," replied Roderigo mockingly, and laughing again, Jason went on his way.

After lunch Serena sent word that she wished to see Jason, and Constancia, who delivered the message, said that Serena was waiting her siesta time for him.

As he walked along the corridor to Serena's apartments, he wondered why she wanted to speak to him. He hoped she was not going to voice some objections about Sarah Winter's treatment of the children. He thought Sarah was proving she could handle them, slowly but surely, and he did not relish the prospect of sacking her and hiring a new governess just because her methods were perhaps a little old-fashioned.

Serena was in her lounge, draped decoratively on a couch, the long cigarette holder between her fingers. She was wearing a sheath dress of a deep red colour, and looked startlingly attractive.

"Hello *amado*," she said, as he entered the room, immediately dwarfing its adequate proportions. "I'm glad you've come so promptly. It was rather important." She waved a hand in the direction of a low armchair. "Sit down. You make me feel so insignificant when you stand."

Jason smiled at this, for never could Serena be described as insignificant. There was something wholly compelling about her, and he could understand Antonio, with his love of dramatic things, admiring the vivid personality he had found in Serena. Jason was quite fond of his sister-in-law, and their relationship was comfortably relaxed and friendly. Serena did not attract him sexually, and he hoped she never thought of him in that way. If she did she certainly never gave any sign, for which he was grateful.

He lowered his bulk now into one of her armchairs and stretching his long legs out in front of him he sighed in a satisfied manner. "This is very comfortable," he remarked, half closing his eyes. "I could quite easily fall asleep here."

The venetian blinds which were drawn against the afternoon sun gave the room a restful, mellow light, and Serena grimaced. "How very complimentary you are! However, I suppose you are quite alert, even if you do look as sleepy as a cat."

"Quite, quite alert," agreed Jason lazily. "I only hope your remarks won't be too distressing. I don't relax often enough."

"Well, that depends a lot on you," replied Serena, lighting her cigarette. "I merely thought you might like to know that Irena has been talking — if you can call it talking — to Miss Winter."

"Oh, God!" Jason closed his eyes fully. "Go on!"

"She cornered her this morning as Sarah was leaving the pool. She didn't exactly lose her temper, but she was telling her the tale about being cursed and hating this place and so on ..." She drew on her cigarette. "You can guess the gist of it for yourself. I think the poor girl was frightened out of her wits. And with good reason, don't you think?"

Jason opened his eyes, and leaning forward helped himself to a cigarette. "Do you want a drink?" asked Serena, gliding off the couch as she spoke. "Beer?"

"Thanks." Jason lit his own cigarette. "Thanks for telling me too. I doubt whether I should have been told otherwise. Miss Winter doesn't strike me as the kind of girl to come running to me with tales, however nervous Irena might have made her." He sighed wearily. "Where is it all going to end, Serena?"

73

Serena handed him his glass and seated herself on the arm of his chair, looking down at him seriously. "You could have the specialist from Port of Spain here again."

Jason twisted his mouth. "No," he muttered. "That wouldn't do any good. I can't send her away, Serena. It would be like condemning her to a fate worse than death."

"That's nonsense, and you know it."

"No, it's not." Jason swallowed some of his beer. "Maybe if I'd never married her she would never have become . . . what she is. She's harmless enough. She merely lives in a dream world."

"Harmless? I wonder." Serena ran a hand down the scar on his cheek lightly, and then as though afraid of her emotions she moved away. "It's true what they say," she murmured. "You've been condemned to a life of misery by your religion."

"*Our* religion," he reminded her quietly. Then he rose to his feet. "I'd better go. There are things to do."

"Are you going to speak to Irena?"

He shrugged. "I don't know. I expect so. But I'm afraid she won't like it."

Serena sighed. "Jason! You're master here."

"Do you think I ever forget that responsibility?" he asked harshly. Then he stood down his glass on a side table. "By the way, I've accepted an invitation from Roderigo to his mother's barbecue party tomorrow evening, and I expect to take Miss Winter along. Would you care to come?"

Serena raised her dark eyebrows in surprise. "You've actually accepted an invitation! Lord, what's happening to you?" She laughed. "But I don't think I will come, thank you all the same. I'm glad you're going. Dolores will be there. But why are you taking Miss Winter?"

"Because I think it's only fair to allow her to meet the young people of the island. To be incarcerated up here all the time gives her no chance whatsoever. We never entertain, and it's not fitting that she should have no social life."

Serena laughed. "I have no social life," she remarked dryly.

"You could have," replied Jason swiftly. "If you would allow yourself to go out and forget about Antonio. I know it was a tragedy, and you'll never love anyone else in quite the same way, but one day you'll want to marry again. You're so young to be a widow."

Serena shrugged. "Perhaps you're right. But there's so much here to remind me of him. If I could get right away . . ."

Jason studied her for a moment, and then he said: "If Miss Winter settles down satisfactorily with the children, there's no reason why you shouldn't go away yourself for a while; to Trinidad maybe, to see your parents. You'd like that, wouldn't you?"

Serena's eyes sparkled. "Could I? Could I really?"

"I don't see any reason why not. Give this young woman a week or so to settle down and then I'll make arrangements."

"Thank you, Jason. You're a darling!" Serena flung her arms round his neck excitedly, and kissed his cheek.

Jason, half embarrassed by her enthusiasm, drew back, but at that moment Sarah, who had just come down from her room and was on her way to find the children, paused at the open French doors and looked into the room.

"Excuse me," she exclaimed in astonishment, and walked hastily on along the verandah.

Serena looked awkwardly at Jason. "That was bad, wasn't it?"

"Very bad," agreed Jason wryly. "Excuse me, anyway. I want to speak to Miss Winter myself."

Serena watched him go with eyes that were a little calculating. She knew she would never have Jason herself, no matter what, for he had never shown any interest in her in that way, but she certainly did not like the idea of him concerning himself with the thoughts or inhibitions of some English nobody who had happened to come here to teach his nephew and nieces.

Jason himself, unaware of Serena's thoughts, saw Sarah disappear among the orange trees that surrounded the stables, and walking swiftly he caught up with her as she reached the gentle incline down to the beach.

"*Señorita!*" he said, and Sarah swung round sharply, caught unawares.

"Yes, *señor?*" Her voice was subdued but cold, and he wondered what she thought she had seen.

"I want to talk to you again," he said. "Shall we sit down?"

Sarah sank down on to a hillock of grass without a word, and he flung his length beside her. "Well," she said. "Is it something to do with the children?"

"No, it's nothing to do with the children," he replied, flicking some sand from the leg of his trousers. He studied her for a moment, and she was forced to turn her eyes away as a flush of bright colour stained her cheeks. "First of all, I want to explain what you've just seen," he went on softly.

Sarah's eyes widened. "That's not necessary, *señor.*"

Jason almost lost his temper. "Damn you, I know it's not," he muttered angrily, and then sighed in exasperation. "But I want to explain anyway. I don't care to have you believe that I'm a man who amuses himself with other women as well as

75

his wife. No matter what you think, I'm not a philanderer."

Sarah smiled suddenly at his choice of words. "That sounds rather old-fashioned," she remarked impulsively.

Jason stared at her, and then frowned. "Nonetheless, I'm serious."

"Yes, *señor*," she agreed, but he had the feeling that she was inwardly laughing at him, and for some reason that infuriated him.

He rose to his feet abruptly, and looked down at her with eyes so tawnily yellow and incensed that Sarah felt overwhelmingly conscious of her own frailty beside such a man. "Tomorrow I'll take you to the lagoon," he said coolly, looking out to sea. "Have the children ready to depart after breakfast. You may have your morning swim there and afterwards return to your lessons. Is that suitable?"

"Yes, *señor*." Sarah felt repentant, and wished he would sit down again, but Jason moved his shoulders deprecatingly and said: "Tomorrow evening, some friends are giving a barbecue party. I have accepted an invitation for you to join them."

Sarah stood up. "Thank you, but I don't think that's a very good idea."

"Why not?" He looked down at her searchingly. "Are you perhaps of the opinion that I'm not a man to be trusted?"

"You? I don't understand."

"Did you imagine I would send you to a party without an escort"

"You're accompanying me, *señor*?" Sarah stared at him.

"Yes. At least, I expected to do so." Jason bent his head and studied the toes of his boots. "I thought it would give you an opportunity of meeting the younger set on the island."

Sarah smiled. "I'm sorry, I didn't understand. Naturally in those circumstances, I should love to go."

Jason's eyes were narrowed. "In truth?"

"Of course, *señor*. I shall look forward to it."

Then she remembered Irena and a cloud passed over her face, but she did not speak her thoughts. What had passed between Irena and herself was not important. In future she would try to avoid her.

Jason sensed her withdrawal, and wondered what she really thought about them all. It was indeed a strange household into which she had allowed herself to be jettisoned.

"Until tomorrow morning, then," he said.

"Yes, *señor*."

Jason turned and walked back towards the villa, and Sarah

sank down on to the sand again, clutching her arms about her knees.

The next morning Sarah, who had told the children of their uncle's decision the night before, found Eloise, Ricardo and Maria only too willing to help her in any way they could. It was gratifying to know that they were beginning to accept her, but the previous day's lessons had been a revelation. Although Maria was well within her age group, Ricardo and Eloise were hopelessly behind, and it would take her weeks, possibly even months, to bring them up to any sort of standard. No wonder their uncle had been concerned for them, she thought. They would never have stood the pace of any ordinary school. In addition to which, both Eloise and Ricardo were apt to find anything she said amusing, and until she had threatened them with exclusion from the following day's activities she had not been able to interest them in the intricacies of simple reading, writing and arithmetic. She did not intend to broach the subject with Jason until she had some definite improvement to report, and she hoped that would not be very far ahead. The children were bright enough, and rather too shrewd in some matters, but they had never been disciplined to take lessons every day and consequently they did not like it very much. Sarah supposed it was understandable. The island was a veritable paradise for children and to sit indoors reading books while the sun shone outside seemed somehow unfair.

Thus it was that they were all waiting on the verandah when a dust-covered station wagon drew up beside them. The children were wearing their bathing suits beneath their shorts and tee-shirts, and carried towels under their arms.

Sarah had hesitated a long time before deciding whether or not to wear a bathing suit herself and swim with the children. She did not know what Jason de Cordova would be doing and it was disconcerting to find that the prospect of swimming in his presence with a minimum amount of covering seemed rather nerve-racking. But she had finally decided that the children might attach some ulterior motive if she refused to swim with them, so she had donned the yellow suit again, and pulled on green denim jeans and a sleeveless yellow sweater to conceal it.

Jason slid out of the driving seat and opened the rear doors for the children to jump in. Then with mocking derision in his eyes he opened the passenger side door and slid in himself. "You may drive us, *señorita*," he said lazily. "I'll direct you."

Sarah eyed him with some trepidation, and then got in beside him, ignoring the surge of purely sensual pleasure she felt at the sight of his lean hard body and tanned complexion. Today he too was wearing denim jeans and the red shirt he was wearing was open to the waist and simply thrust into the top of his pants. Her pulses were throbbing so loudly she did not see how he could fail to hear them, and she stalled the car in her first attempt to move away. The children giggled, and Sarah compressed her lips furiously. "Calm yourself," she thought angrily. "Stop thinking about him. Think about yourself instead. Thinking about him is madness!"

She drove smoothly down the drive after that, and at his request turned right out of the gates. As they left the villa Sarah caught a glimpse of someone standing on the verandah watching them go, and although it could have been Serena, Sarah had the strongest feeling that it was Irena de Cordova.

The drive to the lagoon took them through the interior of the island, along passes between towering cliffs, where crystal-clear streams tumbled down the rocks and showered the shrubs that grew in profusion in spite of the absence of the rays of the sun. The scarlet and blue of the flowers contrasted with the various shades of greenery, making the whole island seem a veritable flower garden. Scents of bougainvillea and poinsettia drifted in through the open windows of the car, and Sarah sighed in appreciation.

Jason glanced at her. "I think perhaps you're falling under the spell of our island," he said softly. "Your face is very expressive. This abundance of colour – it pleases you, doesn't it?"

"It would please anyone," said Sarah, a little defensively.

"No, not everyone," replied Jason, lying back in his seat, and extracting a cigarette from his case. After he had lit the cigarette, he continued: "To some people the island is a prison, an isolated fortress without hope of redemption – an evil place, even."

Sarah glanced at him. "But you don't believe that," she stated firmly.

"Do you?" Jason's eyes were probing.

"No." Sarah shook her head. "No, you're right. I love it."

They descended into a valley, and spread out below them was the lagoon, gleaming in the sunlight, the water clear and transparent. It was surrounded by the towering cliffs of the inner mountain range of the island, and Sarah gasped.

"How on earth did it get here?" she exclaimed in delight.

Jason sat up and stretched. "No one knows. I should imagine it was originally an underground river that ran to the sea and finally wore away the rock until it made itself a basin. There's

78

still an underground tunnel leading to the sea from the lagoon, and the water in the lagoon is salt water."

There was a natural pathway leading down from the road to a sandy cove, while the rocks surrounding the lagoon provided ideal diving areas. The children scampered down the path excitedly, stripping off their shorts and shirts.

"Relax," said Jason, as Sarah was about to call to them to be careful. "The lagoon is perfectly safe for swimming, and even Maria won't come to any harm in there. Have you brought your bathing suit?"

Sarah got out of the car, ostensibly to stretch her legs, and replied: "Yes, I'm wearing it, as the children are."

"Good." Jason slid out too, and began unbuttoning the top of his jeans.

Sarah flushed in embarrassment, and turned away abruptly, but he merely laughed. "I, too, am wearing a bathing suit," he said mockingly. "Do not be alarmed, *señorita,* I am not in the habit of stripping naked in front of children."

She turned round to find him taking off his shirt, and a pair of white bathing trunks, accentuating the tan of his body, were revealed. He was cool and confident, and for a moment Sarah allowed herself the pleasure of just looking at him. And then he said, rather harshly: "Get changed! I'm going into the water."

Sarah watched him dive cleanly off the rocks into the pool, and emerged a few moments later beside Eloise, ducking her unmercifully while she screamed with laughter. Ricardo and Maria swam up to them and began splashing him excitedly and Sarah sighed. It was obvious that the children adored him and it was sad that he had no children of his own. He would have made a wonderful father.

With a nervous shake of her head, she took off her jeans and sweater, and flinging them into the back of the car, she picked up her bathing hat and walked down the path to the sandy cove. Jason climbed out of the water at her approach and watched as she pulled on the ugly rubber bathing hat over her hair.

He frowned and said: "Good God, Sarah, what do you want that for?"

Sarah looked at him, aware at once of his use of her Christian name.

"To keep my hair dry, of course," she retorted coolly.

Jason shook his head. "And that suit! I guarantee that wasn't bought anywhere along the archipelago!"

Sarah flushed. "You're right, of course. I bought it in England."

79

"Several years ago," muttered Jason. "You didn't intend taking *that* to the barbecue this evening, did you?"

"It's the only bathing suit I possess," she retorted, becoming annoyed now. "What's wrong with it? It's quite suitable."

"Really!" muttered Jason, shaking his head, and turning away he dived back into the pool.

Sarah stared after him feeling furious. How dared he make personal remarks about her clothes? It was nothing to do with him what she wore.

Maria climbed out of the water and came across to her. "Come on, Miss Winter," she said eagerly. "The water is gorgeous!"

Sarah climbed on to the rocks and dived into the pool without much enthusiasm, but the silky feel of the water over her sticky limbs removed all her feelings of annoyance, and she moved languidly, allowing herself to float with the gentle current. She did a lazy crawl across the pool, and then turning on to her back she floated, allowing the warmth of the sun to explore her face and neck. She could hear the children and Jason playing noisily, but she felt removed from the problems of the day, in a wonderful world of peace and contentment.

And then her peace was shattered, as a firm hand on her middle pressed her down into the water, and she came up splutteringly indignant to hear the children applauding Jason's action. She met Jason's laughing eyes, and with an angry impulsive movement she brought her hands down on his head, pushing him bodily into the depths of the lagoon.

She laughed herself now, and swam intuitively away, in case he tried the same thing on her again. Turning round, she looked back, but could only see the children, and for a moment her heart almost stopped beating. Where was Jason? Had she hurt him?

Then she felt strong hands around her waist beneath the water's surface, and she was tugged down herself into the brilliant green underworld to open her eyes and see Jason smiling at her in the gloom. She ought to have realised that a man who went skin-diving was hardly likely to be perturbed by an underwater excursion, and smiling herself she twisted away from him, immensely conscious of the strong physical attraction he had for her.

She surfaced again, and Jason surfaced beside her, and breathed deeply. Then before she realised his intention, he had pulled off her bathing hat and flung it far away across the lagoon to land on the rocks at the far side. His swift movement loosened the hairpins which held her coronet of plaits in place, and the plaits fell loosely to her shoulders and floated on the water, pale and silky.

80

She looked at him, feeling a sense of frustration at her own helplessness, when he said softly: "I'm sorry. But it's a sin to hide so much loveliness under a ridiculous rubber cap." His fingers caught one of the plaits and held her prisoner. "I'd like to see it loose," he murmured, as though to himself. "It's very long, isn't it?"

Sarah nodded, not trusting herself to speak.

"And it will take a long time to dry, won't it?"

"Yes."

His eyes were very dark now, and she caught something of his mood and would have turned away, when he said: "Don't ever have it cut, will you?"

"Why?" She spoke tremblingly.

"Because I don't want you to," he replied, half-arrogantly, and then he released her, as the children came swimming up to them to find out what was going on.

Sarah swam vigorously to the cove and climbed out of the water. Reaching her towel, she sat down and wrung out her plaits with both hands. She was about to release them when she decided it would be better to wait until she got home and could do so in the privacy of her room.

Ricardo came to where she sat, and said: "Gosh, your hair is as long as your waist!" He smiled. "It's very pretty, isn't it?"

"Why thank you, Ricardo," she said smiling up at him.

"I've decided I like you," he said, flopping down on the sand beside her. "I just thought I would come and tell you so."

She smiled. "I'm very glad about that. I like you, too."

"And Uncle Jason," said Ricardo solemnly.

"Uncle Jason!" Sarah was startled. "Whatever do you mean?"

"Nothing." Ricardo shrugged. "But we have fun with you, and Uncle Jason likes you, I know he does."

"I don't know about that," exclaimed Sarah weakly.

"Well, I do." Ricardo sounded convinced. "But, Miss Winter, you will be careful, won't you?"

"In what way?"

"Irena." Ricardo was very serious. "She'll hate you if she thinks Uncle Jason likes you. She's very jealous, even if she does hate him."

Sarah stared at him. "Hate is akin to love," she said quietly, almost to herself.

"Now who taught you that? I don't think you leaned that in the convent." Jason's voice, near her ear, startled her, and she realised he had come silently to sit beside them, his lean body dripping with water.

"No, you're right," said Sarah jerkily, standing up. "Er – are

81

we – I mean, is it time for us to go?"

Jason shrugged. "That's up to you, *señorita*. It's . . . let me see . ." He consulted the waterproof watch on his wrist: "Nearly nine-thirty. It'll take us about thirty minutes to get back. What's your decision?"

Sarah hesitated, then she said: "Children, you may have fifteen more minutes, and then we must go."

The children ran excitedly back into the water, for Maria and Eloise had come to see what was going on, and Sarah began to walk up the path to the car to dress. The warmth of the sun was already drying her swim suit and after rubbing herself down she pulled on the jeans and sweater, managing to keep out of Jason's sight as she did so. Then she bound the plaits back round her head, secured them in place and felt more herself.

Jason had come to join her at the car and reaching into the glove compartment, he extracted a flask, and said: "Coffee?"

"That sounds marvellous," she agreed, with pleasure. "I'd love some."

"Good." Jason handed her the flask. "Help yourself, while I pull on my pants."

Conscious of him the whole time, Sarah removed the cups from the lid of the flask and poured out the steaming liquid. Jason pulled on his shirt but left it loose and accepted the coffee from her, his fingers hard and cool against her own. He lit a cigarette and they leaned companionably against the bonnet of the car drinking the hot coffee.

"Have you enjoyed yourself?" he asked, looking at her lazily.

"You know I have," she answered, looking down at her coffee cup. "It's been marvellous."

"Good," Jason nodded. "We must come again."

"Yes," she said slowly. "But the children need a lot of tuition to bring them up to their proper standard, and there are lessons to prepare, and marking to do."

Jason's eyes were narrowed. "I see. You don't want my company."

She shrugged awkwardly. "I didn't say that."

"You are afraid of me! Am I not right?" His eyes were alight with a kind of suppressed fury.

"That's nonsense!"

"Is it? I think not. You think I'm not to be trusted. You're perhaps afraid I'll try to make love to you, aren't you? Do you think because my wife treats me like a fool that I'm searching for some woman to share my bed? Don't you realise, you little fool, that if I wanted a woman there are hundreds in the town I could satisfy my desires with?"

Sarah pressed a hand to her heaving stomach. *"Señor,* please!"

"Oh, you infuriate me!" he muttered.

"And you are rude, *señor!*" Sarah's breath was coming rapidly, and her breasts were heaving beneath the thin material of her sweater.

"Am I? Then I apologise," he said coldly, but she was aware that his apology was nothing more than conventional.

"I'm sorry, too," she said inadequately.

"Oh, God!" He opened the door of the car as he spoke. "The children are coming. We'll have to continue this discussion at some other time."

"Yes, *señor.*"

Sarah stiffened her back and stood up straight. For once she was glad of her height. At least he could not accuse her of playing on her femininity.

CHAPTER SIX

LATER that day it began to rain, and by tea time it was obvious it was no passing shower. Sarah, who had left the children to Max, had tea in her room, and received a message from Constancia to the effect that the *señor* would not be attending the barbecue that evening as it had been rained off and would the *señorita* be prepared to go another evening.

Sarah sat glumly by her open French doors and stared out vengefully at the rain. She had been looking forward, with a frightened kind of anticipation, to the evening's festivities, and now there was to be nothing.

Constancia offered her dinner in her room, and she accepted. She felt in no mood for small talk with Serena, who the previous evening had been sullen and uncommunicative. She went to bed early, but not to sleep. For once sleep evaded her, and it was not until the early morning light was gilding the shutters of her windows that she fell into an uneasy slumber.

The day was cool, but refreshing, and when the sun lifted the clouds it grew hot again. The children rode with her, and afterwards Sarah watched them swim in the pool without taking part herself.

Irena did not appear, and Sarah was glad. That would have been the last straw, particularly as she was feeling so miserable for some reason. It seemed hardly credible that it was less than a week since her arrival. She felt as though she had lived here always, and could not remember clearly the boredom of her life back in England. After the colour of the island, England seemed grey and faraway, and unreal somehow.

Lessons were brisk and successful. Eloise and Ricardo had joined Maria in concentrating, and Eloise actually read a sentence without hesitation. To Sarah, it was as though the children sensed her mood and were trying to do their utmost to lift her depression.

Dolores came to lunch that day. She looked sleek and attractive in green linen, the dress clinging to her small but perfect figure. She was comparatively friendly towards Sarah, and Sarah was surprised. It was so different from her first day on the island, when Dolores had tried to annoy her by being rude. But even Dolores had to comment on the change in the children, and Serena shrugged her slim shoulders deprecatingly.

"Bribery and corruption," she remarked idly as they ate the fresh fruit salad and cream which was served for dessert. "Miss Winter has won the children's hearts by morning rides and use of the pool."

Sarah felt uncomfortable. Although it was true she had used the horses and the pool as incentives, the children's work did not warrant such unkind criticism.

"The children's hearts were waiting to be won," she commented quietly. "And they're nothing if not honest. They work hard and play hard, and that is how it should be. Children are not here to be ignored."

Serena cast her a venomous glance. "Indeed! And you think you've won the battle? My dear Miss Winter, wait until the bribes begin to pall."

Ricardo, who had been studying his mother during the course of this conversation, said: "Miss Winter isn't like Aunt Irena, Mother. She treats us as human beings, and not like stupid children. She's interested in what we do and she doesn't criticise us all the time."

Serena stared at him. "Go to your room!" she exclaimed angrily. "How dare you speak to me like that?"

Thankfully, Dolores intervened, and said, "Now, Serena darling, don't be so touchy. You know Miss Winter has only been doing her job. If Ricardo likes her, this is all to the good, surely. You wanted the chance to get away on your own, didn't you? Soon you will have that chance."

Serena scowled. "I suppose you're right," she said, with ill grace, but Sarah shook her head. She did not understand these women; one moment they were friendly, and the next they were at her throat, metaphorically speaking. She sighed. Why had Dolores suddenly become so friendly? Why was Serena so unfriendly? And was it possible that Serena would refuse to allow her to stay at the end of the month? She had said at the very beginning that she had the final say-so! It was most confusing.

The children disappeared after lunch as they often did, and Sarah did not try to stop them. She thought they ought to be allowed some freedom to come and go as they pleased, and they certainly did not return looking like the ruffians they had looked that first lunch-time.

Left to herself, Sarah went to her room, changed into jeans and a sweater, and went down to the beach. The sun was really warm now, and she settled herself in the shade of a grove of palm trees, and opened the novel she had brought with her. But the unsettled night she had spent had left her exhausted, and in no time at all the book fell unheeded from her hands; she was asleep.

She did not know how long she had slept when she opened her eyes and became immediately aware that she was not alone. Sitting, his back against a palm, was a young man with curling dark hair and dark brown eyes. He was dressed much the same manner as herself, and was sucking a blade of grass.

"Sleeping Beauty awakes," he remarked lazily, rolling on to his stomach to look up at her. "You're Sarah Winter. I'm Roderigo Valente."

"How do you do." Sarah felt at a disadvantage. How long had he been sitting there watching her? "Who are you? Should I know you?"

"No. I'm Manuel Diaz' nephew and Dolores' cousin. The son of Carlos and Luisa Valente of Honey Grove Estate, Cordova. At your service, *señorita*!"

Sarah had to smile. "Then it was to your mother's barbecue the *señor* and myself were invited, is that right?"

"But of course. And it was rained off. We intend to have it tomorrow night instead."

"I see."

"Did Jason tell you?"

"No. I haven't seen the *señor* since yesterday morning."

"I see," he said slowly. "Do you realise how honoured you are to be escorted by the most elusive man since the Scarlet Pimpernel?"

Sarah laughed. She liked this young man. It was such a relief to meet someone with whom she could be herself, without being concerned about undercurrents of hate and jealousy and passion.

"I'm looking forward to it," she said, smiling. "Will there be many guests? And what do I wear?"

"There are to be about twenty guests, and ourselves of course. I have three sisters, Catherine, Helene and Christabel. They are all younger than me; I am twenty-three. And you?"

"Twenty-two," said Sarah easily. "And what about clothes?"

"Clothes are very informal. A swim suit and something to wear over it is all that is needed. It will be very warm, and there will be dancing on the beach."

Sarah thought of the yellow swim suit with loathing. After Jason's words of the previous day it seemed the most ugly garment she had possessed. Her bathing cap too was still lying down at the lagoon, for she had forgotten all about it. But she would have to see about another bathing suit. If she was to swim the next evening, she would not be the object of everyone else's amusement.

"What are you thinking about so solemnly?" he asked, but she shook her head.

"Nothing. Tell me, what do you do with yourself all day?"

Roderigo stayed for an hour and Sarah was quite regretful when he left. She had enjoyed talking to him, but a glance at her watch told her it was nearly tea time. He had apparently arrived in a dinghy with an outboard motor, and left in the same way, so no one encountered him but herself.

She changed into a pink linen dress for the children's teatime, and afterwards walked on to the verandah, taking her book with her. She spent a pleasant hour there, and was about to go in to wash before dinner when the station wagon halted at the foot of the steps and Jason slid out and mounted them casually. Sarah was on her feet by the time he reached her, and nervously caught the parcel he threw into her hands.

"Tomorrow evening," he said, as though she had asked a question.

"The barbecue? I know." She fingered the parcel.

"How do you know?" His eyes were dark suddenly.

"I had a visitor this afternoon – Roderigo Valente."

"Indeed." Jason looked at her askance. "What did he want?"

"Just to meet me, I think," she replied, awkwardly. "I take it you have no objections?"

"No. Only reservations," he replied enigmatically. "Be ready to leave after dinner tomorrow evening, about nine, right?"

"All right. Providing it doesn't rain, of course."

"Of course. If it rains, I'll have to think of some other diversion for you."

"Why should you do that?" she asked quickly, finding it difficult to breathe.

"Because I'm a wicked lecherous man, with designs on your virginity," he replied solemnly, and she wished she had not asked.

Turning, she walked in through the entrance, aware of him close behind her. She could smell the faint odour of sweat from the heat of his body after the day's work, mixed with the indefinable scent of his body, and she felt an overpowering longing to see that he rested after his shower, she longed to smooth away his tension with the tips of her fingers, to touch that scar that disfigured his cheek and put her lips to his mouth that so often mocked her by its indifference.

With a panic-stricken motion, she moved swiftly and ran up the stairs as though the devil himself were at her heels, and she did not stop until she reached the solitude of her bedroom.

Once there, her fingers tore open the parcel he had so carelessly tossed to her, and she gasped in pure amazement at the contents. In her hands she held a bikini bathing suit, of a kind of stretch-nylon towelling material the colour of creamy almonds. It was edged with scarlet beading, and was the most exciting item of clothing she had ever possessed.

But she would never wear it! Of that she was certain. She would never dare expose herself in such a garment! He had bought it to torment her, for he must know she was too timid a person ever to wear so daring a costume.

She thrust the bikini into a drawer and sank down shakily on to the bed. How dare he? He was treating her like a child! Deliberately taunting her to do something she had been brought up to despise. For although the nuns at the convent had been wide in the knowledge of God's will, the fashions at present in vogue back in England appalled them; the short skirts and trouser suits; they would never have countenanced Sarah wearing anything like that.

Serena was more amiable at dinner time. Dolores had departed for a dinner appointment, so they were alone. Sarah wondered what Serena would think of the bikini. She would probably be furious, for it seemed obvious from her attitude that she was only too willing to befriend Jason should he so desire.

"I understand you had a visitor this afternoon," Serena remarked suddenly.

"Yes – Roderigo Valente. Do you know him?"

"But of course. He is Dolores' cousin."

"Yes, of course. He seems very pleasant."

"Roderigo is a nice boy. He is a little wild, but I like him." Serena smiled. "You are going to his mother's barbecue tomorrow evening. Will you be attending Mass in the morning?"

Sarah gasped. She had forgotten it would be Sunday. "I – er – no, I think not."

Serena frowned. "No? But why? Myself, Jason, the children; we all go. You may join us if you wish. Besides, Father Dominic Sanchez will wish to meet you."

"Oh . . . yes. Very well, *señora*. What time do we leave?"

"Seven. The church is down in the town. Do you know it?"

"No, *señora*. I've only passed through the town once."

"Did not Jason take you to town the other morning?" Serena frowned.

"The other morning? Oh!" Sarah swallowed hard, "No, *señora*. We didn't go to town."

"Then where did you go?" Serena was looking angry.

88

"To a . . . lagoon, señora. To swim."

"To the lagoon?" Serena gasped. "Jason took you there?"

"Myself, and the children, señora, yes. Why?"

"Nothing." Serena muttered to herself, and shouted to Max to come and clear the plates away, as though venting her anger on the servant.

Sarah shrugged. What was wrong now?

The following evening was a perfect night for the barbecue. Sarah felt a surge of excitement at the prospect. This would be the first time she had spent an evening out with a man. Albeit, they were attending a party.

She hesitated over the bikini, but decided not to wear it, even though earlier she had convinced herself that she should, if only to show Jason that she was not scared to do so. She thrust it into the canvas bag she was taking with her and did not wear a bathing suit at all. Instead she slipped on a slim-fitting shift of apricot-coloured Tricel which was straight and simple, and ended quite daringly several inches above her knees. Her hair shone from a recent washing and she did not realise how charming she looked.

It was dark when she reached the verandah, and only the glow of Jason's cigarette warned her of his presence. He rose to his feet as she emerged from the doorway, and she saw he was wearing a light tropical lounge suit of a fawn-coloured silk, a cream shirt and dark brown tie. His hair was damp from his shower, and she thought he had never looked more attractive.

"Are you ready?" he asked, sending the cigarette spinning out across the gravel of the drive.

"Yes. Do I look all right?"

Jason smiled, quite a nice smile, without any mocking tilt to it, and said: "I'm sure you're well aware that you look delicious," he remarked casually. "Come on, let's go." His fingers curved about the flesh of her upper arm, and she shivered in anticipation at his touch.

The station wagon had been washed and looked clean for a change. She slid into the front seat, feeling her legs turning to water as he slid in beside her. He set the car in motion, and they turned right out of the drive gates and took the road which wound up into the hills above the villa. It was a beautiful night, and the rain as usual had left everything looking fresh and new. The night scents invaded her nostrils, and her whole body felt stimulated.

"Tell me," he said, as they drove higher into the hills, "why did you not take communion at Mass this morning?"

89

Sarah had been waiting for this question from the moment they had attended Mass, and now it had come she was not prepared for it. She looked at her nails, and said: "Because I'm not Catholic, *señor*."

Jason's fingers tightened on the wheel. "I guessed as much," he remarked slowly. "Why did you let us think you were?"

"Because I was afraid you wouldn't accept me if you thought I was not of your faith," she replied frankly. "And I wanted to come here very much."

"I see." He shrugged. "But you were brought up by nuns. Why was that?"

"My parents were killed in a car crash outside the convent. I was with them, but unhurt. The nuns took me into the convent, which was also used as an orphanage in those days. I had no known relatives, and the nuns were allowed to keep me and bring me up. But my parents had been stout Protestants, and the nuns would not let me take their faith until I was sure that that was what I wanted. You see, I did want to become a novice. That was before I left the convent, and came out into the big wide world." She half-laughed to herself. "I'm sorry if I've disappointed you."

Jason shrugged. "You haven't disappointed me," he said softly. "But I am glad you have told me the truth. So you wanted to become a novice. And are you still of the same mind?"

"No." Sarah looked blindly out of the car windows. "How long will it take us to get there?"

"Half an hour or so. Why? Why are you now unconvinced of your vocation?"

"That's my affair, *señor*."

Jason sighed. "Forgive me. I did not mean to intrude. And please, for tonight at least, you must call me Jason. *Señor* is much too formal."

"Very well, *señor*." Sarah refused to look at him. She was too conscious of him; she would give herself away.

The road had reached the top of a promontory now, and Sarah gasped: "Isn't that the ruin we saw when I first arrived?" The remnants of the old house were vaguely visible at the side of the road.

"Yes," said Jason dryly. "But we don't go there. It's dangerous. There's a hundred-foot drop to the rocks below. Besides, the house itself is in part still standing, and the ruins are dangerous. One day a hurricane will destroy it completely."

"A hurricane? Do you often have hurricanes?"

"Not often. But sometimes, yes. Why? Are you afraid?"

"No, of course not." Sarah was indignant.

"Then you should be. They can be dangerous."

"Yes, *señor*."

"Jason!"

"Jason," she agreed, smiling a little, "and will you call me Sarah?"

"If I have your permission."

"Of course. But the day before yesterday you used my name without permission, *señor*," she said, mocking him now.

"Then I'm sorry, *señorita*. But at times you anger me so much, I think I have cause. By the way, are you wearing my present to you?"

"No." Sarah flushed, glad of the veil of darkness to hide her embarrassment.

Jason shrugged. "Ah, well! You'll see. You'll see."

The partial floodlighting of Honey Grove Beach was visible long before the house came into view as they descended the hills at the far side of the island, and came down to sea-level. Sarah thought it required quite a powerful car to negotiate these twisting mountainous roads, particularly as the road in places was worse than a dirt track.

Jason parked the car alongside several others in the drive, and then cupping Sarah's elbow with his hand, he guided her up the steps into the house where their host and hostess were waiting to greet them.

The Valentes were both in their early fifties, and were a slim, grey-haired couple, who seemed genuinely pleased to welcome a stranger into their midst. "Rod has told us all about you," said Luisa, smiling warmly. "And of course my brother Manuel is quite intrigued by you."

Sarah looked up at Jason awkwardly, and then shrugged deprecatingly. "I'm sure you'll find I'm quite an ordinary person," she exclaimed.

"That is impossible," said a voice close by, and Sarah saw Manuel Diaz advancing on them. "Good evening, *señorita*. Are you well? I'm so glad our little entertainment had not been rained off this evening."

"Manuel was quite prostrate," remarked Carlos Valente dryly, "when we had to cancel the Friday evening barbecue."

Manuel smiled, not a bit disturbed by his brother-in-law's words. "I regretted the delay in meeting you again, *señorita*," he said warmly. "May I say you look delightful this evening, does she not, Jason?"

"Delightful," agreed Jason, and released her arm.

Sarah immediately felt as though she had been cast adrift

on an open sea in a rowing boat, for she was at once surrounded by a cluster of young people, most of whom seemed to be wearing bathing suits, among them Roderigo Valente and Dolores Diaz. Dolores was wearing a bright yellow bikini, very much more daring than the one Jason had provided for herself. The sides of Dolores' bikini were simply laces, and the bra was very narrow to allow the maximum amount of freedom.

Sarah glanced across at Jason, who was talking to their host, a drink in his hand. He caught her eyes, and the direction they had travelled, and gave her a slight bow. She sighed. Most of the young women were wearing bikinis and the only concession to formality were their brightly coloured beach coats.

"I think everyone is here now," said Señora Valente at last, "so shall we go down to the beach?"

Sarah, who seemed to have been monopolised by Roderigo, allowed herself to be led away with the rest, and glancing round she saw Dolores detach herself from the group and go to join Jason. Sarah felt a pain like a knife in her stomach. She was vaguely aware of Manuel trying to get to her side, but she felt too disturbed to speak.

The barbecue was a very well organised affair. The guests were all provided with low loungers or canvas swing couches, and several airbeds had been left from the day's sunbathers for those who wanted to recline more fully. The food, an amazing assortment, was served by white-coated Negro waiters, and on a side table stood bottles of every type of drink imaginable, from the unintoxicating Coca-Cola to the island spirit, rum.

Manuel at last managed to gain her attention, and said: "Come and sit with me, Sarah, I want to talk to you."

Sarah managed to smile and say: "Very well, Señor Diaz," and allowed herself to be led across to a low swing couch near the rotisserie, where a huge beast was being roasted for steaks later.

"Now," he said, "tell me all about yourself. You rushed away so swiftly the other evening I did not really have time to talk to you."

"There's very little to tell," replied Sarah blankly. "What do you want to know?"

While she talked to Manuel she watched Jason and Dolores. They were standing some little distance away, talking, and Dolores was obviously trying to persuade Jason to go swimming with her. They were joined by Rodcrigo, who pointed over at herself, Sarah, and raised his shoulders angrily. It was apparent that Roderigo was talking about Manuel and herself. She half-wished she had not come. After all, if she was to be partnered

92

by Manuel for the whole evening she would be bored stiff. Manuel was such dull company after Jason.

She sighed, and looked imploringly across at Jason. To her relief he caught her look, and nodded almost imperceptibly. Then he strolled across to them accompanied by Dolores and Roderigo. Sarah wondered intuitively whether this was why Dolores had been so friendly to her; because she knew her father was interested in her. It was awful, absolutely awful!

Jason looked down at Sarah, his head slightly on one side. "It's a pity you haven't got your swim suit," he said mockingly. "We're going swimming with the others. You could have come."

Sarah bit hard on her lip. "Oh, but I have got it with me," she exclaimed impulsively, unaware of her confession, only desirous of a way of getting out of Manuel's clutches.

"Have you, indeed?" Jason smiled slightly "Well, go over there into one of those bathing cabins and change, and we'll wait for you."

"Now look here," began Manuel. "I can't come swimming, you know that, Jason. And you're taking Sarah away from me."

Jason shrugged. "Do you want to swim, Sarah?"

"Do I?" she exclaimed fervently, and Jason gave Manuel a lazy smile.

"The lady wants to swim," he said softly. "Sorry, old friend."

The bikini clung to her like a second skin, and even in the dim light which came in through the cabin window she could see how becoming it looked. But so revealing! She felt as though she blushed all over. She emerged cautiously, to find Jason in his bathing trunks again, playing with Roderigo and Dolores with a huge blue beach ball. He stopped playing as she came out and said: "There you are. Come on, let's go," and so did not give her time to feel at all embarrassed.

Sarah was grateful to him. She ought to have realised Jason would not make mockery of her in front of anyone else. There was something too gentle in his make-up to do a thing like that. But now he had ignored her costume she wished, conversely, that he had not. Women, she thought to herself. Were they always so contrary?

The water was still warm and although they were out of the bright floodlighting on the beach, there was sufficient light for them to see quite clearly. Sarah found Jason beside her for a moment, and he said: "It suits you, Sarah. Do you like it?"

"Yes, I think so." She smiled. "I'm sorry I was so rude. I should have thanked you for it before."

"That's all right. Relax, enjoy yourself. What was wrong with Manuel?"

"He . . . well, he rather embarrasses me," she confessed self-consciously, now out of her depth and swimming beside him leisurely. "I think he's a little old for me, don't you? I don't understand him."

Jason nodded. "I see. And yes, you're right. He is too old for you. Roderigo is more of your age group."

Sarah frowned. "You make me sound like a child."

Jason shrugged, and swam lazily, treading water. "You are little more than a child, *pequeña*."

"Are you trying to provoke me?" she asked with asperity, and he grimaced, and replied: "It's not difficult." Then he turned and swam back to where Dolores was still wading at the water's edge.

Sarah found Roderigo beside her, and sighed; but Roderigo merely shouted: "Race you to the raft, Sarah!"

Sarah now saw the raft, moored out in the centre of the small cove. Roderigo had swum on ahead, so with firm strokes she began to follow him, casting caution to the wind. She was a strong swimmer and had nothing to fear and she refused to acknowledge the painful emotions that were stirring inside her.

Slowing, she turned round and looked back the way she had come to see Jason and Dolores swimming lazily together, far behind her. She compressed her lips for a moment and continued swimming for the raft. Roderigo was already there, climbing the ladder and shaking the water from his hair. He was shouting to her to hurry, but her limbs felt lethargic suddenly, and it was an effort to swim at all.

Was this what thinking of Jason de Cordova was doing to her? He was a married man, and a Catholic into the bargain, who although he might mock her sometimes, took his religion very seriously, and certainly would do nothing to break his faith. Even his obvious affection for Dolores Diaz would come to nothing, unless one day Irena died and left them free to marry, if they so desired. Why must she continually break her own faith with the nuns who had placed such trust in her? They had not thought a trip across the world a desirable thing for so young a girl, but they had trusted her, and in return she was becoming morbidly obsessed with a man who treated her like one of his nieces.

The raft loomed up ahead and she was relieved. As her cold fingers caught the rungs of the ladder she admitted to herself for the first time that the deny herself thoughts of Jason de Cordova would be a kind of hell on earth.

CHAPTER SEVEN

THE barbecue supper warmed the younger members of the party, for they had all been in the water, and there was no hot sun now to dry their tanned limbs with its warmth. The night was not cool, but the firelight provided a cheering glow and a steak with salad was just what they needed to fill their empty stomachs. Wine was plentiful with the meal, and Sarah felt quite heady after drinking several glasses provided by Roderigo. Manuel, to her relief, had not rejoined them after they emerged from the water, but Dolores seemed annoyed at Sarah's treatment of her father, and was consequently back to her sarcastic ways.

A troupe of limbo dancers arrived after the meal, and to the throbbing beat of the steel drums they performed their strenuous act, twisting their bodies almost in two, to sweep triumphantly under the low limbo cane. After their performance, many of the youngsters tried to join in, causing a great deal of amusement before falling giggling on to the sand in exhaustion. Roderigo was the most successful, and actually cleared the cane at three feet, but when it was lowered a couple of inches even he was stumped.

Sarah had not joined in. She would have felt too self-conscious, particularly as she was still wearing the bikini. Leaving the others, she went to the bathing cabin and slipped on the apricot shift over her bathing suit, and combed her hair back into place. In the water, the coronet had remained fastened thanks to a certain amount of careful pinning beforehand, but now she reset it and emerged looking cool and reserved.

She found Jason by her side. He was dressed too, and looked relaxed in his light suit. He smiled down at her, and said: "I hope you can dance. Rod is waiting for you."

"And where is Dolores?"

"With her father, I suppose. I think she thinks that you gave him a raw deal." His smile widened. "However, I must admit I'm glad you were not deceived. I regret to say the Diaz family can be rather fickle with other people's emotions."

"In what way?" Sarah asked, a little stiffly.

"Surely it's obvious," replied Jason, in a low voice.

"Are you telling me your friend Manuel would consider me fair game?"

Jason shrugged. "That could be one way of putting it."

"I see." Sarah contained the unreasoning sense of indignation

95

his words aroused inside her. "Does Roderigo think of me this way, too?"

Jason sighed. "That I don't know."

"You surprise me." She turned away from the brightly lit barbecue stands, and hunched her shoulders. "I would like to go home now."

Jason put a hand on her shoulder, but she shook it off impatiently. "Don't touch me," she exclaimed. "Please, I want to go back to the villa."

"You're as prickly as a porcupine," he said, in a low annoyed tone. "I'm sorry I spoke. Perhaps you would have preferred to learn the hard way."

Sarah shook her head. "Are you going to take me home, or is there some way I can get there myself?"

"This is ridiculous!" he exclaimed, in exasperation. "For goodness' sake, girl, I was merely warning you. You're very unsophisticated and I feel responsible for you."

"There's no need for you to feel responsible for me. And I want to go home."

Jason gave her an exasperated look, and then turned and walked away across the sand towards Luisa Valente. He said something to her, and she looked concerned, and followed him back across to where Sarah was standing.

"Jason tells me you are going home," she said lightly. "I am sorry you are not feeling well, my dear. A good night's rest will probably cure you. You must come again, we are always ready to welcome new friends."

Sarah looked at Jason, for a moment, and then said slowly: "Thank you, señora. I have enjoyed myself."

"Good. I am glad." The señora smiled and looked up at Jason. "And we are very glad to see you, Jason. Don't let this be the last time, will you?"

Jason gave no reply, except to express his thanks for the evening's entertainment, and the señora watched them as they walked up the path towards the villa.

The car was awaiting them and Sarah slid in, inwardly dreading the drive home. But she need not have concerned herself. Jason did not speak, and she could only assume that he was annoyed because she had dragged him away from the party so early. It was only a little after eleven, and there were signs that the party would continue well into the early hours of the morning.

The journey was soon over. Jason had driven fast and expertly, and concentrated on the road ahead the whole time, apart from lighting an occasional cigarette. What an ending to such

96

a promising evening! Sarah felt completely depressed.

When he halted at the foot of the steps leading up to the darkened entrance to the villa, she said hastily: "Thank you, *señor*," and springing out, ran lightly up the steps and into the house, not waiting for his reply.

Everywhere was in darkness, but she knew her way easily enough, and was soon in her bedroom, feeling a wave of absolute misery sweeping over her. She sank down on the bed and allowed the tears to engulf her.

After a while she dried her eyes and rose to her feet, stripping off the apricot dress. Studying her reflection in the wardrobe mirror, she saw, quite without any sense of pleasure, that the bikini suited her long limbs, emphasising the curve of her breast, and the smooth line of hip and thigh. She wondered what Jason really thought of her behaviour. It was quite likely that he considered her completely stupid. After all, his warning had been well-meant, and perhaps in other circumstances she would have welcomed it. As it was, she knew that the reasons she was not likely to get involved with the Diaz family were not ones she could explain to Jason. Because he was the greater part of those reasons.

Deciding not to bother showering before getting into bed, Sarah pulled back the bedclothes and began taking off her bra. But before she could unfasten the strap, her body grew numb with horror at the sight of what was in her bed. An enormous spider was walking slowly across the undersheet, black and hairy and ugly. Sarah stared at it for a moment, mesmerised by her own terror, and then with a swift, jerky movement she flung the bedclothes back over it, and stood staring at the place where it was hidden.

"Oh, God!" she whispered, in revulsion. She might have simply stepped into bed without thinking if she had been really weary, and then . . .

She pressed her hands together. She must do something. She could not leave the creature there; it might be poisonous!

"Jason!" she thought, swallowing hard, "*Jason!*"

She wrenched open the door of her room and scurried along the corridor silently, ignoring the implications which were now ringing through her head. The spider had not got into her bed of its own volition; someone had put it there. But who? Irena? Serena? The children?

No, she could not believe it was the children. They would not do such a thing. Then who?

The stairs had never seemed darker or more menacing. All Irena's wild words about witchcraft and voodoo came rushing into her head, and her mind was in a panic of fear. Someone had wanted to frighten her, and had gone to her room in her absence and left the spider in her bed, waiting for her! It was terrifying!

She was barefooted and the stairs were smooth and slippery to her hurrying feet. She was near the bottom when she lost her footing and fell bruisingly down the last few stairs to land in a heap on the marble mosaic of the hall. She realised she had cried out as she fell, and she lay there for a moment in agony, unable to gather her scattered wits together. Too many things had happened in too short a time and she felt exhausted.

Then she heard footsteps crossing the hall and hard but gentle hands were lifting her, into a haven of warmth and comfort. She knew immediately that it was Jason; her heightened senses were fully aware of him, and she allowed her body to relax against his broad chest.

"Sarah!" he muttered softly. "In heaven's name, what are you doing here?"

He did not wait for an answer, but carried her across the hall and along the wide corridor to his study. He pushed open the door and flicked on the light before depositing her on a low arm-hair. Closing the door, he drew the heavy curtains across the windows, and then crossing to the miscellany of bottles on the side table, poured her a drink and carried it across to her. As he had done once before, he went down on his haunches beside her, and said: "Now drink this, and then tell me what's wrong? Yes?"

Sarah nodded, sipping the drink, and as she did so, Jason's eyes surveyed the tear-stained face and untidy hair, the plaits falling about her shoulders. His eyes darkened as he discovered the weals across her shoulders and down the soft flesh of her arms where she had tumbled down the stairs. She was grazed and bleeding in places, and he walked across the room and disappeared through a door into what appeared to be a bathroom, emerging a few moments later with a dish of warm water and a sponge.

Bringing the dish across to her, he begun to bathe her arm, and Sarah willed herself not to grasp hold of him and cling to the reality of him. All the rest was a nightmare!

She finished the drink and put a hasty hand to her hair, but he said: "Forget your appearance for a moment – what happened?"

Sarah ran a tongue over her lips, and then said: "There – there's a spider in my bed!"

Jason frowned. "A spider?"

"Yes, a spider. I don't like spiders."

Jason stared at her. "Sarah, Sarah!" He shook his head. "Are you serious? How did it get there?"

"I imagine it was put there," she said, leaning back in her chair feeling sick suddenly. The whole affair had nauseated her, and she prayed she was not going to disgrace herself utterly by actually being physically sick in front of him.

Jason studied her pale cheeks for a moment, and then shrugging his broad shoulders, he turned and went out of the room, closing the door firmly behind him. Sarah lay there waiting for his return. She had never felt so ill in all her life. She knew she would have to go to the bathroom after all, but getting up she almost screamed with the agony of the pain in her ankle. She must have twisted it in her unexpected fall from the stairs, and she was forced to hop across to the bathroom door and only just reached the basin in time.

She lay against the cool tiled wall afterwards, allowing the chilly surface to reduce the temperature of her skin. She heard the outer door of the study open, and moved awkwardly to the door of the bathroom as she heard Jason's sharp: *"Sarah!"*

He shut the study door and came striding across to where she was standing on one leg, and taking one look at her swollen ankle, he swung her up into his arms and again deposited her on the armchair. "You've been sick?" It was a statement more than a question.

"I'm sorry. I used your bathroom," she murmured, lying back weakly.

"Don't be silly!" he muttered, and reached for a cigarette. "You were right about the spider. I'm afraid I didn't realise its size."

Sarah stared at him imploringly. "Has – has it gone?"

"Yes, it's gone. But you can't sleep in those sheets tonight, and it's too late to wake the servants. You'll have to sleep in my bed." Sarah's eyes widened, and he said: "Don't be alarmed. I mean alone, of course."

Sarah shook her head. "I'm not alarmed," she said, with feeling, but Jason ignored her.

"We'll have to bind your ankle with something cold," he said, thoughtfully. "A towel should do. Just wait a moment, and then I'll take you up to bed."

"Yes, *señor*."

He looked at her consideringly, and said: "The name is Jason. I believe I told you."

"Yes, Jason."

"Bien," he nodded, and went to get a towel from the bathroom.

99

He carried her up the stairs to his room and it was exquisite agony to be so close to him for a while. He carried her as though she was weightless, and her body trembled at the strength of him.

His room was very masculine, with dark green rugs and mustard-coloured curtains and bedspread. She felt intensely conscious of the scarcity of her clothing as he laid her on the wide double bed, and wondered what he would do if she wound her arms around his neck and begged him to stay. For that was what she was tempted to do; his nearness was the only reassurance she had, and she dreaded being left alone.

"Wh – where will you sleep?" she asked, as he straightened up away from her, and ran a hand through his thick hair.

"A chair in my study will suffice," he replied quietly. "I hope you won't find anything here to disturb you. I don't think it's likely."

Sarah's eyes followed his every movement, and he went on: "By the way, the spider was harmless. But I would like to know how it got there." He moved to the door. "Goodnight, Sarah."

"Goodnight, Jason."

With his departure, her earlier fears came crowding back to torment her, but she was so weary, and physically as well as mentally exhausted, that she slept in spite of everything.

Sarah did not see Jason the next day, nor indeed for several days. The following morning Constancia appeared with her early morning coffee as though it was not unusual to find her in the *señor*'s bed, and Sarah silently congratulated her on her diplomacy. Constancia also brought her some clothes, and she showered in Jason's bathroom before dressing in the jeans and sweater which Constancia had provided.

Her ankle was much better this morning, and did not pain her sufficiently to impede her progress other than providing her with a slight limp which would soon wear off as the ankle's swelling subsided. However, she had to apologise to the children for not taking them riding, although she did don the yellow bathing suit and join them in the pool.

Serena was sympathetic when she heard that Sarah had fallen on the stairs, but not knowing the circumstances made no other remarks. It was an effort for Sarah to return to her own room, even though the bed had been changed, and all signs of the previous evening's visitor had disappeared. She could not prevent a shudder of revulsion as she looked at the bed and wondered if she would ever get between those sheets again without first making sure the bed was quite empty.

The week passed without incident. There were no more spiders, nor any other insect for that matter, in her room, and Irena did not appear. Dolores was frequently about the place, but Sarah found she was to be ignored, so she did not have to make conversation with the other girl.

The children were amiable, and once Sarah borrowed the station wagon, with Serena's permission, and took the children to the lagoon. Another morninng they drove down into the town of El Tesoro, and spent an exciting hour wandering round the stalls in the market, examining the many interesting things on display. Sarah bought herself some essential extras and the children some paper and paints so that they could have a painting lesson the next day. They were doing so well with their lessons, she thought a change to a more relaxed style of teaching was indicated, and she decided she would ask Serena whether it was possible to hire a boat to take them out to the reef to study the biological phenomena at first hand. Now that the children were beginning to read quite well, it would make the lessons far more interesting if they spent some time discovering things for themselves.

It was strange, Sarah thought, as the week drew to its close, how so many people could live in one house, and yet never meet one another. The only person she seemed to see, apart from the children, was Serena, and she did not have a lot to say to her. Her bruises had turned all colours before fading and the grazes had healed on her arms, much to her relief. The children had been very concerned about her, and spent a lot of time questioning her on how she had managed to fall.

On the following Saturday morning, she was descending the stairs preparatory to joining Serena and the children for lunch, when Jason appeared in the hall and looked up at her thoughtfully. She was wearing a pink skirt and a sleeveless white blouse, the bruises on her arms visible for all to see. But it was too hot to wear a cardigan, and besides, Serena knew quite well that they were there and did not seem to mind.

But Jason's eyes were drawn to them, and as she drew nearer he flicked a finger at her arm and said: "They are improving, yes?"

"Thank you, yes." Sarah halted a couple of stairs from the bottom so that her eyes were on a level with his.

"That is good. I have an invitation for you, *señorita*. I said I would deliver it."

Sarah cast her eyes down to her sandalled feet "I don't wish to accept any invitations," she said calmly, trying not to allow the hot colour to surge up to her neck and face.

Jason shrugged. "That may be so. Nevertheless, I think perhaps you might like to come."

She looked up. "With you?"

"Yes, with me. To a small island about five miles from here, Coral Cay."

Sarah stared at him. "Are you issuing this invitation, *señor*?" she asked, puzzled. He had said he had promised to deliver the invitation.

"Not exactly," he said, flexing his muscles lazily. "My mother wants to meet you. She lives on Coral Cay."

"Your mother?" Sarah was astounded.

"Yes, my mother. I did have one, you know." His tone was sardonic and now she blushed.

"I – I didn't mean that to sound as it did," she said awkwardly. "I mean – well, I naturally assumed your parents were dead."

"My father is dead. But my mother is very much alive. You will come then? This afternoon?"

"The children . . ."

"Max can see to their tea, and put them to bed. You are at liberty to spend the afternoon as you will. But if, however, you do not care to come, I shall quite understand, and I shall certainly not object."

Sarah stepped down the last two stairs and looked up at him. "I'd love to come," she replied. "What time?"

"In about an hour and a half. Shall we say two-thirty?"

"Very well, *señor*."

He looked at her for a long moment, and then turned and walked away, and she felt a disturbing sense of excitement that would not be denied.

She did not mention her trip to Serena, but apparently the other woman knew, for she said: "I hear you are visiting Coral Cay with Jason this afternoon."

"*Yes, señora.* I hope you don't mind."

"Why should I mind? Your time is your own. Jason pays your salary, not me, and if he says you can go, who am I to object?"

Sarah, nonetheless, felt she did object, and replied: "The children are my first concern, *señora*. If they required my attention, naturally I should have to refuse the *señora*."

Serena studied her speculatively. "What I can't understand is why she should want to see *you*," she said broodingly. "She never comes here and none of us are ever invited over there. Jason sometimes takes the children with him, but only rarely." She frowned. "Be careful, *señorita*, that you do not let your emotions rule your head. The Señora Irena will find out about

102

this trip in some way, and when she does, you may expect trouble."

Sarah pressed a hand to her stomach. "Intrigue," she said, trying to sound indifferent.

"Yes, intrigue," agreed Serena dryly, "but dangerous intrigue, if you are careless with your affections, señorita."

"I don't know what you mean."

"You are not a very good liar, señorita," returned Serena smoothly. "And as I suffer from the same complaint myself, I think I am capable of observing the symptoms in others."

Sarah left the remainder of the crab salad she had been enjoying, and rose from the table. "Excuse me, señora," she said politely. "I think I will go to my room. I have a headache."

"Shall I tell Jason you are not going?"

Sarah nodded her head. "I – I think perhaps you'd better," she conceded, moving to the door "Excuse me!"

She lay on her bed. She was fully clothed, but she had drawn the curtains and the room was cool and dim for her aching temples. It was already half past two and soon Jason would be leaving, without her. She had no doubt that Serena would deliver the message personally. She would enjoy doing that.

There was a gentle tap on her door, and calling "Come in," Sarah looked expectantly to the opening, expecting to see Constancia. But it was not Constancia who entered the room, but Jason, and he looked annoyed.

"What do you mean by asking Serena to tell me you couldn't go because you had a headache?" he demanded.

Sarah sat up, looking hot and flustered. "It's true," she said, with alacrity. "I have a headache. I'm sorry, señor, but you'll have to go alone."

"Nonsense!" Jason crossed to the bed and put a cool hand against her temples. "You're simply feeling the heat. A sail, some fresh air into your lungs, that is what you need."

Sarah gazed at him in astonishment. "Señor, you told me that if I didn't want to come with you, you wouldn't object," she said stiffly.

"You wanted to come a short while ago. Now you've changed your mind. I wonder why? Could it be that Serena said something to change your mind for you?"

Sarah slid off the bed. "Please go, señor."

Jason hunched his shoulders. "Very well, if that is your final decision." He sighed, and for a moment his face mirrored his disappointment. His fingers sought the jagged line of the scar, and Sarah felt her heart melt.

He went to the door and would have gone, had she not said:

"Wait for me! I'll come."

He looked back at her broodingly. "I'm not begging you," he said deeply.

Sarah twisted her hands together. "But you will wait?"

Jason's lips curved sardonically. "Yes, I'll wait – mouse!"

Sarah found her hands were trembling as she stripped off her skirt and blouse and put on a dress with a semi-flared skirt, made of a particularly vivid shade of blue Crimplene. She realised that slacks would be more suitable for sailing, but she did not think they were suitable wear for meeting Jason's mother. Her hair did not require a lot of attention, and as her skin had tanned since her arrival she did not use any make-up, other than some light eye-shadow.

Jason was waiting on the verandah, dressed casually in dark blue slacks and a white shirt, open at the throat to reveal his tanned chest. His hair brushed the collar of his shirt, but Sarah thought it suited him long. He was in a serious mood, and barely glanced at her as they got into the Land Rover to drive down to the harbour. The market was quiet in the heat of the day, and only the barking of a dog disturbed the peace.

They walked along the quay to where Jason's yacht was awaiting them, and he said at last: "I hope you're a good sailor. It might be a bit choppy out in the sound."

"I've never been sick at sea yet," she said abruptly, remembering the embarrassing affair of the spider.

He half-smiled at her. "Don't go stiff on me," he warned her quietly. "And if you are sick, it will hurt you much more than it will hurt me."

"I'm sorry if I disgusted you . . . that . . . that night I was sick," she said, nervously now.

He laid a casual hand across her shoulders, looking down at her. "Disgusted me?" he exclaimed in surprise. "I don't think anything you did could disgust me. And being sick is a natural reaction to something pretty frightening."

Sarah grimaced. "I thought I behaved rather foolishly," she murmured. "After all, a harmless spider!"

Jason shrugged. "How could you be sure? And how would you have dealt with it? Killed it?"

"Oh, no!" Sarah shook her head, shivering

"I thought not. Never mind, forget about it. Here's the yacht. Have you ever sailed before?"

"No. What do I do?"

"I'll explain." He grinned and jumped aboard and turning, helped her to join him in the stern. "All right?"

"Yes, thank you." She subsided on to the low seat near the

104

tiller, and watched as Jason went forward and started the auxiliary engine which would take them out of the harbour, and through the pass in the reef.

It was a wonderful afternoon, and Sarah trailed her hand in the water, looking down and seeing the many-coloured fish swimming just below the surface. "Are there any sharks in these waters?" she asked suddenly, withdrawing her hand from the water.

Jason, seeing her action, laughed. "Yes, there are sharks. But I hardly think your fingers would provide much of a temptation."

"I wouldn't like to put them to the test," said Sarah, smiling, and raising her shoulders in a little gesture of complete freedom and enjoyment.

Beyond the reef, Jason hoisted the sails, and Sarah was given the task of holding the yacht on an even course while he made coffee in the tiny cabin below. Then he came to sit beside her and allowed the wind to take over, at times speeding them along at fifteen knots and at others swinging about and causing the small craft to buck and sway alarmingly. Not that Sarah was alarmed; she thought she would never feel alarmed with Jason.

He smoked a cigarette and Sarah loosened the top buttons of her dress, allowing the sun to get to her skin. She looked at Jason, suddenly, and smiled, as he said: "Are you glad you came?"

"Hmm," she nodded.

"And have you a headache now?"

"No, of course not." She sighed. "But I did have one before."

"Serena had said something, though, hadn't she?" he persisted.

"Yes, but it was nothing." She looked about her. There were hundreds of tiny atolls in the immediate vicinity, and she wondered how Jason could tell one from another. "How long will it take us to get there?"

"Maybe an hour. It depends on the wind. Why? In a hurry?"

"No. I love it." She laughed excitedly. "And the pitching of the boat doesn't bother me a bit!"

"Good. I hoped you would enjoy it. But you've changed the subject, and I want to talk about the reason you said you wouldn't come."

At his words Sarah realised just how alone they were. When they had attended the barbecue, and Jason had driven them there in the car, they had been alone, but she had always known that had she wanted to get out and walk she could do so, but now, here, out in the middle of the ocean, there was no way of escape,

105

and he had her completely at his mercy. But the thought did not terrify her. There was no other man she would sooner be with.

"Why do you want to talk about that?" she asked, tilting her head on one side to look at him.

"Because I'm interested in your reasons for refusal. Was it something to do with Irena?"

Sarah sighed. "You knew it would be." She looked down at her finger nails, and then up at his face, at the scar so close now that she could see the way the flesh was roughly drawn together. "Tell me about that." She indicated the scar. "Will you?" She raised her shoulders. "I mean, what happened?"

Jason's eyes narrowed. "Don't you know?"

Sarah sighed again. "Eloise said Irena did it. Is that right?"

He lay back, and half-closed his eyes. "Yes," he agreed shortly.

She looked at him solemnly for a moment. "You don't want to talk about it, but I want to know. Why did she do it? And when?"

He frowned. "I'm your employer, and you ought not to ask impertinent questions."

"Oh, Jason," she exclaimed exasperatedly, you know very well that you don't always treat me as an employee. Even though we have known each other such a short time."

"I feel as though I've known you all my life," he murmured enigmatically, and Sarah knew he was echoing her own thoughts.

"Then why are we always arguing with one another like this?" she asked, a trifle breathlessly.

"I'll tell you . . . one day," he said, closing his eyes fully, his long lashes throwing a veil over his cheekbones.

"Then tell me about the scar," she murmured, but he did not reply.

Sarah gazed out to sea. They were moving rhythmically and it was a drowsy rhythm, but she would not allow herself to sleep and so miss any part of this wonderful afternoon. After a while she thought Jason was asleep, and she looked down at him. With the tips of her fingers, she did something she had wanted to do since their first meeting – she ran them lightly over the scar. It felt hard and dry to the touch, and when his eyes did not open, she studied him intently. In repose the tawny eyes could not torment her, and he looked younger and more vulnerable. It was an exquisite torture to look at him like this while he slept.

Then to her horror, his eyes opened, and he said: "Satisfied?" in harsh tones.

Sarah would have moved away, but his fingers caught her

wrist, and he said angrily: "Don't ever do that again. Do you understand?"

Sarah stared at him. "Yes, *señor*," she said chokingly, and he sat upright with a little movement.

"My name is Jason," he muttered.

"You're my employer. It's impertinent to use your christian name," she said tersely, unknowingly provocative in her indignation.

"Oh, God, Sarah!" he exclaimed, releasing her. "You're so young; so *young*!"

"And that's a fault?" she enquired unsteadily.

Jason shrugged his shoulders, and rose to his feet. "The island is just visible on the horizon," he said, changing the subject finally. "It won't take us much longer now."

CHAPTER EIGHT

CORAL CAY was a very small island, not more than a mile square, but exotic in its exquisite beauty and colour. A tiny jetty jutted out for the few small craft that visited the island, and on the quay a horse-drawn open carriage awaited them. It seemed remote and unworldly, but Sarah thought it delightful. Here, one could imagine oneself away from the troubles of the world, and back in a time of more leisurely living, before cars and aeroplanes were invented.

Jason moored the yacht, and helped Sarah to jump on to the quay, which was nothing more than a sandy beach spread with wooden planks to prevent their feet from coming into contact with the water which seeped below them. Several native children stood watching their arrival with interested eyes, and Jason said smoothly, "My mother's servants and their families are the only inhabitants here. The men fish and grow vegetables and the women help in the house. The island is almost self-supporting and anything else they need, I send over from Cordova."

"Very feudal," remarked Sarah rather dryly, fully in command of herself again.

"You don't like it?" he queried.

"On the contrary, I think the prospect of living apart from so-called civilisation an interesting one. Your mother must be quite a woman to forsake the kind of life she must have been used to leading to come and live here."

"My mother lives in comparative luxury," replied Jason. "But as you say, she has none of the usual amenities that she could enjoy on one of the larger islands, like, say, Trinidad or even Jamaica."

Sarah noticed he did not say Cordova, and wondered why. After all, that was his mother's natural environment. Why had she left?

The black West Indian who sat awaiting them in the carriage was dressed in a severely cut suit of dark green livery, and Sarah thought how hot he must be in the heat of the sun. She was inestimably glad she had worn a dress after all, and not been tempted by the slacks which would have been so much more serviceable for climbing in and out of boats. If Jason's mother dressed her servants in livery in the heat of the day, it was hardly likely she would have appreciated a visit from her grandchildren's governess dressed as if for the beach.

108

Jason greeted the coachman in his usual casual way. It was enlightening to see the way the faces of the servants brightened at his greeting. Sarah thought she had never known one man emanate so much personality and friendliness. He had, she supposed, what one could call "the common touch" and she thought he would never be unjust no matter how disturbed his frame of mind might be. Looking at him, as she was assisted into the carriage, she wondered whether he would ever lose that mask of imperturbability in her presence. He had been near to losing it in the yacht during that eventful journey, but he had withdrawn again. If only she could have contented herself with the knowledge that he was a married man, with many responsibilities, and she was only the governess.

Seating himself beside her in the carriage as it lurched gently away, he said: "It's not far. But in the heat of the day, it's much more comfortable to ride than to walk." He indicated the track they were gradually mounting. "It's quite strenuous, and the ground is hard for the feet."

The carriage rocked alarmingly at times, but the horse merely plodded along steadily, and after a while Sarah found she relaxed completely and began to take an interest in her immediate surroundings. The track wound between trees and rock formations, and the abundance of colour almost hurt her eyes. Looking back, she could see the sea in the distance, the yacht seeming much smaller from here. Jason had lit a cigarette, and seemed, as usual, completely at ease. She could hardly believe that a short while ago she had had the temerity to actually touch him. Now he seemed as remote as he ever had and his eyes were cool despite their tawny brilliance.

The house belonging to Jason's mother was a Spanish-style bungalow, spread widely over a vast area and built round a central courtyard into which the carriage wheeled. Here a marble Cupid spilled water over a fountain basin, while a litter of spaniel puppies played with their mother, who was lying lethargically in the shade of a stone colonnade which ran round the bungalow. As the carriage stopped, a tall figure rose from the shade of the arches and came to meet them.

Jason's mother was the most imperious and impressive woman Sarah had ever seen. Although she was in her sixties she walked erect, and was dressed fashionably in a slim-fitting two-piece of grey and yellow silk she was fairer than Jason although her hair was quite grey, and her still swarthy complexion showed signs of age. The skin of her bare arms was not as tanned as Jason's, and she looked younger than many women of her age. Jason climbed swiftly down, and handed Sarah down beside him

109

before addressing his mother. Then he said: "Well, Mother, this is Sarah Winter. Sarah, my mother, the Señora Maria Consuelo Venetia de Cordova!"

His mother smiled charmingly. "Ignore my son," she said lightly, in a voice as warm and friendly as Jason's own. "His methods of introduction leave a lot to be desired. So you are Sarah. I am very pleased to meet you, my dear. Jason tells me you have worked wonders with the children. I am so glad. They really are quite friendly souls when they are not continually being used as objects of contention."

Sarah shook hands politely, feeling nervously like curtseying, even though the *señora* had put her at her ease so completely.

"I'm afraid I didn't know of your existence until today," she remarked awkwardly. "Jas – the *señor* had not mentioned his mother before, but naturally I was very happy to visit you when I was invited."

Jason's mother noticed the way Sarah had been about to say *Jason* and said: "Please don't think you have to stand on ceremony here, my dear." She smiled, and took Sarah's arm. "Come, let us go and sit in the shade and Gonzales will bring us some iced tea. Would you like that? Or would you prefer a long, cool drink, of the kind Jason always demands when he comes here?"

"A long cool drink, I think," replied Sarah, walking with the *señora* to the shade of the colonnade, and bending down to fondle the pups who came leaping towards them, barking excitedly.

Low lounging chairs with footrests provided a delightful relaxation in the heat of the day, and Sarah lay back luxuriously. It was incredible to think of her life back in England. Already, everything before the island was fading into obscurity.

The glasses clinked with ice, and the fountain provided a continual sound of falling water. The view over the trees to the sea below them was soporific and Sarah felt her eyes closing. It was an effort to concentrate when Jason's mother said: "Now, tell me: how are you enjoying the life here? Do you find yourself at all homesick?"

"Homesick?" Sarah looked up at Jason who was leaning against a pillar smoking a cigarette. "No, I've not had time to feel homesick. Besides, I don't think I should anyway. I love it here. I prefer the sun to wind and rain, with an occasional warm day if we're lucky. Here the weather is marvellous, the water's warm, and the people are friendly."

"You think so?" The *señora* frowned. "And Serena? What do you think of my daughter-in-law?"

"I ... well ..."

"I think you are embarrassing Sarah, Mother," remarked Jason, flicking his ash lazily.

"But why? Serena is a complex character, as are both my daughters-in-law; Miss Winter as an outsider might see things differently." She turned to Sarah thoughtfully. "Did you know that Serena wants to go to Trinidad to see her family?"

"Well," Sarah frowned, "when we were talking once, she did say she wished she could go back there for a while. I think she would like to see her family, yes."

"Ah!" the señora nodded. "And you, how do you feel about having complete charge of her family here? After all, Jason is out much of the time, you would have a lot of responsibility."

"Yes, I suppose I would. But that doesn't trouble me."

"Not at all? I'm glad to hear it. But there is another thing, and in part the reason why you are here."

"The reason?" Sarah looked puzzled. "But I thought ..." She looked at Jason. "There is a reason?"

"Yes," Jason nodded. "I have to fly to New York within the next few days on business, and I've half decided to take Serena to Trinidad, leave her there for a holiday with her parents, and continue on my way. I may be away over a week, possibly longer. That's why my mother, who wanted to meet you, made the suggestion."

"I see." Sarah's heart had sunk into her stomach. Jason was going away – for a week, ten days, even longer.

But none of this showed in her face as she turned to the señora and said: "But what more is there? Surely I'll stay at the villa with the children as usual, but with the additional task of taking over Serena's duties as well."

Maria de Cordova looked at her son, and then down at the delicate china cups she held between her fingers. "My son does not wish you to stay alone at the villa," she said, and looked up into Sarah's eyes. "Irena will not be going with Jason, and you would be there alone with her, apart from the servants."

Saral felt her stomach turn over. Irena! Of course! She had almost forgotten Irena in the shock of Jason's news. "I see," she managed quietly. "But I don't think –"

"You will come here, with the children," said Jason firmly. "Whatever you think or don't think!"

Sarah looked up at him, her breast heaving suddenly. His eyes were dark and she could not read their expression, but she was aware of the paralysing effect of his personality when he chose to exert it. "Very well, if that is what you want, and," she turned to his mother, "if you have no objections."

111

Maria smiled warmly. "None whatsoever. But I insisted on meeting you before making any definite decision. After all, we might have disliked each other on sight, and this is a small island with little room to hide our feelings."

Sarah laughed. "I think it will make a pleasant change, for all of us," she said, relaxing now and refusing to think of Jason's departure. "When will you be leaving?"

Jason stubbed out his cigarette and straightened. He ran his hands through his thick hair. "Maybe Tuesday of next week," he answered. "Could you be ready to leave then?"

"Of course. Does Serena know?"

"I mentioned it at lunch time. She's thrilled, naturally. She's too young to be tied with a litter of children. Like Sheba over there," he nodded at the spaniel. "She's too young to have had pups, but unfortunately we had no say in the matter."

He laughed, and Sarah found herself laughing too.

It was a wonderful afternoon, and as it grew later, Maria said: "Would you like to see round the house, Sarah? After all, if you're to live here, you might as well know the general layout of the place."

Jason walked away to speak to one of the servants who was watering some plants, and Sarah followed the *señora* into the building. A low, light, airy place, with polished wooden floors which Maria confessed were not as cool as marble tiles, it pleased Sarah enormously. Unlike the villa on Cordova it was not too big so that one could lose oneself in it. The rooms were not overly large, but ample windows and air conditioning system cooled the atmosphere to a temperature of seventy degrees.

"This will be your room," said Maria de Cordova, opening a door into a room designed for a woman with gay chintz and walnut furniture, skin rugs on the floor. "There is an adjoining bathroom," she continued, "but the children's rooms are at the other side of the bathroom, so I am afraid you will all have to share. There are only two bathrooms in the villa and the other is at the opposite side of the building near my room. I hope you will not consider me selfish keeping mine all to myself, but it was more convenient to put you near the children so that you could keep an eye on them."

"Of course," exclaimed Sarah, smiling. "Back home in England, there was one bath between twelve of us!"

Maria studied her for a moment. "You are very young, are you not?"

"I'm twenty-two," said Sarah defensively.

"I am sixty-seven. To me you are very young."

Maria smiled a little regretfully. "And Jason . . . you like my son, do you not?"

Sarah felt her cheeks burning and wished furiously she could control her emotions, "Of course, señora," she replied, with as much assurance as she could gather.

"There is no 'of course' about it," said Maria slowly. "Irena does not find it difficult to hate him. But perhaps she thinks she has reason."

Sarah moved her shoulders awkwardly.

"Ah," Maria sighed, "I am embarrassing you again, I am afraid. I'm sorry. My son is my first concern, you must understand that, and the life he is leading is very bad." She sighed again. "It is so rarely that I can discuss his problems with anyone. Always there are feelings to consider. Only Antonio knew how I really felt."

Sarah bit her lip. "Your daughter-in-law, Irena, you don't like her?"

"Irena is a little mad, I think," said Maria slowly. "She is a fanatic, and cares about no one but herself. She should never have come here, to live among these people, feeling as she did."

Sarah did not like to ask how she felt. It was sufficient to know that Maria knew as clearly as she did herself that Irena was not quite normal. Her talk of *voodoo* and *obeah* had seemed ridiculous, but to Irena's mind it was real, and she really believed she had been cursed for some reason. Not that Sarah ridiculed the ancient ritualistic customs; there was too much evidence to deny the existence of a supernatural force, but she believed that Irena was using the cult as a weapon in her hatred of her husband and his family. But again she came back to why; and as yet she could find no answer.

When they returned to the courtyard, Jason was waiting for them. "We'd better be leaving," he said. "It's almost seven, and it will soon be dark."

"Then stay for dinner," suggested his mother. "After all, you will be too late for dinner if you leave now, and it will be company for me."

Jason glanced at Sarah. "Do you want to stay?" he asked.

"I'd love to," confessed Sarah, smiling. "And it is a wonderful evening. If you don't object to sailing home in the dark."

"He has done so many times before," returned Maria swiftly. "So! I will go and see Benita. Excuse me, for a moment. If you wish to wash, Sarah, you know where the bathroom is."

"Yes, thank you."

Sarah watched her hostess depart, and then turned to Jason with a new-found confidence. "I'm enjoying myself very much.

113

I'm glad you brought me."

"Good," Jason smiled. "I thought you would like my mother. She can be as candid as you at times."

Sarah looked up at him, and he turned away abruptly, hiding the side of his face where the scar was so blatantly visible.

"Why do you always do that?" she asked softly. "I've told you it doesn't disturb me."

"No?" Jason's voice was harsh. "But it is hideous, is it not?"

"Not to me," she replied quietly.

She sighed and put up a hand to her hair, feeling tendrils which had come loose from the plaits clinging to the nape of her neck. Jason turned and looked at her. "Do you ever loosen your hair?" he asked, in a husky voice.

Sarah shivered in spite of the heat. "When I brush it," she replied. "It's easier to sleep with it in the plaits though and takes a lot less grooming afterwards."

"I'd like to see it loose," he said, his nearness causing Sarah to press her hand to her throat. She turned away, unable to prevent the surge of emotion which was gripping her. The facts of his situation, his wife, his position on the island, counted for little beside her overwhelming desire to have him touch her, to feel those hard fingers moving over her soft flesh, and to have his body close against hers. She wondered what a man's body felt like, lean and strong like Jason's, demanding possession.

She linked her fingers together and prayed for the feeling to go away. By even thinking such thoughts she was breaking every rule she had ever lived by, and despite her innate belief in the sanctity of marriage, she could not help but wish that Jason was less of an honourable man. The month she was to spend here in the islands might end during his trip to the United States, and if it did was she right to agree to stay on? The choice was hers, after all, and if she were to keep faith with herself she ought to leave at the end of the month and not think of Jason de Cordova again, but she knew she would not. To leave here now would be like cutting herself in half, and leaving the only half that mattered here with Jason.

She felt him move behind her, and then he said: "You're very thoughtful. What are you thinking about?"

Sarah started. "Oh, I – the month of my probation will probably be up while you're away, won't it?"

"Very likely. Why?" His voice was cool now.

"Will I be asked to stay?"

"I hardly think you need an answer to that," he replied coldly. "You know you're succeeding with the children. That was what you were hired for, so how could we ask you to leave?"

"I see."

She heard his sharp intake of breath, as he muttered angrily: "I take it you wish to stay on, or is this your way of telling me that you've decided to leave?"

Sarah glanced round at him, and then bent her head. "I haven't given the matter a lot of thought," she denied, her fingers crossed.

"Then do so," he said harshly. "After all, if you're leaving, I might find a substitute in New York, mightn't I?"

He could be cruel when he liked, she thought, closing her eyes for a moment. "I – shan't be leaving," she said slowly, despising herself for her weakness.

"Good." His voice was still cool. "Ah, here's my mother. Dinner must be ready.

The journey home in *La Sombre Negra* was a delightful experience. At night the waters reflected the pale light of the moon, and although it was warm, the breeze was sweetly refreshing, mingling with the scents of the flowers which rose nostalgically from every island they passed. The wind was in their favour and they moved certainly across the water, heading relentlessly, Sarah thought, for the shores of Cordova.

Jason was still cool and aloof, and Sarah sat alone in the stern, feeling depressed and unhappy. She had not thought he could become so detached and although he was polite it was obvious she had annoyed him back on Coral Cay. During dinner he had spoken mainly to his mother, and although Maria had introduced Sarah to the conversation, Sarah had remained the outsider for most of the meal.

Realising they would not have far to go, she looked forward to where Jason was standing, smoking, the glow of his cigarette a red circle in the pale moonlight.

As though aware of her attention, he turned and said: "Only another fifteen minutes, I estimate."

"Is that all?" Sarah's voice was small and polite.

Jason sent his cigarette spinning out across the water, and moved back to join her in the stern, seating himself beside her, one arm along the back of her seat. "You're very quiet," he said, looking at her, his face inscrutable in the moonlight.

"Yes." Sarah bent her head. "So are you."

Jason sighed. "You're perhaps unhappy about staying on Coral Cay, despite your averred pleasure at this news."

"Not at all. I shall enjoy it. Your mother is a very likeable person."

"That's good. I wondered whether I'd placed you in a diffi-

115

cult situation, one which you were unable to manipulate because of my rather careless handling. I should have asked your opinion before springing it on you."

"You're my employer. I do whatever you suggest," said Sarah politely.

"Oh, God!" Jason ran both of his hands round the back of his neck. "Sarah, you're deliberately provoking me!"

"I'm sorry. What did I say?"

He rested his arm along the back of the seat again, and looked at her, until she was forced to glance away. "You don't have to say anything," he said. He ran the fingers of one hand down the length of her bare arm. "Such soft skin," he murmured, half to himself, but Sarah's whole body was tinglingly aware of him. He looked at her again. "You wanted to touch me. earlier today," he said, a little thickly. "Do you know what that means?"

Sarah nodded, unable to speak

"And did you think I didn't want to touch you?" he went on quietly. "Your skin, your hair! I wanted to touch you, but with me it couldn't stop there. And you've never been touched, have you? By any man?"

Sarah shook her head.

"So you know nothing of men." He released her and lay back in his seat. "I suppose you do know the facts of life?" His tone was sardonic now.

"Of course." Sarah was stiff and unyielding. His touch had melted her bones, but his words were painful despite their veracity.

Jason studied her for a moment, and then rose to his feet. "We are approaching the reef. We must continue this conversation at some other time."

"I doubt that there's anything more to be said," replied Sarah carefully, avoiding his eyes.

The quay of El Tesoro was deserted as Jason tied up *La Sombre Negra* and helped Sarah to alight. Sarah wished they did not have the journey back to the villa ahead of them. She wanted with all her heart and soul to get away from him, to the privacy of her room, where she could be alone. She did not understand him. One moment he was saying he had wanted to touch her and the next he was mocking her for her innocence. Why did he begin to treat her as a woman and finish by deriding a child?

The Land Rover was waiting where they had left it, although a courting couple now occupied the front seat and had to be moved by Jason before they could climb in. The two dark-skinned West

Indians ran away laughing at Jason's chiding remarks, and Jason himself looked rather wryly at Sarah to see her reaction to such uninhibited behaviour.

Ignoring his questing eyes, she slid into her seat and glanced at her watch. It was later than she had thought, already after eleven o'clock, but time meant little on the islands and as they drove through the town, sounds of music and dancing came from bars on the waterfront, while the throbbing rhythm of the steel bands stirred all that was primitive in her blood. She, who had never danced nor led the usual existence of a girl of her age, now felt the urge to dance the night away, to flirt and provoke jealousy in this man who was sitting so casually beside her, to break down that resistance that surrounded him, to banish the inadequacy of his marriage and come alive in his arms.

She moved restlessly, and had to cling quickly to her seat as the Land Rover turned a sharp corner and almost flung her from her seat. She glared angrily at Jason and said: "Did you do that on purpose?"

Jason shrugged. "What? You ought to know by now that these roads are not meant for dreamers. Just what were you thinking about back there that required such concentration? That perhaps you will leave at the end of the month after all? Or were you speculating on the kind of man who one day tells you he does not indulge in extra-marital relations and the next makes verbal love to the girl who is employed in his house as a governess?"

Sarah did not immediately answer. He always had the power to startle her by his remarks, and she never knew quite how to react. She stared out at the tall walls of the villas they were passing, glimpsing people gathered on verandahs, or around swimming pools, drinking and talking. Although the island was small, there seemed no absence of social gatherings, and the white population seemed to lead very full lives.

The night was all about them as it had been on that other occasion, and as then, they were returning home without so much as speaking to one another Sarah felt guilty. After all, she was mainly to blame. She had acted recklessly, and deliberately aroused his interest.

The villa gates stood wide as usual, and Jason drew up at the foot of the verandah steps with a jerk, pulling on his brake violently. When Sarah would have slipped from her seat, his fingers caught and held her arm in a vice-like grip. "Not yet," he said, in a low voice.

"It's late," she began uneasily.

"I know. And we both have to be up early in the morning. But

117

I won't sleep – will you?"

Compressing her lips, she shook her head silently.

"Come with me, then," he said abruptly, and releasing her he climbed out of the Land Rover.

Shrugging her slim shoulders, she did as he asked and climbed down on to the gravel sweep before the house. Everywhere was in darkness, but the moon provided sufficient light for them to see where they were going. She followed Jason round the house, through the copse of trees and down the slope to the beach, where he flung himself full length on the sand. Sarah did not sit down beside him, but instead kicked off her sandals and walked to the water's edge, paddling in the still warm water. The soft waves caressed her toes, and the sand seeped away beneath her feet in a feathery, slippery motion, so that she was forced to move along the shoreline.

Realising Jason was back along the beach, she continued walking slowly, kicking and splashing in the pools like a child. But only her legs responded to the occupation; the rest of her body was wholly aware of the man who watched her, waiting with a kind of breathless anticipation for his next move. She half wished she had brought a bathing suit; it was the perfect night for a swim. She wondered idly what it would be like to swim without any covering; it could be quite a sensual experience, she thought, the palms of her hands becoming quite clammy at the idea.

Turning, she looked back along the beach and saw she had come quite a long way, reaching a curve where the sand gave way to shingle and small rocks before ending in the sweep of cliff above which towered the deserted ruins of the old Cordova house. There was a flight of moss-covered steps leading upwards, overgrown now but once obviously the means of access to the beach from the old house. It was queer, she thought, that in a place where fires were not often started, a mansion of its proportions should be completely destroyed in such a manner. How on earth had it happened? And where had Jason been at that time? She supposed it must have been about the time he married Irena.

Wrapped in her thoughts, she had not been aware of Jason's approach along the beach, and she started violently when he said: "In a short period of time, you have become completely involved with us, haven't you?"

Sarah swung round. "If by that you mean that as a family you interest me, then yes, you're right."

"I meant rather more than that," replied Jason softly. "I said involved, and involved you have become. You are curious, too;

perhaps too curious is a better way of putting it."

Sarah looked up at him. "Maybe I am at that," she agreed, trying to sound cool. "But you must admit that there are dozens of questions that anyone would find impossible not to ask. Your scar; the house, Irena! It's a mystery, as you well know."

"Is it? But then we all have our secrets, don't we? You didn't tell us that you were not a Catholic, did you?"

"My little secret is nothing compared to yours." She sighed. "Besides, as you said before, it doesn't really come into things, my being a Protestant."

"No, that's true." Jason's eyes met hers searchingly. Sarah became aware that he had loosened his shirt and his lean body was achingly attractive.

She turned away, half afraid she might do something she would regret, but his hands suddenly gripped her shoulders, drawing her back against him, then wrapped themselves around her as though he would never let her go. The heat of his body penetrated the thin material of her dress and she could feel the hard muscles pressing into her soft flesh.

"Now," he breathed in her ear, "is this what you want?"

Sarah let her head rest back against him, her body yielding so that she was moulded to him. "Isn't it what you want too?" she asked softly.

His mouth was hard against her neck, then he twisted her round in his arms, and she saw the agony on his face. The scar was taut and livid, and his voice was savage as he demanded: "Do I terrify you? Doesn't the nearness of this *thing* sicken you? You're so untouched, so innocent. Yet you drive me to distraction!"

Sarah wrapped her arms round his neck, straining against him, all her earlier inhibitions swept away by the power of emotion that was running like a flaming torrent through her body. She did not want him to talk, his mouth was doing astonishing things to her, and she was on fire for him. With a muffled expletive Jason caught her face between his two hands and without preamble put his mouth to hers.

Sarah thought she would never again experience such ecstasy. Without removing his mouth from hers, Jason drew her down on to the sand, and the weight of his body on hers cut out all coherent thought. She was sinking into an oblivion of sensual feeling where all that mattered was that he should go on and on, caressing her, kissing her, making love to her ... She was aware of his urgent fingers loosening the plaits which had loosened themselves from the coronet when he began to kiss her, and then felt a wholly satisfying feeling as he buried his face in her hair

119

and wound it ruthlessly round his hands pulling her back to him. She twined her own fingers in his hair, loving the intimacy of every action, kissing the scar which he so abhorred.

But it was as though her lips against that disfiguration brought Jason back to his senses, for in a moment he had released her, thrusting her roughly away from him, and getting abruptly to his feet. With hands that were not quite steady he brushed back his hair and shook the sand from his clothes. He thrust his shirt roughly back into his pants and reached for a cigarette. After it was lit he drew on it deeply, and moved his shoulders in a weary expression of self-recrimination. Then he looked back to where Sarah lay still on the sand, her hair a glory of silver silk around her, her mouth still parted and inviting.

"Get up!" he commanded her savagely, turning away from such unconscious promiscuity.

Sighing, Sarah did as he said, buttoning the bodice of her dress, and getting reluctantly to her feet. Her senses would not accept his sudden withdrawal, and her body ached with unsatisfied desires.

"Jason," she murmured questioningly. "What's wrong?"

"God!" he muttered, in fury, "don't act so innocent with me, Sarah! Even you, with your limited experience of life, must know what nearly happened just now!"

She twisted her fingers together. As her inflamed blood subsided a little at his words, she wondered how she had ever imagined she could remain mistress of herself with this man. With him she became emotionally absorbed and unable to think coherently. Instead of feeling like this, she ought to be grateful to him for his common sense which had in time prevented something happening which would have been irrevocable. And yet, argued her heart, was it so important to remain untouched, when in her brain she was as strongly committed to Jason as though he had in fact possessed her body?

She put up her hands to her hair and with deft fingers plaited it into a single braid, while Jason smoked his cigarette and stared unseeingly out to the reef.

When it was done, she said: "Are we going back?" in a small voice.

Jason flung away his cigarette and looked down on her, controlled and gentle again. "I guess so," he murmured. "It's just as well I'm going away. At least you won't have to be on your guard all the time. And when I return, if you want to leave, I shall quite understand."

Sarah clenched her fists. "I shall not be leaving, *señor*," she said coldly. "The children are my first concern. I shall not desert them no matter what happens. I'm sorry if you think my presence may disturb you!"

"Sarah! You're deliberately misunderstanding me," he exclaimed, his anger aroused again. "Have you no sense? Next time . . . who knows what might happen? With you, I seem to lose my head; this has never happened to me before."

"How inconvenient for you," she retorted bitterly, and without waiting for his reply, tears streaming down her cheeks, she ran like a wild thing back to the villa, praying he would not follow her and complete her state of ignominy by seeing the tears on her face.

CHAPTER NINE

THE most difficult thing Sarah had ever done was to get up the following morning, after a sleepless night, and act as though nothing had happened. She did not see Jason, of course, but the children's eyes were alert, and she was forced to laugh and eat breakfast with them as usual without showing the misery inside.

Afterwards, Ricardo suggested they drive to the lagoon, but Sarah managed to avoid that by saying that they would not be able to ride if they went inland, and it was a perfect morning for riding.

Lessons passed as usual, and afterwards, leaving the children to wash for lunch, Sarah walked out on to the verandah and accepted a cool lager from Romulus in the shade of the balconies. Dark glasses on her nose, she closed her eyes wearily, tired now in spite of everything.

As it was Sunday, Jason and Serena had gone to Mass and Romulus had told her that as they were lunching with the Diaz family the children had been excused from church. Sarah wondered when the children would be told about their trip to Coral Cay, and hoped it would not affect their companionable relationship. It would be necessary to take all their books and continue their routine as they did here. Perhaps, too, Señora Maria had some horses they could use for riding, and Jason had said the waters surrounding the Cay were ideal for swimming.

She had been sitting there for almost fifteen minutes when a car turned between the gates and drove swiftly down to the villa. She opened her eyes in panic. Was it Jason returning home for lunch after all? But it was Manuel Diaz, and she frowned as he climbed out of the limousine and mounted the steps towards her.

"Ah, my dear Miss Winter," he said, smiling. "The very person I came to see."

Sarah took off her dark glasses but did not get up. "Yes, *señor*," she said politely. "What can I do for you?"

"Rather, what can I do for you?" he returned smoothly. "You will already know that your employer and the Señora Serena are lunching at my house. I came to invite you to join us. Naturally, I thought you would come with the others when Jason was taking such an interest in you, wanting you to meet with the other members of the white fraternity here."

"Thank you, but I would rather not," she replied quickly. "I

— I have a headache, and I would rather not go out."

"Ah, that is a pity. I trust it is not too bad."

"Oh, no, hardly bad at all, but I don't feel like being sociable."

"Yes, I understand." He sighed, studying her thoughtfully. "I don't suppose you would care to have me join you for lunch?"

Sarah tried to think of a suitable reply, and then relaxed. Why not, for heaven's sake? It would take her mind off other things.

"But won't your guests object to your not being there?" she asked.

"Dolores can cope quite satisfactorily," he replied easily. "It would be so delightful if we could lunch together."

"All right, *señor*. I'll just go and tell Romulus of the change in plans."

"Very well, *señorita*." Manuel gave a small bow. "And now, may I sit down?"

To Sarah's surprise she enjoyed lunching with Manuel. He insisted she call him by his Christian name, and naturally she said he could call her Sarah. After their initial formality disappeared, he became friendly and amusing and very likeable. He told her about his work on the island, and as he had travelled all over the world he could tell her stories about places she had always wanted to visit.

Then she asked him about the life the plantation workers led here in Cordova, and he described the villages and the school which was only now beginning to make headway.

"We have an excellent master," went on Manuel, interested in his subject. "Roberto Santana was educated in England, at a public school there, and when he completed his training at university, he came back here to run the island school. He is a brilliant man."

"I should like to meet him," exclaimed Sarah, with interest. "Since I left England, I haven't met anyone with the same interest as myself. And it might be possible for me to help him in some way."

"Now hold on," exclaimed Manuel quickly. "Meeting Roberto is one thing, becoming his assistant is quite another. After all, your duties are here."

"My afternoons are free," she retorted. "Besides, what's wrong with trying to help people less fortunate than ourselves?"

"Nothing at all, nothing at all!" Manuel smiled. "Well, would you like to meet him today? Unlike you, he does not work on Sundays."

"Could I?"

"Of course. We could all go down to the town this after-noon, providing I forfeit my *siesta*."

"And would you?"

Manuel smiled again. "To see you looking so animated after the lethargic way you greeted me, I would do almost anything." He laughed. "I suppose you think that is foolish, an old man like me!"

Sarah shook her head. "I'm seeing an entirely different Manuel Diaz from the one I first met," she replied. "And," she went on candidly, "I must admit I like this one better."

The children were eager for a trip down to the school-house. Roberto Santana occupied the building adjoining the school, and his house was usually full of children. They set off soon after two o'clock. Manuel had rung his home at lunch time to tell them he would not be back, and Sarah wondered what Jason's reaction had been.

Sarah changed into her slim-fitting green dress with the scalloped hemline, and Manuel nodded his approval. The girls wore dresses and Ricardo a cotton suit and Sarah thought how angelic they appeared with clean faces and combed hair.

They scrambled into the back of Manuel's car while Sarah sat beside Manuel in the front. The drive into town was smooth and comfortable. Manuel did not drive quickly, but it was not far and when they reached the outskirts of El Tesoro he turned along a track which led towards the sea front but which petered out before a low thatched building which Sarah presumed must be the school. The house adjoining it was Roberto's and was in slightly better repair than the school. However, Manuel ex-plained as he parked that a new school house was being built not far away.

"It is unfortunate that it is not yet completed" he commented dryly. "You will think us very primitive."

"Lessons are the important thing," she replied. "It doesn't matter where they're taught."

Roberto Santana, hearing the car, came out to greet them, surrounded by some dozen small children, dressed scantily in shorts or brightly coloured cotton dresses, sometimes very dirty, their hair unkempt. He was tall like Jason, but like Serena he was not wholly Spanish, and when he smiled he revealed even white teeth. He was a very handsome man, much younger than she had imagined, not much older than herself in fact, and his English was perfect.

"Good morning, Señor Diaz," he said, in greeting. "To what do we owe the honour of this visit?"

Manuel slid out of the car, followed swiftly by the children and Sarah, who immediately caught the other children's attention by her unusually fair colouring. They crowded round her, and Roberto Santana said: "Hey, Pepe, Consuelo, you others! Leave the lady alone!"

"I'd like you to meet Roberto Santana, Sarah," said Manuel, drawing her forward. "Roberto, this is Señorita Winter who has come to teach the Cordova children."

"Indeed!" Roberto smiled. "And how do you like your work, Señorita Winter?"

"I'm enjoying it," she replied, smiling. "And the children, as you possibly can see, are not quite so unruly as they used to be."

"I thought I had not seen them at the school so often," he admitted cheerfully. "So you are living up at Jason's house, eh? And how do you like it? Do you find it a full-time occupation?"

"No. Actually, that's why I'm here. I asked Manuel if I could meet you. My afternoons are free, and I wondered whether there was any way –"

"Now hold on," exclaimed Manuel abruptly. "I agreed to bring you here to meet Roberto, but I didn't expect you to become immediately embroiled in a discussion about education. Roberto," he looked at the other man, "are you going to offer us a drink? I could certainly use one."

"But naturally," Roberto laughed. "Come along, Miss Winter. You interest me, but if Señor Diaz is thirsty, then I suppose we must satisfy him."

The inside of the house was more inspiring than the outside with low couches and rugs on the floor and modern amenities like a refrigerator and an electric fan. They drank ice cold beers in tall glasses, while the Cordova children played outside with the others, the sound of their happy voices coming in through the screen doors. Manuel and Roberto smoked and after a while Roberto, who was obviously interested in Sarah's attitude towards the school, began asking her questions about her qualifications, and why she wanted to do another job when she already had an occupation.

Sarah explained that her afternoons were free, and then remembered the trip to Coral Cay and said: "I might not be able to help you in the very near future, because I expect to be out of town for some time, but afterwards, if Jas – I mean the Señor, did not mind, I could come here most afternoons, if there was work for me to do?"

"If there was work?" Roberto stared at her in disbelief. "You must be joking. There are dozens of children who are unable to have lessons at all because we simply do not have the teachers.

125

Here we are all overworked, and," he glanced at Manuel, "underpaid, and in consequence, those who do qualify cannot wait to leave the island to gain more lucrative positions in the States."

Sarah smiled. "Well, I would like to help. But until now I haven't had the chance. Perhaps you think I'm only curious, but I can assure you this is not so. I'd really like to help."

"Now wait a minute." Manuel rose to his feet. "Sarah! You haven't discussed this with Jason. What will he say?"

"Jason would help himself, if he had the time," remarked Roberto, standing too. "There are many here who could help if they could find the time. But most of them don't give a damn for the African anyway."

Manuel flushed. "I trust you don't mean me."

"Well, there are times when you could help us more than you do," Roberto pointed out. "You could consider increasing the amount of capital used by the educational system for a start. Jason's money is all tied up in the plantation, and he provides work for many of our families. But you, *señor*, you are rich, as your daughter is not above saying!"

Sarah pressed a hand to her throat. "Please don't let's have an argument," she begged. "Manuel, I'll talk to Jason. I don't plan to do anything without his permission. But he knows I want to help if I can."

Manuel sighed and thrust his hands into his trouser pockets. This was not at all how he had expected their afternoon to turn out.

Jason halted the estate car at the foot of the steps leading up to the villa. Mounting the steps, he loosened his collar and pulled his tie down away from his throat. He was in a singularly bad humour which was rare for him, and he hardly answered Romulus's greeting as the flung open the doors and entered the marble hall.

"Señor Diaz lunched here, I understand," he said, halting in his stride and turning to the old manservant.

"Yes, *señor*. With the Señorita Winter."

"And where is he now?"

"The *señor* and *señorita* and the children went out soon after lunch, sir. In Señor Diaz' car. I do not know where they have gone, *señor*."

Jason hunched his shoulders angrily. "Very well, Romulus. I'm going to my study. Where is the Señora Irena?"

"Resting, *señor*. I believe she is in her bedroom."

"Thank you."

Jason strode away down the marble corridor towards his study.

Where on earth had Sarah gone with Manuel Diaz? It was so unusual, particularly as she had not seemed to like him a week ago. He went into his study and threw his jacket on to a chair before pouring herself a cool beer and seating himself at his desk. Before he went to the States, he would have to see the overseers from the estate and ensure that they knew what their individual tasks were to be. If they left the crop too long to ripen it would not be a good yield. But it would very likely wait until his return. With luck a week should complete his business in New York, and he might find the time to fly to Los Angeles to see a psychiatrist friend of his about Irena, and ask his advice.

He was finishing his beer when the door opened and he looked up in surprise to see Irena herself standing in the doorway. She came in and closed the door with controlled movements, and then crossed to the desk and looked down at him. "You took the *señorita* to see Señora Maria yesterday," she said in accusing tones.

"Yes." Jason's reply was flat.

"Why?"

"Señorita Winter and the children are to say on Coral Cay while I go to New York. Serena is going to spend a month in Trinidad with her family."

Irena stared at him. "And why cannot the *señorita* stay here while you are away?" Her voice was rising on a hysterical note.

Jason shrugged. "It will be easier for her to handle the children with my mother to assist her," he replied carefully. As always, he must not incite Irena's uncontrollable temper.

"You mean she is afraid to stay here with *me*!" she cried now. "I suppose she told you I had been talking to her, telling her of the life I am forced to lead here! Telling her about the curse!" She flung the words at him.

Jason sighed. "There is no curse, Irena. It's your imagination!" He rose to his feet and came round to her, but she backed away. "Don't touch me!" she screamed, and he thrust his hands into his pockets jerkily.

"I wasn't going to touch you," he muttered. "But Irena, can't you see, you're deluding yourself?"

Irena shook her head. "If my father hadn't died he would have taken me away," she hissed at him. "He wouldn't have let me stay here, living with a man I despise!"

"God!" Jason raised his eyes heavenward. "Irena, it's fifteen years since we *lived* together in the true sense of the word, and you know it."

"But I live in this house. I've seen your own brother marry a half-breed!"

127

Jason turned away. "Give it a rest, Irena!" he muttered.

"Why? Why should I?" Irena banged her fist against the chair behind which she had retreated. Then her face changed and grew sly, as she watched him. "But I finished you, didn't I? I spoiled your *pretty* face! What decent woman would look at you now –!"

"That's enough!" Jason swung round, his face pale beneath the tan. "Why are you doing this, Irena? Living a life that can only end in disaster! If you ever loved me, stop it now, and let us at least live like civilised people!" He bent his head. "By this, I don't want you to imagine that I wish to share your bed, but at least act normally towards one another in public."

"I hate you, Jason," she said, in a voice so utterly contemptuous that he shook his head in despair. "And one day I will repay you for all the shame you've brought me."

"Irena, stop it!" He shouted the words, losing his temper with her as he had not done for years. "My God, don't you think you've ruined my life? Living here with a creature who's hardly human, let alone a *woman*! Do you honestly imagine that this is *living*!"

Irena stared at him, and then laughed in his face in pure enjoyment at his torment. She turned to the door, and opened it with delicate fingers, but his voice halted her.

"Irena! Why did you put that spider in Sarah's bed?"

Irena swung round and frowned at him. Her ears had caught his casual use of the word *Sarah* and she clenched her fists tightly.

"A spider!" she said mockingly. "A spider in the *señorita's* bed. How very amusing! But a fitting bedfellow for a fly, don't you think?" She laughed in that tinkling way Sarah had heard on her first day at the villa. "Poor Jason, it seems you have two problems instead of one. But Miss Winter, I am sure, is hardly likely to be interested in a primitive animal like you. I think Manuel Diaz might not fit the bill, but *you*!" She laughed again. "*Amado,* no woman could possibly find you attractive now!"

She went out slowly, looking back at him with a strangely thoughtful expression on her once beautiful face. Then she stopped, and said quietly and deliberately: "And if the *señorita* did find you attractive, then she might find I can be quite a dangerous opponent!"

After she had gone, Jason buried his head on his hands, feeling a throbbing beginning in his head, and the drawing pain of his scar. As always after a session with Irena he felt completely exhausted. No one knew the things they said to one another in private, not even Serena, who was the nearest to knowing the

128

true situation here. His mother had left the island after the fire and gone to live on Coral Cay, never to return to Cordova, and she could only guess at their circumstances. But he was not a man to be self-pitying, and during the agonising years he had spent with Irena, he had learned to regard her remarks as the incoherent reasoning of a schizophrenic.

Controlling himself, he rose to his feet and walked to the doors to the verandah, leaning against the window jamb and staring out at the continual beauty of the view. A shimmering heat haze hung over the palms and the sea looked very inviting. At times he felt the desire to swim out into that blue water and keep on swimming until Irena, Cordova, and his life here, were all left far behind.

His thoughts turned to Sarah, and with clarity he recalled the softness of her skin, the silky texture of her hair, the warm, compelling response of her body. She had not been *repelled* by him, or if she had, she had concealed it well. He recalled his own tempestuous loss of self-control, and the fact that she had not been frightened. Instead she had responded to him completely and had been his for the taking. But he had not taken her, even though his own inflamed senses had caused him an agony of self-denial. He had wanted her – God, how he had wanted her, but he could not ruin her life in that way. He would never be free to marry her; he would always stay by Irena no matter what. It might be kinder to send Sarah away, back to her English convent, where eventually she might meet somebody, fall in love, and marry!

But at this word he baulked. To contemplate Sarah with some other man, living with him, sleeping with him, was more than he could bear. He could not *send* her away. If she chose to go he would not try to stop her, but at least, having her here, under his roof, where he could see her every day if he so desired, was better than not knowing where she was, or who she was with.

He left the window and reaching for a cigarette lit it before moving to the door. It was already after four; he would go and shower and change. Anything to fill the minutes! But where had Sarah and Manuel gone? And how soon would they be back?

Jason was lying on his bed when he heard the car sweep down the drive and the sound of voices filled the quiet afternoon air. He was naked, save for a towel wrapped round his lower limbs, and for a while he did not move. Then, with deliberation, he slid off the bed and dressed in dark, close-fitting slacks and a light-grey sweat shirt. His hair was still damp from his shower as he descended the stairs and came upon Ricardo in the hall, drinking a bottle of Cola.

"Where have you been?" he asked, and Ricardo grinned cheekily.

"Out, Uncle Jason. With Miss Winter and Uncle Manuel."

"I know you've been out," said Jason, with ill-concealed impatience. "Where?"

"Down to see Señor Santana, Uncle Jason. The schoolmaster, you know!"

"Roberto Santana?" Jason frowned. "But why? Had Manuel business with him?"

"No, I had not! But your governess did!" Manuel appeared from the direction of the kitchens, an amused expression on his face. "I told you, Jason. I warned you. Your new acquisition has a definite streak of obstinacy. She has decided to help Roberto run his school!"

Jason stared at Manuel. "You must be joking?"

"No, Jason, on my honour, I am not. She has decided all the children should have an equal chance of education, and if she can help she is going to do so. But she says she will be going away for a while and won't be able to help until she gets back. Is this right?"

"Yes," replied Jason slowly. "The children and Miss Winter are going to stay with my mother on Coral Cay, while I go to New York. Serena is to visit with her parents in Trinidad."

"Ah!" Manuel nodded, and Ricardo stared at his uncle. "Coral Cay?" He jumped up and down. "Yippee! Are we really?"

"Yes, and you all have to do as Miss Winter says, understand?" Jason looked down at his nephew seriously. "I shall ask Miss Winter for a full report when I get back, so you'd better not have caused any trouble."

"Gosh, Uncle Jason, we won't. Can I go and tell the girls?"

"If you like. Where is Miss Winter?"

"She's supervising the children's tea," said Manuel, in reply, as Ricardo skipped away. "Did you wonder where we had gone?"

"Yes, I did. I understood you were lunching at home. That was the general idea when we accepted that invitation. Serena is still there. Dolores asked her to stay on."

"Ah, but I could not resist staying with the charming señorita – and when she invited me –" He spread wide his hands.

"*She* invited *you*?" Jason was sceptical.

"But of course. Perhaps she was lonely, eh?"

Jason bit his lip, and shrugged. "Perhaps," he replied slowly. "And now what are your plans? Are you staying for dinner?"

130

"Are you inviting me?"

Jason sighed. "If you like."

Manuel hesitated for a moment, and then shook his head. "I can see you do not really wish me to stay, so I will go, my friend. Tell the *señorita* I hope to see her before she leaves for the Cay."

"Very well," Jason nodded, and Manuel left him. Then Jason walked down the hall towards the kitchens, and found Sarah talking to Anna as she made some lettuce and cucumber sandwiches for the children, and prepared a fruit salad and ice-cream. He saw the way she jumped at his entrance, and the nervous expectancy as though afraid of what he might be going to say.

Jason felt furious, suddenly. Good heavens, did the girl think he was about to seduce her or something? Or perhaps she was afraid he was going to embarrass her in front of the girls who were eating bananas in the corner, and making a loud noise with wooden spoons and saucepans. Ricardo had obviously delivered his message and gone, for at Jason's entrance both Eloise and Maria cried: "Are we really going to Grandmother's, Uncle Jason? Is it true?"

Jason nodded, and swung them round in his usual manner as they flung themselves upon him, but his eyes were on Sarah, watching her every reaction. She had stopped chatting to Anna and was setting everything on a tray preparatory to carrying it into the children's dining room.

"Miss Winter," he said suddenly, "could you leave that to Anna? I want to speak to you privately."

"Very well, *señor*." Sarah put down the jug of cream she was carrying and walked to the door which he held open for her, passing him coolly and walking into the hall.

Jason closed the door and looked down at her, not attempting to go any further. He was supremely conscious of the delicate pallor of her cheeks as she looked at him, and memories of the previous evening were fresh in his mind. However, his expression revealed none of this, as he said: "Manuel tells me you've been down to see Roberto Santana, and that you've decided to help him at the school."

Sarah nodded. "I would like to, *señor*. Providing, of course, you have no objections. But as my afternoons are free anyway —"

"Your afternoons are free so that you can rest in the heat of the day." Jason's voice was abrupt. "They're not meant to be used for occupations which can only tire you and inhibit your natural vitality. How long do you suppose you can work all morning with the children here, and all afternoon down at that airless rabbit hutch they call a school?"

"When I lived in England I worked all day. Why should this be any different?"

"The climate is different," he stated harshly, conscious of his own motives in all this. He didn't want her to go down to the school every day, tiring herself out and possibly inviting all kinds of infection. Besides, she would never be able to stand the pace, and it was then, when one was tired or weary, that one was susceptible to disease. Consequently, by his rather overbearing tone, he immediately aroused Sarah's sense of independence.

"I think, if you have no other reasons why I shouldn't go down, then I'm at liberty to do as I please," she said shortly, trying to ignore the bronzed skin of his bare arms, the way the dark hairs grew on his flesh, the gold watch with its expanding strap encircling his wrist.

"Damn you, I'm your employer, and I'll say what you do or do not do," he exclaimed angrily. "What do you know of such schools?"

"Nothing. But I'll learn. Is that all, *señor*?"

Jason seethed. Without revealing his own feelings and thus creating a situation he had wished to avoid, there was nothing more he could say. He could forbid her to go down, but that would sound ridiculous, particularly as he liked Roberto Santana and wanted to help him if he could. And if he forced her to obey him and she left – He sighed. His life had been empty before, but it would be even more empty if she left and he didn't know how he would bear it.

"Yes," he said now, "that's all. The children now know about the trip to Coral Cay, so will you be ready to leave on Tuesday morning. I'll get Max to take you over in the launch. The steamer will arrive later in the day and Serena and I will take it to Barbados."

"Very well, *señor*. And now, will you excuse me, and I'll see that the children are all right?"

Jason stared at her for a moment, and he saw the way she trembled beneath his gaze. "I'm not going to apologise," he muttered, knowing she was fully aware of his meaning.

"I don't want you to go," she whispered, and then with a muffled exclamation she turned and ran off towards the west wing where Serena's apartments were situated.

Jason watched her go, and then ran a hand across his forehead wearily. His whole body ached with a kind of insatiable desire, and it was difficult for him to shake off his hunger. How long would he be able to appease his senses by will power alone? Would his natural physical needs one day dominate his reason?

132

CHAPTER TEN

THE morning they were leaving for Coral Cay, Sarah was up very early to complete the children's packing. Although Constancia had made a fair attempt with her own things, Sarah had seen the way Anna was attempting to fold skirts and shorts, suits and dresses into the massive holdalls, and with a smiling dismissal she had sent Anna to pack the school books instead.

Sarah had not seen Jason since Sunday when she had gone down to El Tesoro with Manuel, and in a way she was glad. It was going to be very difficult to reassume their separate roles as employer and employee, and at least this sojourn on Coral Cay would provide a necessary breathing space for them both, and allow things to return to normal.

She was fastening the last suitcase when the door of her room opened and Serena came in. "Have you got everything you need?" she enquired politely.

"I think so." Sarah rose to her feet and smiled tentatively. "I expect you're very excited, going to Trinidad!"

Serena shrugged. Today she was wearing a cerise-coloured trouser suit with flared bottoms, and her hair had been tamed into deep waves. She looked very attractive, and Sarah felt her heart turn over. Was all this for her parents' benefit, or did the fact that she was travelling with Jason have anything to do with it? Serena had practically told her she was interested in Jason; could she possibly be hoping he might spend a few days with her in Port of Spain? There at least they would have some privacy, without the menacing presence of Irena to spoil everything.

As though divining her thoughts. Serena said: "Jason is spending a short visit with my parents before leaving for New York. It will do him good. He needs to get away from here and be lighthearted again. He has become an introvert – Irena's fault, of course."

Sarah managed to nod in agreement, and moved over to her dressing table to gather together her few jars of cosmetics. Thrusting them into a plastic holdall, she was aware that Serena was watching her and waiting, as though she had something more to say. "Er – look after the children for me, won't you?" she added. "I know you probably consider me a terrible mother, but I do have some feelings for them. I think as they grow older we will have more in common; I'm afraid I'm rather a selfish

133

beast, and I resent having been saddled with them, and no husband to support me."

Sarah looked at her, and then said impulsively: "I think I'm beginning to understand. You should have waited before starting a family. After all, you're still very young –"

Serena looked gratified. "Yes, I am, aren't I?" She smiled. "As to the other, sometimes one has no choice in these matters."

Sarah had to smile too. "I expect you're right. Enjoy yourself in Trinidad. If you give me your address, I'll have the children write you and tell you what they're doing. It will be good practice for them."

"All right," Serena nodded. "And now I must go and see whether there is anything I have forgotten."

After she had gone, Sarah lifted the two cases nearest to her, and walked to the door. She was half-way down the stairs when Jason appeared at the bottom, and with one lithe movement he vaulted up the steps and seized the cases from her hands. "There are servants for this kind of thing," he exclaimed impatiently.

"I am a servant," she replied, one hand resting on the banister rail. She turned, and began remounting the stairs to get the rest of the cases, hoping he would go. But instead he stood down his burden, and climbed the stairs after her, reaching her easily as she began to walk along to her bedroom.

"What was the essence of that remark?" he asked, one hand gripping her wrist, halting her.

Sarah wrenched herself away, and walked into her bedroom, but he followed her and stood in the doorway blocking her exit. Sarah would have lifted the other cases, but he said: "Leave them!" in such a commanding tone that she obeyed him. She stood, fingering the tied belt of her dress, feeling rather like a spoilt child who has been chastised.

Jason studied her for a long moment. Sarah thought he had never seemed more attractive to her. He was wearing a beautifully tailored charcoal grey silk suit and a brilliant white shirt, while the tie slotted beneath his collar was the dark grey and red of a famous public school. The narrow cut of his trousers accentuated the lean muscular length of his legs, and the broadness of his shoulders owed nothing to padding. Her heart turned over with longing, and with trembling movements she turned away from him and walked slowly across to her balcony.

"Are these the last cases?" he asked, indicating the three that were left alongside her own holdall.

"Yes, señor. And I'm quite capable of carrying them downstairs, thank you."

"Nevertheless, you will not do so." Jason frowned, and Sarah who had turned to look at him, suddenly found her tongue.

"Don't order me about!" she exclaimed angrily. "Just because you're omnipotent here, don't imagine I'm subservient to you." She cast aside the gentle teachings of the nuns who had always practised tolerance, and continued: "If I want to carry suitcases downstairs, or up them for that matter, I shall do so. Now go away, and stop treating me like an imbecile. On Sunday you told me I might not do what I liked during my free afternoons, and today you're actually attempting to inhibit my normal activities. What will your next commands be, I wonder?" Her breast was heaving, and so absorbed was she in her own speech, she had taken no account of Jason's expression, which had gradually darkened as she went on with her tirade.

Her first indication of his reaction, was when he came deliberately into the room and closed the door behind him with controlled violence. Realising how rude she had been, she was immediately penitent. But she could not utter the words of apology that trembled on her lips. Instead she stood her ground and waited for the axe to fall.

Jason folded his arms and said, with cold emphasis: "You will do exactly as I say, is that understood? You will neither attend the school in the afternoons, nor carry suitcases, or do anything else that I may deem it necessary to forbid!"

Sarah stared at him in surprise. Surely he could not be serious! Did he really imagine he could control her movements by orders?

"*Señor*, I think you're overreaching yourself," she said indignantly. "You may be my employer, but you're not my keeper."

"I'm whatever I decide to be, and if you don't choose to adhere to my edicts, you're at liberty to leave."

Sarah clasped her hands together. "Then perhaps you'd better make arrangements for a new governess while you're away," she said shakily. "I won't be treated in this way. I must be allowed a little independence."

"A few moments ago you told me you were a servant."

"I am. That is –" Sarah paused, "I'm your employee, if that sounds better." Her nerves were reaching breaking point.

Jason shook his head and straightened. "So you wish after all to sever our association. I regret this very much."

Sarah stared at him. Could this be the man who had held her in his arms so passionately only a few nights ago? Was this the gentle, understanding Jason she had grown to love? For she did love him, that much she knew. But this man was suddenly a stranger – a cold, unfeeling stranger! She looked down at the

135

ice green of her dress, but saw nothing but a blinding flood of hot tears. She could not look up now; he must never know of her humiliation.

"When do you wish to leave?" he asked abruptly. "Is it too much to expect you to stay until I return from the States?"

Sarah could not answer. Her voice was lost in the surge of misery emanating from her throat. She wished he would just go and leave her, she did not want to see anybody. After a few moments she shook her head.

"I don't recall saying that I *wanted* to leave," she murmured chokily. "But if that's what *you* want ..." Her voice trailed away.

Jason's fingers sought the handle of the door, and he wrenched it open unceremoniously. Standing in the doorway, he said: "I think, *señorita,* we'll leave this discussion until my return. I don't care to make snap decisions. I'll consider the matter and let you know my feelings then, *Adios.*"

The door slammed behind him and Sarah sank down on to the bed feeling physically sick. "Oh, God!" she thought achingly, "I can't go! I simply can't go! I can't leave him now!"

From the very beginning, Sarah found living with Jason's mother the most relaxed time she had experienced since her arrival at Cordova. To begin with, the señora liked her and was therefore only too willing to talk to her and make her feel at her ease. The children, to whom it was a great adventure, were more than usually obedient, and obviously offered their grandmother the love which Serena so carelessly ignored. Señora Maria explained that the reason she so seldom had the children visit her was because she herself did not get along with Serena, and continuing, she said: "I felt rather guilty, inviting the children and not their mother, even though I know Serena does not care to come here."

"Don't you have any desire to return to Cordova?" asked Sarah curiously.

"Not while Irena is there," said Señora Maria thoughtfully. "I am afraid I must appear a very hard person to get along with, of alternatively you may think I resent my sons' marriages, but I can assure you this is not so. Irena killed any feeling I had for her years ago, and Serena ... as I have said, Serena is not the easiest person to know. At times one thinks one knows her, and then she does something completely illogical and you realise you never knew her at all."

Sarah looked down at the plate of fruit which had been placed in front of her and allowed a soft sigh to escape her. She ought to be feeling completely happy, here amongst people she liked and was genuinely fond of, but instead the remembrance of the morning's argument was there to turn the food to sawdust in her mouth.

The children had been put to bed in their rooms and now Señora Maria and herself were dining on the terrace. Candles had been lit, instead of the usual electric lights and it was very romantic with the cicadas making their nightly din, and the sounds of the small creatures coming out for the night rustling in the undergrowth. The scent of roses and lobelia mingled with some stocks which the *señora* had planted beneath the windows wafted in on the gentle breeze, and Sarah reflected that Coral Cay was a much more intimate island than Cordova.

After the meal was over, they seated themselves in low loungers and Gonzales served them coffee and tiny fingers of absinth in glowing ruby glasses. The *señora* lit a cigarette, and then said: "Tell me all about yourself. I understand you were orphaned and brought up by nuns."

"When you've said that, you've said it all," remarked Sarah dryly. "I'm afraid I've led a very prosaic existence compared to the exotic life here."

"You like it here?"

"Of course. I adore it. I think I'd like to live here always."

The *señora* smiled. "Are you sure you wouldn't find yourself hankering after the bright lights? After all, apart from the outdoor sports indulged in by the younger set, there is very little to occupy you. Of course, some of the older members of the community form bridge fours and have parties, and so on, but I hardly think you look the type for bridge for a few years yet. What would you do if you lived here?"

Sarah smiled. "Well, I haven't actually given the matter a lot of thought. I expect I should live a life much the same as I'm living now. I would hope to be married and have children of my own, so my position wouldn't be so very different, would it?"

"No. But honestly, don't you think you would prefer to live in say Jamaica, or Trinidad, or one of the other islands with night life for those who want it? And how do you know until you've tried it?"

Sarah sighed. "Well, back home in England, there are night clubs, you know, but I've never been tempted to visit them. So why should I start now?"

The *señora* smiled. "*Touché.*"

137

There was silence for a while and Sarah sipped the liqueur and watched an enormous moth fluttering dangerously close to the candle flame. What was it that attracted the poor dumb creatures to ultimate disaster? she wondered idly. And wasn't she herself in much the same position as the helpless moth? Wasn't she courting disaster by allowing her feeling for Jason de Cordova to override all her innate sensibilities? Where was he now? Was he at the hotel in Port of Spain with Serena, dining with her, dancing with her? Holding her in his arms, as he had held herself only three nights ago?

The *señora's* next words startled Sarah back to cold reality. "How long have you been in love with my son?"

Sarah stared at the *señora* and went hot and then cold, rubbing the palms of her hands against her elbows. "I beg your pardon, *senora*?"

The Señora Maria smiled, and drew on her cigarette. "Do not try to deny it, my dear. It was perfectly obvious the last time you were here that Jason meant something more than an employer to you. The way you looked at him, the way you spoke to him; to me it was very evident. But again, I am sorry if I have embarrassed you. I seem to make a habit of doing that, but I wish it could be different. I would like to think that you felt you could confide in me, for I assure you the knowledge of your feelings does not appal me as it should."

Sarah rubbed her cheeks violently, and then studied the pale ovals of her nails. "I feel I ought to tell you that I may be leaving when Jason returns," she said quietly. "We – we – had an argument this morning. I'm afraid he expects me to leave, and maybe he will engage someone else to take care of the children while he's in the States."

Señora Maria frowned. "But why, for heaven's sake?" she snorted angrily. "You are doing eminently well with the children. You can't leave!"

Sarah hunched her shoulders in an attitude of complete dejection. "To be quite honest, I don't understand Jason," she sighed. "You're right, of course, I am in love with him. And I thought ..." She swallowed hard. "On Sunday afternoon Manuel Diaz took me down to meet Roberto Santana, the schoolmaster, you know, and I offered my services down at the school during the afternoons I was free. When I got back and told Jason he was furious! He said my afternoons were for resting and not for tiring myself out down in the town. Oh, he said lots of things, and we left it at that. And then this morning an argument blew up over absolutely nothing. He practically asked me to leave, and then said we should leave it until he returns."

"I see." Señora Maria grimaced. "That doesn't sound at all like Jason."

"I know." Sarah flung herself back in her chair. "Oh, lord, what am I going to do?"

The *señora* looked at her for a moment, and then she shrugged and changed the subject. But she did ask Sarah what she thought of Roberto Santana.

"I liked him. I think he's doing a wonderful job. And I would like to help him. I don't take a *siesta* in the afternoons, and I could be of some real assistance to him."

Señora Maria nodded. "That you could," she agreed. "And of course, if Jason does decide to fire you, you could stay on and help Roberto. And visit me, of course," she laughed. "But I think the chances of Jason dismissing you are very slight. I don't think he can have been himself this morning. Perhaps Irena . . ." She stopped and glanced at her watch. "It is getting late, and we must be up early with the children. Do you mind if I retire?"

"Of course not." Sarah shook her head. "It's been quite a day!"

In her room, Sarah undressed slowly. She had not considered Irena as being in any way responsible for Jason's treatment of herself, but perhaps Señora Maria was right. Irena was quite a problem.

She lay awake watching the stars in the curve of velvet sky above the bungalow. She wondered whether Jason was in bed, perhaps looking at the sky too. But as it was only a little after ten she thought it was highly unlikely. If he was in Port of Spain, there was little chance of his being in bed much before dawn.

Life on Coral Cay moved at a leisurely but satisfactory pace. In the mornings the children swam as usual, and afterwards they had their lessons outside under the shade of a huge date palm. Lunch was at one-thirty and then the children rested or went to play with the children who lived in the small settlement to the rear of the bungalow. They had tea at five and were usually in the bath by six-thirty and in bed for seven. Sarah had taken it upon herself to bath them, and consequently she usually emerged soaked to the skin and breathlessly flushed from her exertions. But the children loved it and she felt she was in part giving them a feeling of security which until now they had lacked.

When the children were settled, Señora Maria provided cocktails before dinner, and after it was over they sat and talked or discussed various mutual interests. Sarah discovered the *señora* was keen on books as she was herself, and they discussed literature and music and art.

Sarah had been on the island for four days when Roberto San-

139

tana surprised them by appearing just before dinner. He and the Señora Maria were obviously old friends and he was invited to stay to dinner. Sarah wondered why he had come, and when the meal was over Señora Maria said: "Now tell us why are you here. Is it to do with Sarah wanting to work at the school?"

Roberto smiled easily. "As usual, you are astute, *señora*. And why not? Actually, Enrico Vares has broken his leg, and as you can imagine things are a bit tight at the moment. I wondered whether the fair *señorita* was serious, and if she was whether she would care to come and help us out for a few days."

Sarah sat up in her seat, and trembled a little. She had not imagined she would have to make a decision like this while Jason was away. It put her in an invidious position and she was not prepared for it.

"Of course I was serious," she said now. "But I can't help you until I return to Cordova, can I?"

"If you wanted to, you could help us tomorrow," he replied. "That would give you an afternoon of work and then Sunday to get over it." He looked rather mocking.

Sarah hesitated. "But how would I get there and back?"

"The same way as I have done — by launch. It takes only a little over half an hour. Surely you could manage that!"

"Now wait a minute," Señora Maria interrupted them. "Roberto, this may sound all right in theory, but this child has been forbidden by Jason to do anything about it until he returns from New York. Now what can she do?"

"Forbidden!" Roberto laughed. "Indeed, has she? Then what more can I say? The mighty has spoken! God, I never thought Jason would do such a thing. What's he afraid of? That she'll get infected with some filthy bug or something?"

"Roberto!" Maria's voice was husky. "Try to understand. It is not Sarah's decision to make."

"Isn't it?" Roberto grimaced and rose to his feet. "I had better go. It's getting late, and I have to get back before I say something I'll regret. Sorry to have troubled you, *señorita*. I ought to have known your protestations were too good to be true!"

"Now wait a minute!" Sarah rose to her feet. "I was utterly serious when I suggested helping you and I'm serious now. I'll come — that is if you can provide someone to take me there and bring me back. I can't steer a boat and I don't know the way."

Señora Maria rose too. "Do not allow Roberto to hustle you into doing something you will regret," she said slowly. "If Jason doesn't want you to go, I don't think you ought to, at least until he returns at any rate."

"He may be away another week," exclaimed Sarah impatient-

ly. "It's only a job, señora. Please, won't you see it my way?"
She looked at her appealingly.

Señora Maria hesitated a moment and then spread wide her
hands. "Very well, Sarah. If that is what you want to do, I won't
stop you. A person must find his own way in life, I have always
known that. And as to the means, Gonzales can take you and
wait for you and bring you back. He will enjoy the trip to Cordova. He doesn't have much excitement here with only his family
for company. He will be able to look up his brothers and sisters.
Yes, I can provide transport."

Roberto stared at them both. "Wonderful!" he exclaimed.
"Then I may expect you tomorrow, señorita?"

"Yes. What time would be best?"

It was arranged that Gonzales should leave the island at two
o'clock with his passenger, and return in the evening about six.
That would give Sarah over two and a half hours at the school.
and during that time she would have to achieve as much as she
possibly could with a class of fifty.

After Roberto had gone, Señora Maria sank down rather
weakly into her chair and said: "I hope you know what you are
doing."

"I think I do. Why? Do you think Jason might dismiss me
for going against his word in his absence?"

"I don't know what to think," Señora Maria sighed. "In
other circumstances I would say – go ahead – do as you like. But
with Jacob, I don't know. He has had a lot to contend with in his
life."

"But why should it matter?"

"You love my son. Try to understand him. I don't know whether or not he loves you, but I suspect he might. Whatever his
feelings, he can never leave Irena. Regardless of the fact that her
condition is nothing to do with him, he feels responsible for her
– and to her."

Sarah tucked a strand of hair behind her ear. "But – but why?
Why is she like – like she is?" Then she flushed. "I'm sorry, that
was impertinent. Please forgive me."

Señora Maria touched her hand. "Don't be silly, Sarah.
You've been here some time now. You deserve to know."

"I – it's nothing to do with me."

"Of course it is." Señora Maria was firm. "It's no secret. Our
family skeletons are no worse than anyone else's."

"Has – has this something to do with – with the fire?"

"The fire? Oh, yes," Señora Maria nodded, "it has everything
to do with that. But first I should tell you how Irena came to the
island." She frowned. "That happened about sixteen years ago,
141

Her father was an impoverished member of the aristocracy – from Spain, you understand. They had no money, but they did have friends on the island, and they came for a prolonged visit. I think they lived at that time by sponging on others. In any event, that was how Jason met her." Señora Maria's eyes grew distant. "He was only a boy then, of course, little more than twenty-one or two. He was fascinated by her. She was – and still is, I suppose – a beautiful woman. He was not long returned from school in England, with high hopes of modernizing the plantation and becoming master here." She smiled reminiscently. "Carlos, my late husband, was an old man. We had our children late in life, and he was only too willing to hand over the reins to Jason. Irena's father realized that Jason was the most eligible young man on the island and determined to marry Irena off to him."

Sarah's nails dug into the palms of her hands. It was hard to hear of Jason being fascinated with Irena, in spite of the years between.

Señora Maria went on: "We were against the match. I could see, even then, that Irena was not quite normal. She recoiled from the servants, she was terribly superstitious and apprehensive, and she clung to Jason like a leech, once she had got her claws into him. So – they were married. They had a brief honeymoon and returned to live with Carlos and me at the old house."

"On the cliffs," put in Sarah softly.

"Yes, on the cliffs. It was a huge place, you see, and there was plenty of room for all of us."

"Yes," Sarah nodded.

"Within a couple of months Irena found she was pregnant." Señora Maria sighed. "Jason was delighted, but Irena seemed – indifferent. We all thought it might provide her with an interest – something to arouse her from the lethargy which seemed to engulf her at times." She shook her head. "She used to do strange things even then. I can remember occasions when she used to lock Jason out of their room, when he had to sleep in a dressing room. He hated those scenes. The servants used to talk, you see, and although he had to get used to it, he hated it."

Sarah bent her head. She could imagine Jason's feelings. He was a proud man, and Irena's actions must have humiliated him terribly.

"Well, anyway, for a time things seemed all right, but there is always someone who can't bear to let opportunities to cause trouble pass them by."

Sarah looked up. "Who? Jason's brother?"

"Antonio? No, he had already left the island. He went to live in Trinidad for a time. That was how he met Serena, of course."

"Of course," Sarah nodded. "Please – go on."

"Well, this person was Manuel Diaz' wife, Camilla."

"Dolores' mother?"

"Yes, that's right. Camilla was an unscrupulous woman. Although she was married to Manuel, and the mother of a young daughter, she had always been attracted to Jason, and infuriated when he refused to reciprocate. She had never liked Irena – she would never have liked any woman who married Jason – but she pretended to do so, insinuating herself into Irena's confidence, poisoning her mind with talk of witchcraft and black magic, curses and death rites!"

"So that was where Irena got all that from!"

"Partially, although she was a more than willing pupil. She was already prepared to believe almost anything about the West Indians, and Camilla fed that superstition and hatred."

"How terrible!" Sarah was appalled. "But didn't anyone know?"

"Not then. It wasn't until much later it all came out."

"Go on."

"Irena was about six months pregnant. Her father had unfortunately died some weeks before, and perhaps that had helped to unbalance her, that and the extreme state of nerves she was suffering. In any event, no one could have guessed how Irena would react when Camilla casually mentioned that none of the white families on the island would dare to trace back their history. She intimated that Jason's ancestry was tainted, that the child Irena was carrying might conceivably have coloured blood! It was the cruellest thing anyone could have said, and it was sufficient to drive Irena to distraction. When Jason arrived home from the refinery that evening she confronted him with what Camilla had said. Jason denied it, of course, but she wouldn't believe him. She had reached the point of no return, I suppose. She seized some scissors, and attacked him . . ."

Sarah covered her face with her hands, but she couldn't blot out the mental image of that terrible scene.

Señora Maria was not finished. "Jason managed to take the scissors from her. He tried to reason with her, but it was useless, and eventually he had to lock her in her room. Remember, he was only twenty-two. He had no idea how to deal with a schizophrenic. Besides, he was bleeding profusely, and although we called the doctor he refused to tell him what had happened.

"Doctor Baring fixed his face as best he could. Jason should have gone to Trinidad and had surgery, but he refused, knowing he couldn't leave Irena in that state. We thought she would calm down. I know Jason wanted to spare his father and me the scandal which would have erupted if Irena's condition was made known. But that was not the end of it. In the early hours of the morning Irena climbed out of her room on to the balcony –"

"But she was pregnant!"

"I know. But she was without fear. She systematically fired the whole house, and however any of us got out alive, I shall never know. The shock was too great for my husband. He died in hospital a week later, and I left the island never to return. Irena lost the baby, of course. She refused even to look at it. Jason saw the poor little thing, but he has never spoken of it to any of us. He should have had her certified as unfit to remain in society, but he refused. In spite of everything he blamed himself for not realising how unbalanced she had become and trying to help her. But we all know that Irena would never have accepted help from him."

"And – and this – this curse she talks about?"

"Oh, that's just an obsession brought about by the disasters which she sees to have befallen her since she came to Cordova. Antonio marrying Serena and bringing her back to the island was the last straw, of course."

"I suppose to a certain extent, then, her behaviour is unpredictable."

"Yes. Although her hatred seems concentrated upon Jason himself. And he knows while he is there he can take charge of her. That's why he brought the four of you here while he is away."

Sarah rose. "And do you think he'll be angry when he discovers what you have told me?"

Señora Maria shrugged. "Who can tell? It is better that you should know the truth. Better than insinuations whispered in your ear by Irena."

"And you think because of what has happened, Jason is less tolerant of disobedience in others?"

"I think Jason does not want you to run any risks – to involve yourself too closely with the affairs of the island. And maybe, too, he is jealous. Roberto is a very attractive man. You must have noticed."

Sarah linked her hands together. "I'm not interested in Roberto. I only want to help."

"I know, I know." The *señora* looked at her frankly. "And Jason? Has he – has he given you any reason to think – how is the situation between you developing?"

Sarah pressed her hands to her burning cheeks. "Jason is not committed to me – in any way," she said.

"So? I am not surprised. My son regards his responsibilities towards his wife too strongly to allow his emotions to rule his head."

Sarah felt strangely breathless as she recalled Jason's wholly uncontrollable lovemaking. Only his scar had brought him to his senses.

But if the scar had not come between them, what would have happened? Was his mother right? Would his brain have controlled his passions before the inevitable happened? Sarah was unsure. Despite his treatment of her since then, Sarah was convinced that for some reason she disturbed him immensely, and with her he was not wholly master of himself. The thought was quite a heady one, intoxicating in the conclusions it evoked.

Unknown to Sarah, the Señora Maria had been watching the play of emotions on her face, but now she said softly: "He is not free, my dear. Jason – all of us believe in the sanctity of marriage; he can never be free of Irena." She gave a weary gesture. "And Jason knows this better than any of us!"

Sarah felt a cold, chilling breeze cool her hot skin at these words. For a few moments she had been indulging in wild fancies. But Señora Maria's words brought her abruptly to her senses.

"Perhaps it would be as well if I did leave," she said slowly.

Señora Maria shook her head. "You don't have to leave. You are here for the children's sake. Think of them. Think how they would miss you! They have just become accustomed to a routine. Would you break your faith with them?"

Sarah felt selfishly aware of her limitations. "I am sorry, *señora*," she answered, biting her lips. "I was only thinking of myself, I am afraid. Of course I must stay, for the children's sake, providing of course Jason doesn't ask me to leave."

"I somehow think that is unlikely," said Señora Maria dryly. "You are forgetting my son is first and foremost a Latin. His blood runs hotter than the blood of cold Englishmen." She smiled a little. "It is very sad that there will be only Ricardo to carry on the family name. It is Jason's duty to provide an heir for Cordova. The child Irena lost was a girl."

Sarah felt a pain in the pit of her stomach. "I think it's time I went to bed. Will you excuse me, *señora*?"

"Of course. And do not worry, Sarah. As God wills it, so will his purpose be."

Sarah climbed into bed with these thoughts in her mind, but that didn't prevent the pity and compassion she felt for Jason.

Hadn't he suffered enough already? Was he for ever to live a life without love, or even the hope of it?

"Oh, Jason," she breathed achingly, "I love you!"

CHAPTER ELEVEN

JASON read his newspaper at the breakfast table of the hotel in Bridgetown without really noticing its content. Sighing, he laid the paper aside and after pouring himself another cup of coffee he lit a cigarette and looked out at the exotically colourful scene that met his eyes. Donkey carts vied with luxurious automobiles in the busy street below, causing considerable noise and confusion, while the brightly coloured dresses of the Barbadian women mingled with saris and dhotis and the more conservative dress of the European. Overhead the blue sky looked down benevolently, the sun just beginning to add its heat to an already humid day.

Jason was glad to be back in the islands. New York had been cold and wet, and he had had to wear an overcoat for the first time since his last visit there. He had looked tanned and fit amongst the pale skins of the Americans, who had just suffered a severe winter and were looking forward to the spring. His business in the States had taken longer than he had expected and it was over a fortnight since he had left Cordova. He had only stayed overnight in Trinidad with Serena's family and had then flown on to New York the following day.

But it was wonderful to be back, even though his first thoughts had been of Sarah, and of the immediate problems at hand. All during his stay in the United States he had been overwhelmingly aware of his need to return to Cordova. It was a madness in his blood, but he could not dispel it. He remembered everything about her so clearly, and most particularly the way he had hurt her on the day he had left.

He had been jealous, that was the whole trouble; jealous of Manuel, jealous of Roberto, jealous of anyone who could conceivably take her away from him. It was a new sensation for him; he had never known what jealousy was until now. But it was a destructive emotion which gnawed at him continually.

Thrusting back his chair, he rose unceremoniously to his feet, and strode out of the restaurant. He mounted the stairs to his room, ignoring the lift which stood empty, requiring the action to dispel his feelings. Here he was behaving like a lovesick adolescent; it just would not do! He must get a hold on himself. And maybe, when he reached home, he would have the strength of mind to ask her to leave.

But he doubted whether he could do this. Apart from anything else, the children depended upon her. He could not destroy their newly-born security, and with a sense of frustration he realised he was glad. He wanted a reason for her to stay; he did not want to let her go. Just at this moment, he thought irresponsibly that if she went he would go with her, and beg her to live with him! They could find somewhere where he could work – he was no idle drone. They could be happy . . .

But the thought died as soon as it was born. He knew he could never leave the island. Apart from the children and Serena, there was Irena, and no matter what, she was his wife, and she would stay that way. He could have her taken to Barbados or Trinidad, put her into a hospital there, but it would not be fair. No matter what she had done, she was not responsible. She was ill, mentally ill, a creature to be pitied, not despised. And things might have been so different.

His room was cool, and he flung himself on the bed, closing his eyes against the problems of his world. Images of Sarah and Irena plagued his mind, and rolling on to his stomach, he recalled with sudden clarity the baby which Doctor Baring had shown him that early morning all those years ago. He had never cried; his pride would not allow him such a luxury, but he thought he had never hated anyone as he had hated Irena that morning. He had wanted to kill her, before reason reasserted itself and he was made aware of the bitter truth of her condition.

With a weary exclamation he slid off the bed. Time was hastening on, and although the weekly steamer was not going to Cordova today, he had hired a launch to take him, rather than wait several more days here. He changed into a dark suit, packed the remainder of his belongings into his suitcase, and went down to the quay to find Pedro Amendes, the boatman.

Cordova had never looked lovelier than it did that afternoon, as the *Tia Maria* negotiated the reef and moved surely across the water to the quayside. Jason leaned on the rail feeling pride in his homecoming. Whatever his own position might be, the island remained the same, and he loved it as much as ever. The white dwellings above the harbour glinted in the sun, while the usual activity on the quayside and the busy market beyond welcomed him in a purely sensual way. He could smell the aroma of fish and rope, the salty tang of ships and nets, the shrill cry of the seabirds. He was home!

He vaulted easily from the launch as it reached the jetty, paid the boatman who was coming ashore for a drink before returning to Barbados, and walked lazily across the quay, his jacket slung over his shoulder. Abe Smith came out of the harbourmaster's office, and grinned his welcome.

148

"So you're back! It's good to see you, Jason." He slapped him on the shoulder, and Jason grinned, casting all his doubts and anxieties aside for the moment. "Could you use a drink? I've got a nice lager on ice."

Jason raised his eyes heavenward. "Could I not! Lead me to it!"

They sat in the cramped office, and drank lager and smoked cheroots. Abe was as garrulous as ever, and just as candid in his speech. For a time they discussed the business Jason had negotiated in New York, and then, without warning, Abe said: "I see your pretty governess every day now, eh? She likes to come here, I think. I am surprised you permit it! After all, she travels both ways with Gonzales, alone. Not that Gonzales is not to be trusted, you understand —"

Jason was staring at him, his face as black as thunder. "What in hell are you talking about?" he bit out savagely.

Abe raised his eyebrows. "Ay, ay, my friend! I am only telling you the truth. Your Señorita Winter is helping Roberto at the schoolhouse!" His tone was injured, but Jason ignored it, he was too angry to think coherently.

"Since when?" he demanded.

"Since a few days after you left." Abe shrugged. "Enrico, he went sick, and Roberto went across to Coral Cay and saw the *señorita*. She said she would come, of course, so Gonzales brings her afternoons. That is all." He shook his head at Jason. "Why are you so angry, my friend? The little governess has come to no harm! She likes Roberto, and Roberto — well, I think he more than a little likes her —"

"The devil he does!" Jason finished his lager and slung his case into a corner of the room. "I'll collect that later. See you!"

Abe walked to the door and watched Jason stride along the quay, hardly noticing the welcoming greetings he received from passers-by. Leaving the harbour, he pushed his way through the market and reached the track at the end of which stood the school building. It was almost teatime already, and it was likely that classes would be nearly over. The building looked ramshackle and overheated, and he reflected that he would have to try and get the new building completed sooner than expected. There were three classes in the old building, and the children were closely seated and prevented from much serious learning by the lack of interest shown by a recalcitrant few which in the overcrowded conditions spread like wildfire.

Jason's jacket was still over his shoulder, as he banged open the rattan door which led into the first classroom, but as he had half expected, it was empty. The children had gone. After a

149

swift look round, he discovered that the whole building was empty, so where was Sarah? In Roberto's house? His anger was absolute. How dare she disobey him like this, and then actually go to Roberto's house?

Roberto's door was open and from within he could hear voices; Roberto's and Sarah's. His bulk filled the doorway, silencing the two within. Roberto was the first to regain his composure, and he said: "Ah, Jason! So you are back! What a pleasant surprise." His tone was slightly derisive, and Sarah looked as guilty as if she had been committing some heinous crime.

Jason leaned against the doorpost and said: "Well, well! So you decided to come after all, *señorita!*"

Sarah rose awkwardly to her feet, brushing down the skirt of her dress. She was wearing pink, a dress he had never seen before, which clung to the full curves of her slender figure, and revealed the tanned length of her legs. Her hands twisted together nervously, and her eyes darted from himself to Roberto and back again.

"I – I – your mother was agreeable," she confessed at last. "At least, I – wanted to come. Oh, well," she sounded resigned, "I can't deny it, can I?"

"Hardly," he agreed coldly. "Come! I want to talk to you."

"Jason, won't you stay for a drink?" Roberto half-smiled, "Surely you aren't going to refuse my hospitality!"

Jason shook his head. "I don't want a drink. *Señorita!*"

Sarah was obviously in a quandary. She didn't know what to do. Her brain told her to stay and ignore Jason's imperious commands, but her senses and emotions cried out for her to go with him, and try to make her position clear to him.

Roberto looked insolently at Jason. "I don't think you have the right to order the *señorita* about," he remarked coolly. "After all, this is still the afternoon, and her time is her own."

"I suggest you keep out of this," muttered Jason, his voice hard and unyielding. "*Señorita*, are you coming?"

Sarah spread wide her hands. "Roberto, I must go. I . . . I'll see you tomorrow."

"I shouldn't bank on that," said Jason angrily, allowing Sarah to pass him through the doorway. "*Adios*, Roberto."

"*Adios, amigo!*" Roberto's tone was mocking, and Jason's eyebrows drew together darkly.

Sarah walked ahead of him down the road, but his long strides soon overtook her, and he caught her arm in a vice-like grip.

"Don't make a scene," said Sarah, looking up at him. "Not here, at any rate."

Jason's tawny eyes were dark with rage. "What's the matter?

150

Are you afraid I might embarrass you?"

"No, yourself!" Sarah shook her arm angrily. "Let go of me!"

But Jason refused to release her, and they reached the main street of the town.

"Where are we going?" she asked. "Back to the Cay?" She looked down towards the harbour. "Gonzales will be waiting for me."

"Yes. We'll go back to the Cay," he agreed harshly. "But not with Gonzales. On the yacht."

Sarah's stomach turned over. "No," she said clearly. "I'd rather not."

"Why? Are you afraid of me?" Jason's voice was husky now.

"Not of you; of myself," she replied, looking back at him. "I – I'll see you back at Coral Cay, señor."

"What the hell do you mean, you'll see me there? You'll see me now."

"Then you can come with myself and Gonzales," she said, and with a swift movement she twisted out of his grasp, and started down the road at a run, hardly daring to look back to see if he had followed her.

Jason watched her go, then slinging his jacket back over his shoulder again, he followed her more leisurely. She was so young, he thought moodily. By even touching her he was spoiling her life. She should remain untouched until she fell in love with someone suitable, someone like Roderigo Valente, who although he had lived rather a wild life in the past, would probably make a perfectly suitable husband.

With these tortuous thoughts in his mind, he walked down to the harbour. He ought to get the Land Rover and drive up to the villa, but just now he could not leave Sarah alone. It was weak and sensual, but he couldn't help it. He knew that he would touch her again, make love to her again; he would not be able to stop himself.

Sarah and Gonzales were waiting in the launch for him after he had collected his case from Abe Smith. Abe had asked him why he was bothering to take his case over to the Cay, and Jason had said that he would probably spend the night there before returning to the villa. Abe had given him a strange, knowing look, and he had felt doubly conscious of his own selfish needs. He wished he had time to go and see Father Sanchez. Perhaps he would have listened to his confession and cooled his overheated blood, but it was too late for that now.

He sprang into the launch, and Gonzales grinned at him, and started the engine. The breeze cooled his feverish brow, and he moved away from Sarah, and seated himself in the stern, lighting a cigarette. He loosened the top button of his shirt, and pulled his tie away from his neck, running a hand through his hair. He felt impotently furious with himself, but never before had a woman controlled his actions in this way. Always he had been in control of himself, and he disliked the way his body throbbed when Sarah was near him. He would see his mother and return to Cordova that evening, he decided. Max could go over for the children and Sarah the next day, and that way he would avoid the necessity of speaking to her, of being near to her for too long.

But, to his surprise, she came and seated herself beside him and said: "Did you have a good trip?"

Jason frowned. "Well, it was reasonable. It was very cold in New York, about forty degrees."

She shivered, and said: "How awful! I should hate to go back there – I mean to a cold climate. I've become accustomed to the heat and the colour and the sun! I love it here!"

Jason allowed his fingers to trail over the nape of her neck, feeling the silky hair against his skin. It was a purely involuntary movement, and he withdrew his hand when he became aware of it.

"Oh, Jason," she said, turning to him, unable to pretend any longer, "I have missed you!"

Jason's eyes half-closed. "So it seems," he said, his voice cool and detached. "So much so that you actually go against my wishes, knowing how I would react. I suppose your comments are intended to mean that you do not want to leave my employ, and consequently I should forgive you for your disobedience."

Sarah stared at him, her face paling beneath her tan. "You know that's not true," she exclaimed hotly. "All right, so I don't want to leave. But I'm not one of the children, you know. I did what I could to help Roberto, because I like and admire him. I should have thought you would have had time to reconsider your overbearing remarks!"

"Why?" he demanded fiercely. "You are already looking tired! Your face is thinner. Is this the behaviour of a sensible young woman?"

Sarah sighed, shaking her head. "So! What is to happen now? Am I to be dismissed? Am I to leave as soon as we return to Cordova?"

Jason stared at the tip of his cigarette broodingly. "I don't know," he said thoughtfully. "I will let you know."

"Thank you." Sarah's tone was scathing now. "Oh, you infuriate me!"

"And you forget your place," he countered angrily. "If you

wish to remain on Cordova you will do as I say!"

Sarah scowled out to sea, and would not look at him. He sat there, so disturbingly attractive that all she wanted to do was press herself against him and promise him anything so long as he allowed her to stay near him. She had never before known the purely physical pleasure to be gained from just looking at a man.

Jason himself would not analyse his feelings. He dared not do so. He was relieved when Gonzales, who was completely unaware of their conversation, came to join them and to ask him about his trip. Sarah left them to talk and went to sit in the forward part of the boat, and Jason forced his mind into impersonal channels. The launch clove cleanly through the waves, and the sun was warm on his arms. Coral Cay was not much further now, and then he could make his apologies to his mother and leave. It would be as well, anyway, to return to Cordova tonight. It was possible that Irena had caused some minor upset during his absence and the servant relied on him for her good behaviour.

He threw the end of his cigarette away, and turned his attention to Gonzales, his charming smile unindicative of the weight of his problems.

Benito was awaiting them in the carriage as usual when the launch reached Coral Cay. He smiled a warm welcome when he recognised Jason, and Jason asked him about his family, his interest absorbed in the problems of the West Indian. It was always like that, thought Sarah. Jason could devote himself entirely to you, so that you felt he was really concerned about nothing else at that moment.

The journey to the bungalow was accomplished in silence, apart from an occasional remark from Gonzales, who had seated himself beside the coachman, and was attempting to begin a conversation.

When they reached the house, the Señora Maria was waiting on the verandah to greet them. When she saw Jason, she sprang up with pleasure lighting her face, and exclaimed: "Why, Jason! You didn't let us know you were coming!"

"Perhaps it's just as well," remarked Jason dryly, following Sarah's example of climbing down.

Sarah greeted the señora, and then turned and ran into the villa, while the children, who had heard the carriage, came busting out of the house to find out what was going on. Sarah ran past them, but when they caught sight of Jason they did not try to follow her. Instead, they flung themselves upon their uncle, screaming excitedly, and begging for attention.

153

Jason picked up the two younger ones and said: "I do believe you've grown, Maria! Have you been enjoying yourselves? Or have you driven your grandmother and Miss Winter a little mad, eh?"

"They have been extremely good," said his mother, smiling. "And I have enjoyed having them. I feel quite young again. It's good to have children in the house."

"Yes," agreed Jason slowly, standing the children down again and going down on his haunches beside them. "Well, seeing that you've all done so well, I'll have to see if there are some things in my suitcase which might suit you all, eh?"

The children squealed, and Jason rose to his feet again. "Now, run along for a little while. I want to speak to your grandmother in private."

The children went away obediently, looking back a little reluctantly at Jason's suitcase which Gonzales was just carrying into the villa. "Leave it here, Gonzales!" said Jason, stopping the man. "I shan't be staying."

"Not staying? But why?" Señora Maria was disappointed. "You are going back to Cordova tonight?"

"I'm afraid so, Mother. I must find out whether there's been any trouble in my absence."

Señora Maria frowned. "If there had, we should have heard of it. News travels fast in the islands."

"Nevertheless, it's my duty to return home. Irena is entitled to know I'm back."

"Very well," his mother shrugged. "Come, sit down. We will have a drink at least, and you can tell me about your trip."

They sat beside a glass-topped table, and the *señora* poured Scotch for her son, and a rum punch for herself. After Jason had lit a cigarette, she said: "You're annoyed, aren't you, because Sarah has been teaching at the school?"

Jason's eyes were guarded. "Naturally. Did you expect I wouldn't be so? You gave her permission?"

"To a degree. I warned her you would be angry. She is an independent little thing. You cannot expect her to conform to your way of thinking, just because you would like her to. She is not one of the servants, Jason. She is a governess! That is something else."

Jason raked his hands through his thick hair. "She's just what you've said, Mother — a governess, for my three wards! Not for the children in El Tesoro!"

"But why? You have always tried to help these people. Why should the thought of Sarah helping Roberto be so abhorrent to you?"

"If she had wanted to do that kind of work, there are plenty of missionaries in South America!"

"Jason! You are acting out of character! It doesn't suit you."

Jason rose restlessly to his feet. "I'm sorry."

"No, you're not. That was just politeness; not a real apology. What you really fear is that she will discover the truth about Irena! Well, you need fear no longer. She knows!"

"She does *what*!" Jason exploded. "You've told her?"

"Yes, I have. She deserved to know. After all, you brought her here, amongst a collection of the most complex characters she might find anywhere, and you expected her to live, knowing only snatches of a story which once rocked the island! She was curious, naturally so. And I satisfied her curiosity!"

"It was not your place to do so." Jason's voice revealed his anger.

"But why? Good lord, Jason, why? Why shouldn't she be told?"

Jason stood grindingly on the end of his cigarette, and lit another. The darkening trees around the bungalow seemed oppressive. So Sarah knew the truth, knew of the humiliation of his life, the horror of that night so many years ago. And no doubt she would pity him, but he didn't want her pity! He thought of their quarrel on the launch, which had not been of her making, and wondered what she had been thinking.

He turned back to his mother, and shrugged his shoulders. Lifting his suitcase, he said: "I'll go in and see the children, and then I'll leave."

His mother looked exasperatedly at him. "Oh, Jason," she exclaimed, "are you sure you won't stay?"

"Positive," he replied firmly. "Besides, it wouldn't be fair to Irena for me to stay away longer than was necessary."

"Irena!" His mother sighed, in annoyance. There was nothing she could say which would change her mind. She knew that of old. Jason, once his mind was made up, could not be moved.

Dinner that evening was a silent meal. Jason had left, long before Sarah emerged from her room. The children had swarmed into Sarah's room, eager to show her the wrist watches Jason had brought for them from New York. Sarah had been forcedly bright and interested, but she had been torn by the longing to go out and see him again before he left. She was afraid that by disobeying him she had completely alienated herself, and that he might, in fact, ask her to leave. She was terrified that this might happen.

Señora Maria was also a little subdued, and after they had

poured coffee and liqueurs she said: "What happened between you and Jason, back on Cordova?"

Sarah's colour deepened. "Nothing much. We argued a little. He was annoyed because I was working at the school. I expected that." She sighed. "But I couldn't just allow Roberto to struggle on alone. It would have been less than justice. Besides, I have enjoyed my work there. The children like me, and it's very rewarding when I find I have actually helped them to learn something important. Education is important. I was always taught that knowledge of any kind could not only help me to understand the meaning of life. These children who grow up in ignorance of literature, art, sciences: they miss an awful lot."

The *señora* smiled. "Always the philosopher," she commented smilingly. "Does it ever occur to you that what is never known is never missed? Perhaps that is a short-sighted attitude!" She shrugged. "I don't know. But can we be sure that the sophisticated, educated world is a happier place than these islands where the people follow the pursuits of their ancestors, and believe their lives to be full and contented? I have always found that the civilised, or so-called civilised, peoples are never satisfied with their lot and are continually searching for new ideas, new sensations, new entertainments ... Surely this is not a sign of happiness or contentment?"

Sarah smiled now, unable to prevent her amusement at the *señora's* ironic words. "Well, one of us is right," she replied. "And you've certainly lifted me out of a state of melancholia."

"Ah, that is good! But with me it does not work so easily. Just now, Jason troubles me."

"But why?" Sarah was curious. "Surely things are no different now than they've ever been. Irena is not worse, is she?"

"Not so far as I know. But certainly she is no better, and will never be so. This is bad; very bad. Jason is a normal, healthy man. The life he leads is less than normal!"

Sarah nodded. "I know." She rubbed the palms of her hands against her cheeks restlessly. "Was he very angry with you? For allowing me to go to Cordova with Gonzales?"

"He was not very pleased," remarked the *señora* dryly. "But I told him I had told you about Irena, and that pleased him less. I think you may find your life a little difficult for a while after you return to the villa. But I really believe, Sarah, that he is more concerned about your health than about the story. After all, the heat can be enervating, and you're not used to it really, are you? You are looking a little tired."

"Maybe so. Tell me, *señora*, do you think I'm to be dismissed?"

156

Señora Maria looked at her strangely for a moment. "In spite of Jason's attitude, I would say that was less than likely," she replied slowly, and Sarah's heart leapt. "You have been very successful with the children. He tells me that in spite of her tempers and tantrums Serena really likes you. It's hardly likely that he'd dismiss someone who appears to be succeeding so well."

Sarah's heart subsided again. "I think I'll go to bed," she said, rising to her feet. "I'm rather tired."

"Of course. By the way, my dear, Jason has suggested that you and the children return to Cordova with Gonzales in the morning, and he will arrange for you to be met at the quay and taken up to the villa."

"A necessary evil," remarked Sarah wryly, and with a sigh she turned and walked into the villa.

CHAPTER TWELVE

MAX was waiting to escort Sarah and the children back to the villa the next morning, and Sarah stifled the feeling of disappointment she felt to find that Jason himself had not bothered to come to meet them.

Everything at the villa was much the same as usual. Everywhere smelled sweetly of jasmine and roses, bougainvillea and poinsettia, and as all the bedroom shutters had been opened to admit the cooling breezes, there was no atmosphere of disuse to point to their ever having been away. And it was nice to be back, thought Sarah, as she hung a couple of dresses away in the tall wall cupboards in her room. After all, the house on Coral Cay had been a little confining for the children after the first novelty had worn off, and they had missed the horses and the piles of toys and books which filled their bedrooms at home on Cordova.

She had given the children permission to go down to the stables after their arrival to greet the ponies and take them sugar lumps, while Sarah herself showered and changed into dark blue slacks and a pale blue and white checked shirt. She descended the stairs a little after twelve and was disconcerted to find Irena standing in the hall apparently awaiting her.

"Ah, Miss Winter," she said, her smile not quite reaching her eyes. "I have been waiting to speak to you. Will you come along to the lounge? We can speak privately there."

Sarah hesitated. She had no real reason to refuse and she did not want to antagonise the other woman. The slightly repellent quality Irena possessed was also mesmerising, much like the rattle of the snake. "Very well, *señora*," she agreed now. "Will you lead the way?"

Irena nodded, and walked ahead down the marble-tiled corridor towards a charming lounge furnished in blues and greens with pinky-orange rugs strewn about the polished floor. Irena pointed to a low couch, upholstered in a delicate olive green damask, and Sarah subsided into it a little breathlessly.

All the way along the corridor her mind had been buzzing with thoughts, trying to guess why Irena wanted to speak to her, trying to foresee what they might have to discuss. She could only think of Jason – or the children! Her heart stopped its suffocating pounding. Of course it must be the children. It *couldn't* be Jason.

158

Irena offered her a drink and Sarah accepted a lime and lemon cordial, wishing Irena would get to the point. It was all very well inviting someone to have a drink with you if that was all there was to it, but Irena had something on her mind, that much was obvious.

"Now!" Irena twisted her glass between her fingers and paced rather slowly across the floor in the restless manner of a nervous, highly-strung person. Sarah found that Irena's manner was succeeding in making her feel nervous as well. Which was *ridiculous*!

"The drink is to your liking, *señorita*?"

"Thank you, yes. *Señora,* why did you wish to speak to me?"

"It has come to my ears that you have been visiting Cordova in spite of the fact that you have been staying on Coral Cay. And that you have been teaching at the school in El Tesoro."

"That's right." Sarah sipped her drink apprehensively.

"Why did you do this, *señorita*?" Irena's tone was controlled.

Sarah shrugged. "Why, to help them, naturally. They're short of staff. Money is not so forthcoming for schools anywhere."

"But why should you wish to help them? How did this come about?"

Sarah frowned. "Señor Diaz took me to meet Roberto Santana – he is one of the masters –"

Irena's eyes narrowed. "Yes," she said explosively, "I know the Señor Santana! He may be a relative of my husband."

Sarah stared at her. Irena's sudden switch from moderation to anger was startling, to say the least. She was nonplussed, but Irena mistook her confusion for something else.

"Ah!" she exclaimed, pointing at Sarah. "That shocks you, does it not? That the Señor Jason Ricardo Vincente de Cordova should be related to a man like Santana!"

Sarah bit hard on her lips. She did not know how best to reply. The *señora*'s mercurial moods made normal conversation almost impossible, she realised, and she was unused to dealing with such a volatile creature. "I think that's unlikely," she managed at last, and Irena stopped her pacing in front of her, and stared down at her.

"Why? How could you know? Unless . . ." her eyes were calculating. "The Señora Maria has told you about me. I see it all now. That was why Jason took you to the Cay, so that his mother could persuade you to go and work at that filthy hut they call a schoolhouse –"

"No, *señora*, you're wrong!" cried Sarah, getting to her feet. "The *señor* rejected my suggestion that I might help Roberto himself."

159

Irena ignored her last remark and merely stared through her. "The Señora Maria hates me; she hates me for killing her husband, for disfiguring her son, for destroying her grandchild! Yes! I did all those things!" Irena's voice was triumphant now. "I paid them all back for the misery they brought me!"

Sarah was stunned, horrified by Irena's words, but behind her repugnance she felt an overwhelming sense of pity for this poor deranged woman, who had spent the whole of her married life fighting a danger that did not exist. She was married to one of the gentlest, kindest and most understanding of men, and yet she had allowed her fears and prejudices to gain the upper hand, and create a second being within herself who was all too willing to destroy any confidence she might find.

"Señora," began Sarah quietly, "won't you try to forget the past, and live for the present? No one bears you any resentment for what happened. But you won't try to associate yourself with the world around you."

Irena turned away from her, her fingers so tightly clenched round the slender stem of her glass that Sarah felt sure it would break. "Why are you talking to me like this? What do you care?" She looked back at Sarah. "Has Jason put you up to this?"

"Señora, you asked me in here; I didn't invite myself."

"So I did." Irena compressed her lips momentarily. "But I should have known that no one here is to be trusted. Not even you! No one who will allow themselves to teach at that school for scavengers could be trusted, even though it is likely you were coerced into it."

Sarah sighed. "I've tried to explain. It was my own idea."

It was hopeless. Irena just would not listen.

"I thought you might have been a friend to me," said Irena, her mood changing to one of self-pity, her voice low and dejected.

"I am your friend." Sarah felt herself becoming exasperated, and tried to contain her urgency to make this woman understand her. "Señora, the school is not a place to be despised. Children are children the world over. They deserve an equal chance of education. And when the new school house is finished —"

Irena's mood of dejection was gone as swiftly as it had come. "A new school house!" she exploded. "*A new school house!*"

Sarah clasped her hands together nervously, and found they were damp with perspiration. Oh, lord, she thought desperately, what have I said now?

"Jason has not told me of this!" Irena was furiously angry, and the glass she had been holding so precariously was flung vio-

160

lently into the grate where it splintered into a thousand tiny pieces. And with the action Sarah's hopes of speaking naturally to her were just as surely shattered.

"*Irena!*"

Jason's voice arrested both of them, and Sarah felt an overpowering sense of relief at his arrival. Her conversation with Irena was fast getting out of hand, and she was half afraid to say anything after Irena's uncontrollable fit of temper when she mentioned the new school. She linked and unlinked her fingers, feeling schoolgirlish and out of place, and she was not assisted in her efforts to remain calm when Jason said, coldly and disconcertingly: "What in hell are you doing here?"

"I – er – the *señora* invited me," she managed awkwardly, and then felt angry with herself for allowing him to speak to her and reacting like a mouse. After all, she had done nothing to be ashamed of.

"Yes, I invited her," put in Irena, looking half-mockingly at her husband. "Does that surprise you? That occasionally I should want the company of another decent human being, *querido*?"

"Nothing surprises me any longer," replied Jason heavily. He looked at Sarah. "You can go."

Sarah took her dismissal with a sense of frustration. True, she had been relieved to see Jason, but it was not pleasant to be dismissed like a naughty child.

"Yes, *señor*," she said coolly, and walked swiftly towards the door, her head held high, but Irena's voice halted her.

"Don't let my husband frighten you away," she taunted. "I know he is not a pretty sight, my dear, but he won't bite you!"

Sarah pressed a hand to her churning stomach, her legs growing weak at the knees at the look in Jason's eyes. Her antagonism towards him vanished at Irena's cruel words. How could he stand to be treated in this manner, no matter how pitiful Irena might be? Little wonder that his temper seemed to be running low with this continual abasement.

"The – the children are waiting for me," she said, excusing herself. "*Adios, señora, señor!*"

Once outside the door, Sarah leaned back against the cool wall feeling a wave of nausea sweep over her. Was it possible that it was only a little over a month since she came here? In so short a period was one able to become so intensely involved in other people's lives? And was she to stay? Or was Jason going to send for her this afternoon and ask for her resignation?

Straightening up, she began to walk back to her own wing of the villa, adjusting herself to the emotional torment she was experiencing. She could not join the children in such a state. Although it was almost lunch time she felt far from hungry, but the children, returning from the stables, were ravenous, and their excited chatter helped to disguise her own anguish.

"Are we having any lessons today?" asked Ricardo, tackling his fruit salad with gusto.

Sarah shook her head. "I think not. Perhaps you could swim in the pool this afternoon, and entertain yourselves, yes?"

"Oh, goody!" exclaimed Maria, smiling. "It's been so long since we really swam at all, I'm just dying to get into the pool, aren't you, Elly?"

Eloise nodded. "Yes. You can't really swim in the sea, can you, Miss Winter? But we all have to remember to put our watches away in a safe place first. They'll be ruined if they get into water."

"That's right." Sarah commended her thoughtfulness. "You can give them to me, and I'll keep them safe for you."

After the children were changed and splashing in the pool, Sarah got out one of the loungers and placed it beside the pool, on the smooth turf, and tried to concentrate on the magazine she had brought with her. Dressed in a sun-top and shorts, she looked young and attractive, her head protected from the sun by a wide coolie hat which Constancia had provided for her.

The children played happily, and she felt some of the tension leaving her body. Things were much the same as usual, she told herself impatiently. But she did feel an annoying sense of helplessness when she thought of Roberto down at the school, waiting for her in vain.

Someone crossed the grass to where she was sitting, and looking up she saw that it was Jason, tall and forbidding in a navy blue knitted shirt and blue, tight-fitting slacks. The children saw him too, and started shouting, but he said: "Stay where you are. I want to talk to Miss Winter a moment."

Sarah dropped her book to the grass and said: "I can't ask you to sit down, because there's nowhere for you to sit, unless you sit on the grass." She clasped her hands awkwardly. "For goodness' sake, do sit on the grass; I'm at too much of a disadvantage at the moment."

Jason shrugged, and went down on his haunches beside her, his arms brown and muscular, only inches from her own. "Now," he said, "I see you have not gone down to the school today. Do I take it you have abandoned the scheme?"

Sarah flushed. "No, you do not!" she said hotly. "But as my position here is so nebulous at the moment . . ." Her voice trailed away. "When is Señora Serena returning?"

"I'm not sure. It's not important. In her last communication

162

to me in New York, she made it plain she was having a whale of a time, and as there are plenty of men to amuse her, I should imagine it will be some time before she can tear herself away."

"But – the children!"

"They are my concern. I'm their legal guardian, in spite of the fact that their mother is still alive. Serena is not old enough to accept that kind of responsibility, and by that I don't necessarily mean in years, but in outlook. She feels she's missing out on life. Now she's making up for lost time. Do I make myself clear?"

"Yes, but – well, what about me?"

Jason's long lashes half veiled his tawny eyes. "Yes, what about you? That's really what we have to discuss, is it not?"

Sarah swallowed hard, and tried to ignore the way her pulses were racing at his nearness. The scar which he so obviously detested merely enhanced his masculinity, harsh and undisguised. Looking away from him, she said: "If you could tell me whether I'm to be dismissed or otherwise I would be grateful." Her tone was cool in spite of her nervousness.

Jason studied her intently for a moment and then he rose abruptly to his feet, thrusting his hands into the pockets of his slacks. "Do you want to leave?" he asked, looking down at her bent head.

"Of course not. I like it here. But I don't intend to be treated like an inferior being."

"I don't treat you like an inferior being," he snapped, half angrily, his temper aroused by her attitude. "If you're referring to what happened this morning, I was merely concerned on your behalf. You have obviously no conception of Irena's changes of mood." He moved restlessly. "You apparently had some mistaken idea that you could speak to my wife normally. That's practically impossible these days." His voice was bitter.

"How do you know what we were talking about? You came through the french doors; how long had you been there listening?"

"Not long, but long enough to overhear you trying to reason with Irena. Anyway, forget it. That's over now. Only don't seek her company, will you, with aspirations towards psychoanalysis? It's all been done by experts."

"Of course not," replied Sarah stiffly.

"Good!" He walked down to the edge of the pool and then, turning, looked back at her. "As to the other matter, I suggest we forget about it for now. You may stay."

Sarah rose to her feet. "And the school?" she asked pointedly.

Jason turned away, and shrugged his broad shoulders. With his back to her, he said: "I won't attempt to stop you, if that's really what you want."

She could have hugged him, so relieved did she feel. Instead she was forced to remain where she was, and say: "Thank you, *señor.*"

He swung round. "My name is Jason. As I think I've told you on many occasions."

Sarah wrapped her arms round herself in a display of uncontrolled pleasure. She was to *stay!* And she was to be allowed to go on helping Roberto. Could it really be true?

"What did you think of Roberto?" asked Jason, suddenly and unexpectedly, walking back to her side.

"I like him," she averred easily. "Don't you?"

Jason half-smiled. "Of course I do. But I'm afraid Roberto and I are forced into untenable situations by our individual positions here on the island. Actually, we attended school in England together. My father paid for Roberto's training, but that's not common knowledge. He was fond of him. His mother used to work for my mother and when his father was killed in an accident my father brought him up. It was this as much as anything which gave emphasis to Camilla's accusations. I understand you've already been told, by my mother."

"Do you mind?" Sarah tilted her head back to look up at him.

"No, not now. I'm relieved." He turned away, obviously embarrassed now, and half regretting that he had begun this conversation.

"Like your mother said, Jason, it means nothing to me," murmured Sarah quietly.

"Doesn't it?" He was sardonic. "Very well. And now I must go. Manuel is expecting me at the distillery."

After he had gone, leaving her feeling somewhat dejected, the magazine lost its appeal. The children were still playing merrily, but the sun seemed less bright than before, and she wondered whether it would rain. It was very warm, and she drowsed a little in the heat, trying to see where it was all going to end. Was she behaving foolishly by staying here? Even if Jason was not indifferent to her, and there was no indication at all of his true feelings, they had no future. Jason would never divorce his wife, or leave her either. And if she, Sarah, stayed, what would happen? The years would pass by, the children would grow older and not require a governess any longer. The longest she could expect to be employed was three, maybe four years, and after that, what? She could possibly get a job down in El Tesoro, at the new school. Teachers were always in demand, and she might even be able to afford a home of her own. But what kind of life was that for a woman, living alone, with no family around her as she grew older, and only the prospect of infrequent meetings with Jason to keep her alive. How could she bear it? Seeing Jason growing older too, with no children of his own, no real wife or family, when it could have been so different. Life was so unfair!

Gathering her things together at last, she called to the children to come up to the house to change for tea, and then went on up to her own room. It was not until much later in the evening that she remembered she had left her small canvas bag outside, by the lounger near the pool, and inside the bag were the three watches belonging to the children. They had been tired when she and Constancia put them to bed, and as they had only had the watches a little over a day they had not missed them. During dinner, a lonely meal in the small dining salon on her own, Sarah had been too engrossed with her own thoughts to think of the watches.

"Damn," she thought now, leaving her room again, and descending the stairs slowly. "I hope I don't meet Irena tonight. After this morning's episode it would be less than coincidence if I did!"

Jason poured two whiskeys and handed one to Dolores, ignoring the way her eyes devoured him with every alluring gaze. Then after offering her a cigarette and lighting it, he said: "What brings you here this evening, Dolores?"

Dolores looked incredibly beautiful in a sleek black cocktail dress, which enhanced her olive colouring and very dark hair. She had arrived, unheralded, after dinner, and they were now sitting in the lounge, Dolores on the low couch, and Jason in an armchair opposite.

"Well, *querido*," she exclaimed, in a low voice, "someone had to welcome you back, and who better than me? Tell me, how was the trip?"

Jason shrugged. He had not changed for dinner, and was dressed in the same blue shirt and slacks he had been wearing that afternoon. Just before Dolores' arrival, he had been anticipating with pleasure a cool shower and a change of clothes, but now she had baulked him, and he was not altogether pleased that she should have come here like this while Serena was away. He liked Dolores, she was a good companion, an amusing person to be with, but he had never seen her as anything more than Manuel's daughter, *Camilla*'s daughter! It was strange, he thought, how some women, no matter how beautiful, could leave a man cold emotionally, but to him Dolores was such a one. Sarah was different. Despite her fair complexion and cool appearance,

165

she was warm and passionate and exciting to be with, a challenge both in body and mind.

Recalling Dolores's question, he said now: "The trip was fine – successful, I mean. Everything is in readiness for the harvest. How have things been while I've been away? Have you done anything exciting?"

"Not particularly. Just the usual round – picnics, barbecues, cocktail parties, dinners. Sometimes I think I will run away from the monotony of it all."

Jason drew on his cigarette. "Most women would think you led a very full life," he remarked mildly. "After all, what would you rather be doing?"

"Oh, I don't know. I suppose I should like to be married ... have a family of my own. Maybe even travel – I don't know."

"Well, marry then. Good heavens, Dolores, I'm sure there have been no shortage of proposals here. The men outnumber the women by about three to one, don't they?" His tone was light and chiding, but Dolores looked annoyed with this turn of the conversation.

"You know that is irrelevant," she murmured insinuatingly, but Jason rose to his feet and walked over to the wide windows which overlooked the lawns and pool. The moon had risen and its light provided an illumination that revealed Sarah near the pool, a pale wraith in her lemon dress, standing there in the milky light. Her hair, still bound in its plaits, hung over her shoulders and in flat sandals she looked about sixteen.

Stepping into the aperture of the open french doors, he called: "What are you doing, Sarah?"

Dolores jumped to her feet at his unexpected words, and came to join him by the window, sliding an arm possessively through his. Sarah, who had retrieved her bag, walked towards them with obvious reluctance, but Jason released himself expertly from Dolores and said: "Come inside and have a drink. The grass must be damp, and your feet are bare."

Glancing down at her tanned legs, Sarah allowed herself to be drawn into the room, and accepted the glass Jason offered her. She seldom drank at all, but the raw spirit he had poured warmed her, and relieved the numbed feeling she had experienced when first she saw Jason and Dolores together.

Dolores was evidently not pleased by her appearance and to relieve her own annoyance she began asking Sarah questions about the children, mocking questions which Sarah found it difficult to answer. She wished wholeheartedly Jason had not seen her in the garden and had allowed her to return to her room undisturbed. She had to explain about the children's watches, and to suffer Dolores' remarks about her negligence.

Jason, too, seemed restless, and paced about the room like a caged animal. The atmosphere seemed strangely tense, and Sarah could only attribute it to her own overworked nerves.

"Did you enjoy your stay on Coral Cay?" asked Dolores suddenly.

"Thank you, yes," Sarah replied. "I enjoyed it very much. Jason – the *señor*'s mother was most kind to us."

Dolores had noticed this slip on Sarah's part – the casual use of Jason's name, and she felt infuriated. "So!" she said. "Did you then come back to Cordova for entertainment? I understand you have been spending your afternoons with Roberto Santana."

"Hardly with him, exactly," said Sarah politely. "I was teaching at the school, yes. Is there anything wrong in that?"

Dolores grimaced. "That is for Jason to say, of course. You were brought here to teach the Cordova children, not anyone else."

"I have time to do both," said Sarah calmly, in control of herself.

"You think so?" Dolores shrugged her slim shoulders. "You must be a very versatile young woman, mustn't she, Jason? Do you agree with her? Don't you mind that she may bring disease or some horrible bug back into your house?"

Sarah clenched her fists, and Jason said slowly: "Miss Winter's motives are laudable. Who am I to stop her?"

Sarah stood up, and placing her glass on a side table she said: "Excuse me, *señorita*, *señor*. I think it's time I went to my room."

"Now wait a minute," began Jason wearily, his fingers curving round her wrist almost familiarly, as though he was used to touching her.

Sarah stopped and looked at him, seeing the tiny lines of exhaustion about his eyes as though he was not sleeping very well, and felt her antagonism subside again as it had done that morning. She could not despise Jason, whatever he said. She loved him too much for pretence, and her whole heart was in her eyes as she looked at him.

"*Sarah!*" he muttered hoarsely, hardly aware of Dolores' presence for a few exulting moments, and then, without warning, the doors opened to admit Constancia, who looked perturbed and very upset.

Releasing Sarah abruptly, Jason strode to the door, and said: "What has happened? What's wrong, Constancia? You're distressed!"

167

"Oh, *señor!*" Constancia glanced at the two women and then looked back at her master. "It is the Señora Irena, *señor*. She is not in her room. She is not in the house. She has gone, and the car from the garage – it has gone also."

"What!" Jason stared at her for a second. "When did she go? How long has she been gone? And where?"

"I do not know, *señor*. Ana went to her room several minutes ago to give her her usual evening drink, and she was gone!"

The tension which had been in the room was intensified a hundred times. Sarah could sense Jason's apprehension, and her own fears were nothing compared to his. That it was unusual for Irena to leave her room was accepted; for her to leave the villa was a catastrophe! It was impossible to judge her motives, or to speculate what might happen to her out in the car at night. The roads around the villa were narrow and unmade, to drive on them at all required skill and concentration as Sarah had found for herself. Irena could not surely negotiate such hazards.

Jason now thrust Constancia aside, striding swiftly out into the hall. Dolores ran after him, followed more slowly by Sarah and Constancia.

"Jason, where are you going?" asked Dolores quickly. "Where do you think she has gone?"

"I have no idea." Jason's voice was curt. "Max, Max! Where are you, man!"

"Here, *señor*." Max appeared from the other wing.

"You have heard about the *señora?*"

"Yes, *señor*."

"Did no one hear her leave?"

"Well, I heard a car a little while ago, *señor,* but I thought it was the Señorita Dolores leaving."

Jason snapped his fingers irritatedly. "Well, as you can see, the Señorita Dolores is still here. How long ago was this? Fifteen minutes, twenty?"

"About fifteen minutes, *señor*." Max's dark eyes were round with astonishment. It was a long time since the *señor* had been in such a state. Knowing he must have heard the Señora Irena leaving, he felt partially responsible. "But I was not to know it was the *señora, señor*," he protested. "She has never gone out before."

Jason moved impatiently. "I know, I know! All right, Max, don't upset yourself. Could you be certain in which direction the car turned?"

"No, *señor*." Max was regretful.

Jason sighed heavily, and glanced round at the girls standing behind him. "Dolores, will you stay here with Sarah, while I go

168

down to the town? It is possible she has gone to El Tesoro. I don't know why." He raked his hands through his hair. "I must try to find her!"

"All right, Jason, if that is what you want," Dolores nodded.

"Good." Jason gave Sarah a cursory glance, his eyes enigmatic, and then turning left the villa. They heard, a few minutes later, the sound of the Land Rover accelerating away, and the swish of the tyres as Jason turned out of the drive gates.

After he had gone, the silence in the villa seemed oppressive and Sarah shivered suddenly. The island, beautiful though it was, was primitive and untamed at night, the sound of the animals and the insistent buzz of insects adding to the sensation of unreality she was feeling. She looked at Dolores, and saw that even she was affected by the electrification of the atmosphere, and tiny beads of perspiration were standing on her upper lip.

"Well!" Dolores recovered her composure. "There's no point in standing here. We may as well make ourselves comfortable."

"Comfortable?" echoed Sarah, in astonishment. "I couldn't relax."

"Why? Are you scared Irena has blown her top at last?" Dolores laughed, albeit a little nervously. "It had to happen one day, I suppose. Violence always comes full circle. Didn't you know that?"

Sarah hugged herself. "I don't think one ought to speculate about things like that. After all, there may be some perfectly reasonable explanation." But even as she said the words, she realised how unlikely they sounded. What possible reasonable explanation could there be?

"Well," Dolores shrugged, "I, for one, don't imagine she has gone down to the town." She walked slowly along the corridor to the lounge again. "After all, why should she go down there?"

Sarah followed her reluctantly. "Where else could she have gone?"

Dolores gave her a secretive smile. "Haven't you heard that criminals usually return to the scene of their crime? I think she is gone up to the old Cordova house."

"But why?" Sarah looked surprised. "There's no possible reason for her to go up there. You're making it up. Besides, if you thought that, why didn't you tell Jason?"

"How long have you called your employer by his Christian name?" Dolores' voice was cold with dislike.

Sarah shrugged. "Is that important?"

"To me, yes."

Sarah ignored her, and walked over to the french doors and looked out into the night. Where had Irena gone? And why?

Would Jason find her before she – What? She sighed. What might Irena do?

Dolores came up behind her, and with angry hands swung her round to face her. "You're in love with Jason, aren't you?" she cried accusingly.

Sarah's cheeks burned. "That's my affair."

"So! I was right. Little idiot, do you imagine he cares any thing for you? Why, he and I have been *lovers* for almost two years!"

Sarah stared at her disbelievingly. "I don't believe you," she said, a sick feeling in her stomach. "You're lying!"

"Am I? Am I?" Dolores laughed. "Do you really think Jason has been celibate all these years? When Irena has been no wife to him!"

Sarah wrenched herself away from the other girl. She couldn't listen, she wouldn't! It wasn't true! Jason wasn't like that. He would never betray his wife in such a manner. Dolores was angry and jealous; she was taking what revenge she could.

"I'm going to my room," said Sarah, walking to the door. "You can tell Jason where I am when he returns."

Dolores gave her a vicious smile. "I'll tell him, all right. And I should think he will find it all rather amusing, don't you?"

Sarah ran down the corridor, reaching the stairs thankfully, and rushing up them to the sanctuary of her room. She lay on her bed for a while, refusing to think about what Dolores had told her, unable to assimilate the happenings of the last half hour with any degree of clarity. But, as her heartbeats slowed to normal, things came back into perspective again, and she began to conjecture sensibly about where Irena might have gone. Now that she had time to think about it, Dolores' remarks about the old Cordova house were not as irresponsible as she had at first thought. After all, they were not dealing with a normal person, and who knew what strange thoughts might have invaded Irena's head. But why tonight? What would make her go up there tonight? So far as she knew there had been nothing to spur her into that kind of behaviour. And what was up there, after all? Just a pile of old stones, a crumbling edifice.

She turned restlessly. But what if Irena was up there? How dangerous that would be! It would be so easy for her to take an uncertain step and fall to her death on the rocks below.

She sat up abruptly, and sliding off the bed she left her room. Downstairs she found Max in the hall.

"Is there any news?" she asked eagerly.

"No, *señorita*." Max shook his head mournfully.

"Do you think it's possible that the *señora* might have gone up to the old Cordova house?" she asked.

Max's eyes grew enormous. "That old ruin? I don't know, *señorita*. The place is haunted! No one go up there any more!"

"Now, Max, you know that's ridiculous," exclaimed Sarah, exasperated. "I don't believe in ghosts!"

"Me, I know there are such things," said Max with conviction, looking about him fearfully. "You oughtn't to talk like that, *señorita*. You inviting trouble!"

Sarah sighed. The superstitions Max had voiced were rampant all over the island, and she had heard before of the curse which was supposed to hang over the old ruin above them on the cliffs.

"I think we ought to go up there and find out," she said, ignoring the way her stomach plunged at the thought.

"Not me, *señorita*. I ain't going up there for nothing. You wait until the *señor* came back, and he go and find out."

"But that might be too late," exclaimed Sarah. "The *señora* might get killed up there, or fall to her death. Max, we must go!"

Max rubbed his hands together in trepidation. "*Señorita*, you not going to make me go up there! I mighty afraid! I be no good to you."

"Nonsense, Max. Pull yourself together. We can take a short cut and go up the steps from the beach. You know where I mean."

Max groaned. "*Señorita!*" he beseeched her. "Don't make me go!"

Sarah sighed. She could not *make* Max go, of course. She had no authority over him. Turning away, she walked to the front doors and looked out, but there was no sign of any car returning, and this hanging about was playing more on her nerves than action would have done.

"Come," she said softly. "It will only take us a few minutes. And it may save the *señora*'s life."

Max hunched his shoulders. "If I do not go, will the *señorita* go alone?"

Sarah made the decision. "Yes, Max."

"Then I come. But you promise, only a few minutes!"

Sarah nodded.

They went out of the rear entrance, past the pool and the stables, down to the beach, Max shivering and moaning as he followed her. He thought it was madness going up to the old house. It was not safe. Only bad things could come of it . . .

CHAPTER THIRTEEN

THE small town of El Tesoro was buzzing with its usual evening activity. The bars along the waterfront were giving out their usual noisy music and laughter, while in the streets groups of men told ribald stories and guffawed with laughter as they drank from kegs of raw spirit. Children still swarmed about, followed by some of the mangy dogs that went everywhere with them, and the smell of fish and rope, salt water and rum filled the air. Ordinarily, Jason found the uninhibited behaviour of the West Indians exhilarating, but tonight, his nerves drawn to fever pitch, they jarred on him, and he drove through the main street blowing his horn and startling people half out of their wits.

He found Abe Smith coming out of one of the harbour bars, staggering a little from the amount of liquor he had consumed, which must have been an enormous amount, thought Jason, knowing the capacity of the harbourmaster.

"Ay, ay, Jason," he exclaimed, slapping him on the back. "Have you come to spend an hour with us?"

"No," said Jason shortly. "Abe, have you seen Irena, or the station waggon?"

"Irena?" Jason's tone sobered Abe. "She has come down to the town? But why?"

"God knows!" Jason hunched his shoulders. "Abe, I don't know where she is! And I'm rapidly becoming frantic!"

Abe laid an arm across his shoulders. "Calm yourself, my friend, I will help you look for her. Why should she come down here tonight? Has something happened?"

Jason shook his head. "Nothing more than usual as far as I know. We were arguing this afternoon, but that's nothing fresh." He ran a hand over his brow wearily. "I'm trying to find some sense in all this. Why should she leave the villa tonight of all nights?"

Abe shrugged his heavy shoulders. "Perhaps it is something to do with the Señorita Winter, yes?"

"No," said Jason firmly. "There's been nothing like that – except – *the school house*!"

"The school house!" Abe hurried after Jason, who was striding swiftly up the narrow main street of the town, towards the old school building. "What has the Señora Irena to do with the school house? Is it that the *señora* did not like the *señorita* teaching at the school and living in her house, yes?"

"Yes." Jason was abrupt. "She might have gone to see Roberto."

"Roberto?" Abe frowned. "You do not think she may have – did she have a weapon?"

Jason looked at him wearily. "Do you think I know that? I don't even know where she is."

The school house was empty, but Roberto was in his house as usual, and he looked up from some papers he was marking in surprise at Jason's entrance.

"Jason!" he exclaimed. "What's wrong?" He could tell from the look on Jason's face that this was no social call.

"Irena! Have you seen her?"

"Irena? Me?" Roberto was astonished. "No. Should I have?"

"Oh, God!" Jason slumped. "I wish I knew. Roberto, Irena has left the villa. We don't know exactly when, or where she's gone. We thought, at least I thought, that maybe she had come here to find you. She was angry that Sarah was teaching at the school. Maybe she coined some crazy notion to come to you, God knows what for!"

Roberto shook his head and rose to his feet. "Jason, oh, Jason!" he exclaimed with feeling. "Do not, I beg of you, risk your life for that creature again."

"She's my wife," said Jason heavily.

"She is no wife," muttered Abe, in a deep voice. "Roberto, can you think of anything she might do? Any reason why she might leave the villa? Our ideas are at an end!" He frowned. "Unless . . ."

"Unless what?" Jason turned to him. "Come on, Abe, what?"

"Unless she went up to the old Cordova house. After all, she might have had some reason for going there. Who knows what, of course!"

"It's possible," Jason nodded. "It's just possible! And worth a try at least. Roberto, would you –"

But what he was about to say was interrupted abruptly, as several children came darting into the room, screaming excitedly, and rushing up to Roberto and Jason with panic-stricken haste.

"*Señor, señor*, the school house, it is burning!"

Brushing the children aside, the three men dashed outside, but the old school house was standing quietly, still in the moonlight. Jason turned back in anger, his apprehension aroused and doused in seconds.

"You lie!" he exclaimed, his face white with anger, but the children came dancing out, shaking their heads.

"No, *señor*. Not the old house, the new house . . ."

Jason ran down the street, conscious of Roberto at his heels, and as they reached the main street the flames leaping from the three-quarters-built new school building were plainly visible. The building, which flanked the shops but stood in a clearing all its own, was a mass of flames, the tinder-dry wood needing little to ignite it. That this was Irena's doing Jason had no doubts. But the immediate danger was that the flames would reach the other buildings and within minutes set the whole town alight.

Abe, with a swiftness of mind belied by his bulky figure, ran hastily down into the town, shouting for help, and the manually-operated hose and pumping equipment was pulled out of its warehouse and immediately set in motion.

Jason and Roberto ran to the school, Jason praying they would find Irena and prevent any more damage or danger. But there was no sign of the station wagon, and the building was fast becoming dangerously near to crashing down on to them. They were forced to stand back and watch the demolition helplessly, Roberto unable to prevent his rage at such wanton destruction from showing.

"I could kill her," he muttered angrily. "This will take months to rebuild. What arrant waste!"

Jason shook his head. "I know, I know, Roberto. I'm sorry."

"You're sorry!" Roberto gave a harsh laugh. "My God! Do you think that makes me feel any better? And who is to say that should we rebuild she won't come and do this all over again?"

"She won't get the chance," said Jason wearily. "I suppose something will have to be done after all."

"Something should have been done years ago," exclaimed Roberto angrily. "Fifteen years ago, to be precise."

Jason bent his head and kicked at the stones at his feet. "Yes, perhaps you are right." And then he became conscious of the fact that if Irena was not here she must have returned to the villa, and his pulses began to race. Sarah and Dolores were at the villa, and they were vulnerable.

"I must go," he said, glancing round as the men began to arrive with the pumping equipment. "Can you handle things here?"

Roberto nodded, and then said impulsively: "I'm sorry, Jason, if I sound bitter. But I couldn't have lived with her all these years if she had done to me what she did to you."

Jason shrugged. "Do you call it living?" he asked wearily, and walked away to get the Land Rover.

Roberto watched him go, and shook his head. "Poor Jason!" he muttered compassionately.

Dolores was pacing the hall when the headlights of a car swept the terrace. She walked swiftly to the door expecting to meet Jason, but she backed away aghast when Irena appeared in the doorway. Dolores had seen Sarah and Max leave the house earlier and had guessed their destination after what she had suggested, and had felt assured they would find Irena before anyone else. What happened then she couldn't have cared less.

But now Irena had returned, and Dolores knew she had to act naturally and allay any suspicions Irena might have of herself. Irena was a frightening sight, her eyes burning with excitement, her hair in wild disorder, her dress oil stained and smudged with soot. Her face, blackened as though by smoke, completed the picture, and Dolores thought: "Holy Mother, what has she been doing now?"

"Why are you here?" Irena asked at once. "Where's Jason? I want to see him."

"He – he went to look for you," stammered Dolores. "Where on earth have you been?"

Irena looked down at her dress and laughed. "I've been to town," she said. "Yes, to town."

Dolores backed away down the hall. Irena frightened her in this mood, and she could not help but recall the last time Irena had gone berserk and the catastrophe that had occurred. Her fingers went to her face. She was terrified something of what was in her mind was communicating itself to the other woman.

"D – don't you think you ought to go and wash?" she asked hopefully. "I mean – your face –?"

"My face? What is wrong with my face?" Irena was acutely strung up, and something in Dolores's voice confused her. She could sense that the other woman was frightened – but of what? There was nothing here to be afraid of. That Dolores might be afraid of her did not occur to her. "My face," she said again. "Why are you staring at me like that?"

Dolores shook her head. "N – nothing," she gasped. "I merely thought you would like a wash. Er – would you like a drink?"

Irena shook her head. She was convinced now that something was seriously wrong, and she thrust Dolores to one side; running down the corridor to the lounge and confronting herself in the mirror. The sight that met her horrified eyes was petrifying. Her face was *black*! She was black! Like them! In her confused brain the fire was forgotten, and only her own horror remained. All the fears and prejudices she had suffered all these years became manifest in her troubled mind, and she was convinced the curse she had feared had overtaken her. It was impossible for her distorted brain to distinguish fact from fiction.

She turned away in a panic, her eyes alighting on Dolores,

175

who was standing nervously in the doorway. "My face is black!" she said, in a curiously sane voice.

"Oh, nonsense," exclaimed Dolores, in astonishment, astounded at Irena's change of mood. "Your face is dirty, that's all."

"No, it's black." Irena touched her cheeks wonderingly. "Now what am I going to do?"

Dolores sighed, "Irena, you're wrong!"

"Always I am wrong," said Irena, her voice rising a little. "Do you think I wanted this to happen? But they have done this to spite me. And now I don't know what I am going to do."

"Oh, God! Irena, you're m – a – d –" Her voice trailed away.

"You think so, eh?" Irena found this amusing. "And what would a mad person do in a situation like this, I wonder?"

"Irena, please! Look, Jason and Sarah will be back in a moment. Try and keep calm until they arrive."

"Jason – and Sarah?" Irena frowned. "They are together?"

Dolores hesitated, but her own fears were uppermost in her mind, and of all things she wanted Irena out of the house again, away from *her*.

"They have gone looking for you," she said, unable to tell a complete lie, and yet equally unable to tell the whole truth. She was still incensed herself at Jason's concern for the other girl, and she was half afraid Sarah was going to succeed where she herself had failed.

"Sarah has gone up to the old house," she said, uncaring at this moment for the other girl's safety.

"So they thought I had gone up there!" Irena laughed. "How foolish!" Her eyes narrowed. "And they are together, they left you here alone?"

Dolores shrugged her shoulders, unable to reply.

"The fair governess is perhaps in love with my husband," said Irena wonderingly.

Dolores still did not speak, and Irena took her silence for acquiescence as Dolores had known she would. But just then Dolores did not care. She would have agreed to anything to get Irena to leave her alone.

"So! We will wait for their return."

Dolores clasped her hands together. "Don't you think you should let them know you have returned?" she suggested slyly. "I mean, they may be *hours* yet!"

Irena shrugged. "I can wait. There is nothing more to do now."

Dolores shook her head. She couldn't understand Irena. She would have thought she would have been incensed to think of Sarah and Jason together, but just now she seemed not to care.

176

Her own nerves had reached breaking point and she felt suffocated in this room with this wild, unpredictable woman whom she could not understand. She must get *away*!

Edging her way to the french doors, she looked longingly out on to the lawns and the freedom of the beach beyond. If she could just get away!

With an agile movement, her nerves panicking her into action, she suddenly slipped out of the french doors and ran madly for the clump of trees surrounding the stables. If she could hide for a few minutes, she might be able to double back and reach her car. Once in her car she would be relatively safe. She could drive back to civilisation!

But she had not considered the unbalanced state of Irena's mind, and Dolores' action, brought about, Irena was sure, by fear of herself, reactivated Irena's own panic. Like a shadow she followed Dolores across the lawns and into the trees, making it impossible for Dolores to stop and hide. Instead she was forced to go on, her legs growing tight with exhaustion and trembling with real fear now.

The beach stretched ahead of her, and she knew its only outlet was the steps to the old house. Following the footprints made earlier by Max and Sarah, she reached the foot of the steps.

Irena was close behind her now, and the slippery steps, moss-covered and weather-worn, could not be negotiated with the speed she needed. She felt several times Irena's hands clawing at her feet, and half sobbing she scrambled on, uncaring of her torn nails and bleeding hands. The steps seemed never-ending and despite her anger Irena seemed to have a better grasp of the rocks than she had. But at last she reached the top, and saw Sarah and Max coming towards her, attracted no doubt by the frightened cries she had been emitting.

"Irena!" she gasped tremblingly. "She's following me. Oh, help me, please!"

Sarah saw the other woman reach the top, as Dolores flung herself behind Max, and leaving the others, Sarah walked towards her. Although she was frightened herself, she could see that Irena looked more puzzled than angry, and in a gentle voice she said: "Irena, what is it? What's wrong?"

Irena looked at her wonderingly, and then at Max. "Jason," she said. "Where is Jason?"

"Jason?" said Sarah, in surprise. "He's not here. Whatever made you think he was?"

Irena pushed her back. "Of course he's here. You're lying."

Max was as helpless as Dolores. To him, in this outlandish place, with only the moonlight for illumination, Irena looked

177

like the epitome of all his fears, and he cowered back.

"I am not lying." Sarah put a hand on Irena's arm. Her skin was cold and clammy, and Sarah felt her own skin creep a little at the look in Irena's eyes, piercing the gloom with their brilliance.

Irena surveyed them all intently, and then releasing herself from Sarah's hold, she walked slowly across the long grass, letting her fingers trail over the crumbling stones which were all that was left of the old house.

Turning back to them, she said gloatingly: "This is all that is left! A ruin – and there won't even be a ruin left of the school house! It was built of wood; I don't think it will survive at all!" she laughed.

Sarah stared at her in horror. "You mean you've destroyed the new school building?" she exclaimed. "Oh, no!"

"Oh, yes, dear Señorita Winter." Irena spread wide her hands. "You did me a service when you told me of the new building. I had not known. But once I did it was my duty of course to destroy it, just as they have destroyed me! Did you think I would allow them to become educated people, and take over the island completely, for that will come, *señorita,* make no mistake."

"Oh, why can't you accept that we're all the same here?" cried Sarah despairingly.

Irena shook her head. "Poor deluded girl!" she said, and walked through an ivy-hung archway which was all that was left of the old main entrance of the building. Above the open space which had once been the hall hung crumbling beams, left to rot and disintegrate with age. Past hurricanes had brought down most of the building that had been left standing, and only the old hall had any roof left.

"*Señora!*" Sarah stepped forward after her, ignoring Dolores' hoarse: "Let her go!"

"Don't go in there, *señora,* it is not safe! While Max and I were looking for you, part of the wall crumbled at our touch."

Irena looked back at her. "*You* are concerned for *my* safety?" she exclaimed, looking at Sarah in astonishment. "Don't you know that no one cares for my safety?"

"They do. *I* do." Sarah stepped forward again.

Irena shook her head. "No, *señorita,*" she contradicted her harshly. "You are just like them." She waved a hand at Max and Dolores. "They hate me; and perhaps tonight they fear me. Who knows?" She walked into the centre of the hall and stood looking up at the splintered roof above her. "See!" she said chidingly. "It is safe, is it not?"

178

Sarah clenched her fists. "*Señora*, I beg of you."

"What?" Irena laughed, and her shrill voice echoed hauntingly around the ruins.

Whether it was that piercing laugh Sarah did not know, but as she stared with horrified eyes at the beams above Irena, she saw a large splinter of wood detach itself with almost deliberate slowness and begin to fall on the unseeing woman below.

With almost superhuman strength Sarah flung herself forward at Irena, knocking her sideways out of the path of the missile, but at the same time putting herself in Irena's place. She felt an agonising pain across her thighs as the beam fell heavily across her and she was pinned to the ground, unable to move for the weight of the wood, and the pain in her legs.

Irena, at first angry, unaware of the danger she had so narrowly been saved from, sprang up, but when she saw Sarah and the beam across her hips she shouted: "Come here, Dolores, Max! Help me!"

Kneeling down beside the almost unconscious form of the girl on the ground, she tried with feverish fingers to prise the wood from Sarah's hips, but it had wedged itself between two heaps of rubble and would not be moved.

"Sarah," she said, her voice sounding normal to Sarah's half-conscious ears, "are you all right? Can you hear me?"

Sarah could only groan in reply. She was barely aware of her surroundings, and even Irena's anxious face thrust close to her own could not arouse her.

Irena shouted to the others again, but neither Max nor Dolores were there any longer. When the timber crumbled they had fled, leaving Sarah to her fate.

Irena was frantic. Even in her distressed state she could understand what might have happened to herself, if Sarah had not tried to save her, and she would not leave the girl alone here. She looked round, trying to see something that she could use as a lever, and seeing a spar of wood protruding from the wall, she pulled at it savagely, uncaring that the bricks were soft and crumbling and needed little to set them falling.

Sarah, at last recovering from the first agonies of her fall, managed to raise her head a fraction and looked over to see Irena tugging at the spar of wood. Her lower limbs seemed numb, and the pain had receded to the background of her mind. And much more than Irena she was aware of the preciousness of their situation here among such dangerous ruins.

"Irena!" she called vigorously, trying helplessly to free herself. "Irena, do be careful! Just leave me, go and get help!"

But Irena ignored her and Sarah could not be sure she had

heard her at all. She was so intent on her occupation, she could not hear Sarah's pleas to her to leave the wood alone before the whole roof came tumbling down on their heads.

And then it happened; Irena pulled the wood cleanly from its resting place, and as she did so the wall subsided into the place where the wood had been, and the whole side of the roof crumbled down with the speed of years of decay.

Sarah screamed: *"Look out!"* but it was too late. The rubble hit Irena, knocking her to the ground, and burying her beneath a crumbling mass of rocks. A lump of rock bounced sideways, hitting Sarah, and she knew no more.

CHAPTER FOURTEEN

WHEN Sarah recovered consciousness again she was lying in the soft silk sheets of her own bed, and it was daylight outside. The balcony doors were open to admit a cooling breeze, and a white-clad West Indian nurse was sitting beside the bed knitting.

She could only open her eyes half-way, the light seeming overpowering after the darkness she had experienced. She could not remember what had happened at first, but then with horror she recalled the ruins, the pain of something hitting her, and oblivion.

The nurse, seeing the flickering of her eyelids, said softly: "Hello, are you feeling better?"

Sarah tried to smile, but her face felt tight and putting up a hand she touched the bandage that encircled her head. "Am I – am I badly hurt?" she asked carefully.

"Well, you've had concussion, and you've slept for about three days, but you're on the mend now," replied the nurse calmly. "You have a fractured leg, but that will soon heal. It was a clean break."

Sarah frowned. "But how – I mean, how did I get here? I can't have slept for *three* days!"

"Oh, yes, you have. As to the rest, I expect Señor de Cordova or the Señora Serena will tell you." The nurse smiled reassuringly. "And now I'll go and see about getting you something to drink. Perhaps a little soup, eh?"

But already Sarah felt tired with the effort of talking, and she felt herself drifting away again into unconsciousness.

When she awoke again it was dark outside, and the room was dimly lit by a bedside lamp. The chair beside the bed was occupied by the Señora Maria, Jason's mother, and she leaned forward when Sarah awoke, and said: "Hello, my dear. How do you feel?"

Sarah felt much stronger, and tried to struggle up in the bed, but the *señora* restrained her.

"Take it easy," she said softly. "You have been very ill. You must rest. There is plenty of time for that."

Sarah sighed. "Is it – I mean, how long is it now since it happened? Have I slept again for a long time?"

"No. It was this morning you woke. But when the nurse brought your soup you had fallen asleep again. Doctor Martinez from Trinidad says you are coming along very well, so you have no cause for concern. Doctor Martinez is a very important man. He knows what he is talking about."

"I'm sure he does. *Señora* –" Sarah turned her head restlessly. "The Señora Irena ... she was trying to rescue me when the roof caved in. Was she – is she –?"

"Irena is dead," said the *señora* firmly. "And you might have been dead too, if Jason hadn't come upon you as he did. After he got you out the whole building subsided."

"Oh!" Sarah closed her eyes. She could see it all, Irena tugging at the spar of wood, trying to get her free ... "Where were Dolores – and Max –?"

"Dolores and Max ran away. Dolores went straight home, but Max waited for Jason and told him what had happened. I am afraid Dolores has come out of this very badly." But she did not sound afraid; in fact, thought Sarah, she sounded rather pleased.

"I see." Sarah rubbed a hand over her forehead. "When will I be able to sit up?"

"Tomorrow, I should think. And soon you will be able to get about again, although the cast on your leg will inhibit your movements for a while. I expect you will be able to walk with the aid of a crutch."

Sarah smiled a little at this, and the *señora* stood up. "But I talk too much," she said. "I will tell Nurse you are awake and she will decide whether you can have something to eat."

The soup they brought her was delicious, but now that she was properly awake again Sarah wanted to see Jason, and she wondered whether he had been to see her while she was lying here unconscious. She became aware that her hair, even in the plaits, was untidy, and when the nurse had gone and only herself and the *senora* were left, she said: "Did – did Jason come to see me? I mean, while I was unconscious?"

Senora Maria smiled. "But of course. He was very concerned about you."

Sarah half-closed her eyes. "And I must look such a fright. My hair ..."

"Don't be silly, my dear, you look very young, and very endearing. I am sure Jason didn't care one way or the other. He was too distressed over the accident. Irena was buried, of course, two days ago. She was buried in the family burial ground near the plantation, and almost the whole island turned out for her funeral. Even Roberto," she said reminiscently.

"Oh, yes. Was Jason very upset – I mean –" She sought about in her mind for words to express her meaning, and the *señora* smiled a little sadly:

"My dear, you must understand. Jason is a good man, and he
182

would never intentionally destroy anyone or anything. His faith is important to him, but he would be the first to admit that any feeling he had for Irena could only be pity. He could have had her sent to a mental hospital in Port of Spain, but being a religious man he did not wish to separate Irena from humanity." She sighed. "No one knows better than I what a charming, emotional creature Jason used to be, but he has staunched all his emotions for years, and it is not easy for him to release them again. Do you understand?"

Sarah stared at her. "Why are you telling me all this?"

Señora Maria shrugged. "I don't know. Let us talk of something else. The children are all longing to see you. They have not been allowed in here in case they disturbed you, but tomorrow perhaps they will be permitted to come. Would you like that? Of course, Serena came home to look after them the day after the accident, and she is still here, naturally, but I understand she is thinking of making her home in Trinidad with her parents, and taking the children with her."

"What does Jason think of this?" Sarah's heart was pounding. If the children were to leave, there would be nothing left to keep her here.

"I think he is prepared to let the children go, if that is what they want, of course, and I believe Eloise may be able to attend a school there which would be more suitable for her position. The younger ones can attend a kindergarten. You see, there is nothing here for them except the small school in the town, and as you know that is crowded already. Besides, children are better with their mother, and I shall have them to stay with me for holidays."

"And me?" Sarah could not prevent the question.

The señora shrugged. "Well, of course, if the children are to go to Trinidad there will be no need for a governess, of course."

"But I thought Serena's parents hadn't enough room for the children," Sarah murmured faintly.

"Jason is giving Serena enough money to buy a house of her own, and he is going to make her a monthly allowance from the estate. She will be free then to do as she likes. She really is too young to be cut off from people of her own age completely."

"I see." Sarah felt her small world was gradually disintegrating.

The señora rose to her feet. "And now I must go. It is almost dinner time, and Jason will wonder where I am. Sleep well."

Sarah nodded, but privately she thought she would never sleep again. So she was to be dismissed after all. She was to leave the island, never to return? The knowledge broke her heart, and

183

she felt hot tears sliding down her cheeks.

Sarah did not see Jason the next day. The harvesting of the crop had begun, Serena told her, when she came to visit her with the children, and he was too busy to see anyone. Sarah accepted it with cold logic. After all, why should he trouble about her? She was only an employee, and soon she would not even be that.

By the next day Sarah was sitting in a chair by her balcony windows, looking out over the lawns watching the children playing and romping wildly in the pool. Now there was no one to stop them, they seemed to have lost all their inhibitions, and she could see Serena with them, diving into the pool and enjoying herself with her family.

Sarah was dressed in a wild silk dressing gown which Serena had lent her, its deep purple colour accentuating the colour of her rather shadowy eyes. Despite the drugs Doctor Martinez was giving her, she was not sleeping at all well, although she denied this when the doctor tackled her. Her hair was plaited into a single braid and hung over her shoulder, and her restless fingers plucked continually at it.

Doctor Martinez had said that the plaster would be off her leg in about six weeks, and then it would take a little while longer for her to regain the strength to walk on it. At most, in three months, she would be free to leave the island. Tomorrow she was to be allowed to get dressed and go downstairs, although just how that was to be negotiated she had no idea. Unless someone carried her down; Jason perhaps! But at this her mind baulked. If Jason could not concern himself to come and see her now that she was able to have visitors, why should he care to carry her downstairs?

She sighed a little wearily. She had written to the Sisters at the convent and told them of the accident, and she expected they would be writing to her soon. When they learned that Serena was to take the children to Trinidad they would probably expect Sarah to return to England. The prospect was a grim one. Sarah could not imagine life now without Jason; it would be intolerable!

So engrossed was she with her thoughts, she did not hear the tap at her door, nor hear it opening to admit Jason. Closing the door, he stood looking at her for a few moments, and then said: "Well, are you feeling better?"

Sarah turned round swiftly in her chair, her face suffusing with colour. "Jason!" she exclaimed. "I didn't hear you!"

He walked slowly across the room. "No? You seemed rather thoughtful as I came in. And worried, too." He frowned. "Tell

184

me, are you really feeling better?"

Sarah looked away from him. "I was watching the children with Serena and envying them in the pool. And yes, I feel lots better."

Jason pulled a chair across to her and straddled it, his arms folded across its back. "But you're looking tired," he said, with concern in his tawny eyes. "Are you not sleeping well? Are you perhaps uncomfortable in this?" He flicked a hand at the cast, just visible below her gown.

Sarah looked down at her hands. "I'm sleeping well enough," she replied off-handedly. "How – how is the crop coming along?"

Jason half-smiled. "It's coming along very well. Of course, the harvest takes a long time to gather in. It's many months before completion. But for now, that is immaterial." He studied her intently for a moment. "I'm glad you're feeling better."

Sarah felt angry inside. How could he say that, when he had not been to see her in all of the three days she had been conscious again.

"Do you really care?" she flared, and then hunched her shoulders as though regretting her impulsive tongue. "After all, I understand Serena is to take the children to Trinidad, and they'll no longer need a governess, so I'm superfluous."

Jason looked angry. "Of course I care," he muttered harshly. "I don't care to see anyone in pain, or hurt – because of me!"

Sarah shrugged, "It wasn't your fault."

"Of course it was my fault. If I'd never married Irena, none of these disasters might have occurred!"

Sarah looked at him. "That's impossible to say!" she exclaimed. "It seems evident, apparently, to everyone except yourself, that Irena would eventually have shown symptoms of her condition –"

Jason sighed. "Maybe. Maybe not. But that doesn't alter the fact that had you not gone looking for Irena you wouldn't be in this state today. And I'm sorry."

"Oh, Jason," Sarah moved restlessly, "do you think I care about myself? It's you – I – I –" Her voice trailed away, but Jason had risen peremptorily to his feet and kicked the chair aside.

"What was that?" he asked huskily.

She looked up at him, momentarily frightened at the look in his eyes. She was still unable to read his expression, and she was afraid she had said too much already. "It was nothing," she lied awkwardly. She glanced down at the watch on his wrist. "What time is it? Is it almost lunch time –"

"God, Sarah!" His voice was hoarse. "Do I have to get down

185

on my knees before you'll commit yourself?"

Sarah tried to stand, but she was too weak, and with a groan Jason gathered her up into his arms and buried his face in the scented warmth of her neck. She was aware that he was trembling and she wrapped her arms round his middle and clung to him tightly as though she would never let him go. There was a momentary pain in her leg and she stifled a sob, but Jason, realising how ungentle he had been, lifted her bodily into his arms and deposited her unceremoniously on the bed, sliding on it beside her, and finally finding her mouth with his own.

To Sarah, who had spent the last three days living under the sword of Damocles, this was heaven on earth, and the possibility of spending the rest of her life with Jason did not seem so fantastic after all. Surely the warmth of his mouth and the trembling emotion of his body proved that this was no passing infatuation for him no more than it was for her. She loved him, and she did not care who knew it.

At last Jason forced himself to sit up, but retained possession of her hands and would not let her smooth back her hair or wrap the silk dressing gown closely about her. There was a half-smile on his lips, as she tried unsuccessfully to free herself, and he said : "Does this not frighten you? This feeling of possession? Because if it does you'll have to get used to it. What I have, I hold. Will you marry me? As soon as it's decently possible? These are quite unusual circumstances, and no one expects us to observe a long period of mourning."

Sarah stared at him incredulously. "Oh, Jason!" she cried weakly.

"Well? What's your answer?" He leaned over her again, pinning her hands to her sides.

"You know it's yes," she murmured softly. "But why did you make me wait three days before asking me?"

Jason's mouth caressed the creamy softness of her throat, and then releasing her hands, he took her face between his fingers and said : "For two reasons. Firstly I wanted you to recover completely before I spoke of such things. I could not have borne it if, in the horror of the recollections you had, you had rejected me. And the second reason was that, beast that I am, I wanted you to suffer a little for all the suffering I've had because of you."

"You? Suffering because of me?" Sarah frowned, and allowed her hand to stray along the line of his scar, this time producing no result except that he turned his mouth to her fingers and kissed them lightly.

"Yes. Do you imagine I'm without jealousy? Did you think I could watch you with Roberto, or Manuel – without feeling an

186

overpowering sense of frustration because I was not free to have you." He sighed. "Even now, I'm not sure that I have the right —"

"The right!" Sarah's voice was indignant. "Jason, please, don't say things like that! You have every right — so far as I'm concerned. I adore you — and I can't wait to get out of this plaster and become your wife!"

"And there is one other matter," he said quietly. "Will you take my faith?"

"If that's what you want. It's strange, isn't it, that I should have waited all this time to do something I could have done when the nuns first took charge of me?"

Jason kissed her deeply and lingeringly, arousing her body to unknown desires and delights, and finally, unable to stand any more without losing his self-control, he rose from the bed.

"So," he said, a little thickly. "It's settled."

"Yes, *señor*," she murmured mockingly, and he put both hands up to the back of his neck and stretched. "You didn't say why you wanted to marry me," she continued gently. "Or am I simply to imagine what you mean?"

"Sarah!" he exclaimed in exasperation. "You know I love you, I worship you, I desire you, and I need you, but I'm not going to touch you again." He turned towards the door. "This room is too inviting," he said, looking back at her. "And your bed is very comfortable." His eyes were a little amused as at last he succeeded in embarrassing her, and her cheeks burned with colour. "And I would like to stay, very much. But I'm hot, and I need a cooling shower before lunch. It's best that I don't linger too long or my good intentions may melt away in the heat of the moment."

Sarah propped herself up on her elbows. "Then will you have lunch with me?" she pleaded.

"So long as we have a *duenna*," he agreed dryly.

"Is that necessary?" she asked provocatively.

"I think so," he replied. "And this afternoon I have work to do."

"Oh!" Sarah looked dejected, and he smiled.

"Don't be downhearted. In three months, we will go away together. We might go to Europe and visit the good Sisters of the faith and assure them of my suitability. Would you like that?"

"So long as we're together, I don't care where we are," confessed Sarah candidly, and Jason's eyes darkened.

"I must go," he said, rather huskily. "I love you."

The door closed behind him and Sarah sank back on her pillows. She was so happy, and she spared a thought for Irena, that

187

poor demented woman who had inadvertently given her this happiness. At least she was released now from the torments of her own mind, and the island could look forward to the future, free of her superstitions and resentments.

Sarah clasped her hands behind her head. Suddenly the day seemed much brighter. She was loved – by Jason, and soon they would be married. She would bear his children and one day they would have a son to carry on the family name. What more could any woman ask?

Mills & Boon's Paperbacks

MARCH

THE BLACK EAGLE BY ANNE HAMPSON

Because she resembled his long-dead fiancée Roxanne was carried off by the mysterious Mexican Don Juan Armando Ramirez. In time, Roxanne's hatred of her husband turned to love . . . but what chance had she of reaching his heart?

CASTLES IN SPAIN BY REBECCA STRATTON

Holly was delighted to have the chance of visiting the Spanish castle where her aunt had lived since her marriage. Don José Delgaro gave her a charming welcome, but it was his son Marcos whose attitude really puzzled Holly. Was he trifling with her until he married the attractive Helena Mendez?

THE MAN AT KAMBALA BY KAY THORPE

Sara lived with her father at Kambala and was accustomed to doing as she pleased there. She certainly didn't reckon much of the ideas of Steve York, the impossible man who came to take charge in her father's absence. "It's asking for trouble to run round a game reserve as if it were a play park," he told her. Was Sara right to ignore him?

THE SILVER STALLION BY IRIS DANBURY

Lucie Durrant went to the Canary Islands on a working holiday looking for new ideas for the jewellery that she designed. Her call on the attractive Joel Barron was of a purely business nature, but later, as she came to know him better, she began to wonder if that was all he meant to her . . .

THE GLASS CASTLE BY VIOLET WINSPEAR

"Out in the East they say that the mind of a woman is a jungle, and it is the one jungle in which a man should never get lost." That was the code by which Edwin Trequair lived – or so he told Heron. Why then did he ask her to marry him? Could Heron ever understand such a strange, arrogant man?

20p net each

Mills & Boon's Paperbacks

MARCH (contd.)

THE MAN AT LA VALAISE BY MARY WIBBERLEY

Sacha Donnelly decided to holiday in Provence on her own and certainly didn't bargain on having to share her cottage with three strange men. How she longed to escape from Nikolai, dark and dangerous, who had forced her to remain there. But soon Sacha was to wonder if she really wanted to get away . . .

THE TREE OF IDLENESS BY ELIZABETH HUNTER

When Caroline went to visit her aunt in Cyprus she looked forward to renewing her acquaintance with the country and the people. But how was she to deal with Philip Klearchos, dark and disturbing, who warned her, "I may take your education in hand and give you a taste of what being a woman can mean . . ."

A SENSE OF BELONGING BY LILIAN PEAKE

When Carina fell in love with Marcus de Verrier, the man who was grooming her voice for stardom, his reaction was predictable. "Many students fall in love with their teachers. It's nothing unusual. An occupational hazard, in fact. But I prefer to call it infatuation, which will pass with time." How could she make him realise that this just wasn't true?

SHADE OF THE PALMS BY ROBERTA LEIGH

To Stephen Brandon, Julia was no more than Miss Watson, his unflappable, highly efficient secretary. A dowdy woman wearing unfashionable clothes, sensible shoes and spectacles, he would have thought if he'd considered the matter at all. But he was to discover that appearances can be deceptive and that there was a totally unexpected side to Julia.

PEPPERTREE LANE BY LINDEN GRIERSON

Jean Delaney was very grateful to her Uncle Gerald, who had given her and her mother and young brother a home – but Gerald's foster-son Rob was convinced that the whole affair was a confidence trick and that the whole family were out to make what they could from the old man. Was he right to be suspicious?

20p net each

FREE!

YOUR COPY OF OUR MAGAZINE OF
MILLS & BOON ROMANCES NOW AVAILABLE

If you enjoyed reading this MILLS & BOON romance and would like a list of other MILLS & BOON romances available, you can receive a free magazine by completing the coupon below and posting it off today. This opportunity to read more about MILLS & BOON romances should not be missed. Your free magazine will be posted off to you immediately.

Over the page are listed 50 selections from our current catalogue. Why not contact your local stockist to obtain these books? However, should you have any difficulty please write to us at MILLS & BOON READER SERVICE, P.O. BOX 236, 14 Sanderstead Road, S. Croydon, Surrey, CR2 0YG, England, ticking the titles you require, and enclosing your remittance. All Mills & Boon paperbacks ordered through the Reader Service are 20p. Please note to cover postage and handling, will United Kingdom readers add 2p per book. Overseas readers are asked to add 10p per book and use International Money Orders where possible.

Please send me the free Mills & Boon Romance magazine ☐

Please send me the titles ticked ☐

I enclose £.. (No C.O.D.)

Name .... Miss/Mrs.

Address ....

Town/City ....

County/Country........................... Postal/Zip Code..............

MB2/74

HAVE YOU MISSED ANY OF THESE MILLS & BOON ROMANCES?

- ☐ 229 To Catch a Unicorn
  Sara Seale
- ☐ 240 Price of Love
  Rachel Lindsay
- ☐ 268 South from Sounion
  Anne Weale
- ☐ 292 Venice Affair
  Joyce Dingwell
- ☐ 294 The Dutch Uncle
  Margery Hilton
- ☐ 296 And Then Came Love
  Roberta Leigh
- ☐ 302 Beloved Sparrow
  Henrietta Reid
- ☐ 323 A Kiss in a Gondola
  Katrina Britt
- ☐ 325 The Surgeon's Marriage
  Kathryn Blair
- ☐ 364 The Drummer and the Song
  Joyce Dingwell
- ☐ 376 The Garden of Don José
  Rose Burghley
- ☐ 381 Unwary Heart
  Anne Hampson
- ☐ 383 Rising Star
  Kay Thorpe
- ☐ 397 Crown of Flowers
  Joyce Dingwell
- ☐ 399 The Legend of Lexandros
  Anne Mather
- ☐ 401 Dancing on My Heart
  Belinda Dell
- ☐ 406 Enchanted Autumn
  Mary Whistler
- ☐ 411 A Wife for Andrew
  Lucy Gillen
- ☐ 420 The Silver Fishes
  Lucy Gillen
- ☐ 450 The Grotto of Jade
  Margery Hilton
- ☐ 454 Sweet Revenge
  Anne Mather
- ☐ 455 Take the Far Dream
  Jane Donnelly
- ☐ 465 Bitter Masquerade
  Margery Hilton
- ☐ 494 Love Hath An Island
  Anne Hampson
- ☐ 532 The Valley of Illusion
  Ivy Ferrari

- ☐ 537 Dark Enemy
  Anne Mather
- ☐ 551 Wide Pastures
  Celine Conway
- ☐ 566 Sweet Kate
  Lucy Gillen
- ☐ 576 Summer Season
  Lucy Gillen
- ☐ 584 Red Feather Love
  Suzanna Lynne
- ☐ 595 Sandflower
  Jane Arbor
- ☐ 602 The Way Through the Valley
  Jean S. MacLeod
- ☐ 608 South Island Stowaway
  Essie Summers
- ☐ 610 Dark Hills Rising
  Anne Hampson
- ☐ 632 Portrait of Susan
  Rosalind Brett
- ☐ 643 Wife to Sim
  Joyce Dingwell
- ☐ 649 There Came a Tyrant
  Anne Hampson
- ☐ 669 Dear Deceiver
  Doris E. Smith
- ☐ 688 Happy with Either
  Ruth Clemence
- ☐ 693 Victory for Victoria
  Betty Neels
- ☐ 695 Dark Avenger
  Anne Hampson
- ☐ 705 Pirate of the Sun
  Gwen Westwood
- ☐ 720 Nurse at Ste. Monique
  Juliet Armstrong
- ☐ 723 Bride of the Rif
  Margaret Rome
- ☐ 766 The Pied Tulip
  Elizabeth Ashton
- ☐ 767 The Sophisticated Urchin
  Rosalie Henaghan
- ☐ C730 The Stars of San Cecilio
  Susan Barrie
- ☐ C984 Island in the Dawn
  Averil Ives
- ☐ C1107 They Met in Zanzibar
  Kathryn Blair
- ☐ C1114 Trevallion
  Sara Seale

ALL PRICED AT 20p SEE OVER FOR HANDY ORDER FORM PLEASE TICK YOUR REQUIREMENTS